Praise For
The Barefoot Followers of Sweet Potato Grace

"*Sweet Potato Grace* is a spirited, humorous exploration of small-town traditions clashing with a group of eccentric, time-warped travelers. Set in fictional Tombstone, Texas, the novel's witty dialogue and colorful characters examine themes like family dynamics, gender, the tension between nostalgia and progress, and the desire for freedom. As the townsfolk rally against these disruptive outsiders, they confront their own fears about change, home, and self-identity. With heart and humor, this story reminds us that sometimes, letting go is the only path to truly finding oneself."

—Sara Arnell, author of *There Will Be Lobster: Memoir of a Midlife Crisis*

"What begins with Pinky Swear, a young woman mourning the death of her beloved cat, Sweet Potato Grace, and searching for the courage to come out of the closet in Tombstone, Texas, quickly turns into a comic, heart-rending romp when a group of barefoot time travelers drop out of nowhere into the staid, conservative community, alarming the locals but opening the door for Pinky. Under Megan Okonsky's hand, Pinky's voice—her hilarious colloquialisms—rings clear as a bell and has the reader rooting for her to take off her shoes and follow her heart."

—Yvonne Osborne, author of *Let Evening Come*

THE BAREFOOT FOLLOWERS OF SWEET POTATO GRACE

THE BAREFOOT FOLLOWERS OF SWEET POTATO GRACE

BY MEGAN OKONSKY

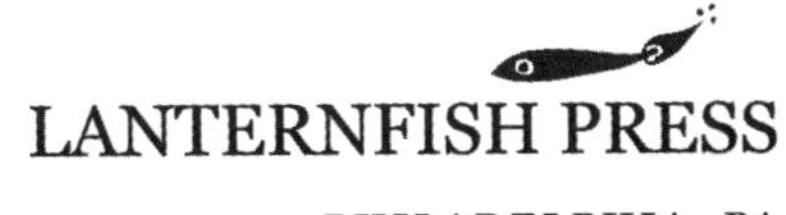

LANTERNFISH PRESS

PHILADELPHIA, PA

THE BAREFOOT FOLLOWERS OF SWEET POTATO GRACE

Lanternfish Press
P.O. Box 34569
Philadelphia, PA 19101
lanternfishpress.com

Cover design by Kimberly Glyder
Interior layout and typesetting by Hadley Hendrix

Printed in the United States of America
27 26 25 24 23 1 2 3 4 5

Library of Congress Control Number: 2024949538
Print ISBN: 9781941360897
Digital ISBN: 9781941360903

To my parents

To Katelyn

To Bonnie, Clyde, Tigger, Duke, Belle, and Binx

To Pinky Swear

And, of course, to Sweet Potato Grace

ONE

I don't *think* you can get heart palpitations from online shopping. No one in Tombstone, Texas, has ever heard of such a thing. Then again, it's hard to trust anything people in Tombstone have to say after what happened with the barefoot strangers.

Everyone has their own twisted version of the story. I'm not one to brag, but: only mine is the truth. And my story—the true and honest story—begins with me, Pinky Elizabeth Swear, rattled with indecision, shopping online for an alarm clock to distract myself from grief.

I started by searching *alarm clock* in Google. I'd never owned one before. My younger sister Fanny once bought one without me, a vintage pink thing that rings like a school bell in the morning. When it goes off, she probably removes her eye mask, releases her hair from a silk scrunchie, and floats through her closet like a cartoon princess. (I can't confirm my suspicions, as Fanny and I haven't shared a room since our family moved out of the trailer.)

I'm no beauty queen like Fanny. Her ringing timekeeper is too pretty for me.

Mama doesn't have an alarm clock. Never has. She wakes

to no man and no man-made item. "Find me an alarm clock that sings Loretta Lynn and maybe I'll consider getting up before sunrise," she says. "I prefer the feminine rebellion of sleeping in."

I'm not sure my grandmother Nene Miriam sleeps at all, on account that she's told me she always keeps one eye open for the following: home invaders; Texas state representatives; thank-you letters from her wayward, ungrateful nieces and nephews; the boogeyman; the mailman; the milkman; Ed (who, according to Nene, assisted her in the production of Mama); and the second coming of Jesus Christ. With so much keeping Nene awake, alarm clocks are not necessary.

What sort of alarm clock suits a twenty-two-year-old woman who wants to put off the task of writing a eulogy for her cat?

What happens after we die, and does it apply to grey-and-white tortoiseshell nightmares like Sweet Potato Grace?

I did not know the answers to those questions. That was why, on July 3, 2022, the day before the barefoot strangers appeared and changed everything for Tombstone, I found myself shopping.

Sweet Potato Grace had been my best friend for over five years, before, during, and after the COVID pandemic. Her villainous stare was so comical that I hadn't minded the isolation when it came. Her bones—she was just about ten when she passed, still so young—were tired from outdoor adventures around Tombstone, and all she wanted in her later years was to eat, snuggle, and maybe claw my arm open if I tried to pet her below the neck. Her insistence on getting what she wanted out of life reminded me that once the world opened up again, I might be able to plan my escape route from Tombstone.

One might say she was a good role model. But after what

happened, saying that around Tombstone is likely to get the gossip train chugging down the track of judgment.

Every day since I came back from college, at 5:58 a.m., Sweet Potato Grace would holler in my ear and swat at my face. At 6:00, her automatic feeder would rotate with the sound of grinding gears, alerting Miss Potato that soup was on and alerting me that the sun was arriving to smile upon the free state of Texas.

Without that routine, I needed something else to wake me up.

Thousands of alarm clocks presented themselves online. Before Sweet Potato Grace's death, I might have sent myself to the funny farm thinking about all the options this big old world has to offer. On July 3? I had no other focus besides completing this silly task. Did I want an alarm clock that lit up like the sun? One that bounced around the room like a toad so I had to leap out of bed and catch it? I had more options than a bigamist and I had to narrow them down to one. Only *then* could I start the eulogy I was preparing to give at the Fourth of July Goat Cheese Memorial for Sweet Potato Grace.

(Sweet Potato Grace loved goat cheese.)

Buy the alarm clock, *then* write the eulogy, I told myself. Maybe this to-do list is what quieted the heart palpitations. Maybe I was just a blank slate of a new woman after losing the pet who had shaped my identity, personality, and Instagram feed since my late teenage years.

Buy the alarm clock, *then* write the eulogy.

If Mama had caught me browsing alarm clocks on the internet, she'd have hollered, "Pinky Elizabeth Swear! Don't you have more important items on your agenda?" If I'd had more of a spine back then, I would have told Mama it was her fault I needed an alarm clock in the first place. Before college, the sound of Mama rustling and grunting past my childhood bedroom was enough to bring me out of my unconscious state. But in the short time I was away at Blinn College, Mama took it upon herself to move my things into the mother-in-law suite on our property and move Nene Miriam into my room. Fanny could have easily given her room to Nene, but Mama said Fanny was too sensitive for such independence. And if a courting fellow came knocking on Fanny's window with a case of beer and an invitation to sin, Mama wanted to hear his grubby little knuckles so she might stand her ground with a flat palm and the threat of Concelia the pistol.

When the COVID-19 pandemic shut Blinn down, I returned home to discover that the mother-in-law suite was a beach lover's paradise—a studio decorated in pale blues and glass vases, meant to accommodate visitors passing through Tombstone who needed a relaxing place to stay. There had never been such visitors to Tombstone, but Mama had the delusions of a seasoned entrepreneur and more hope than a nun outside a tomb on Easter.

Decorative wooden signs still hung around the mother-in-law suite on July 3, 2022:

A GOOD CRY, A DAY AT THE BEACH, AND A MARGARITA FOR BREAKFAST: SALT SOLVES EVERYTHING!

I WISH I WAS AN OCTOPUS, SO I COULD SLAP MY HUSBAND EIGHT TIMES AT ONCE.

If I didn't think too hard, it was like I was on vacation.

COVID didn't change my life too much. It only reversed the changes I had been enjoying. Wanda, June, Ashley, and I had shared a suite at college and they'd moved back home to Tombstone, too. It was like we were back in grade school again.

Just with the threat of a deadly virus looming over grocery stores and old folks' homes.

The boredom of isolation encouraged June to marry her high school sweetheart and Ashley to have a baby with hers. I had nothing to show for myself but a ten-year-old cat named Sweet Potato Grace, whom I'd found licking her chops around the dumpsters of Lethal Peppers BBQ when I was seventeen. Mama begrudgingly took care of my kitty while I was away at school in exchange for the promise that I would come back after graduation. I entered into the agreement for the same reason any seventeen-year-old signs up for student loans: because we don't know any better.

In the building-your-own-family department, Sweet Potato Grace was the card I was dealt. Marriage and children were not in the cards for me, I believed, as I was born with an attraction to women and women only.

In some other parts of the world, I know this isn't a big deal. But Tombstone isn't like those parts of the world. Its doors aren't open to everyone. They were barely open to Roger way back when, and to this day, his name is only met with sad headshakes and "what a shame."

If I had my way, Sweet Potato Grace would've had two human mamas, but as it was, she only had me. So I peered out through the shutters of the closet and kept my mouth shut.

Buy the alarm clock, *then* write the eulogy.

Buy the alarm clock, *then* write the eulogy.

My search results yielded what you might expect: ads, ads, ads. I clicked on the "Images" tab and scrolled with the intentionality of a zombie as my conscious mind thought about cat food shipments and picking up Potato's remains and the to-do list of grief. I stopped only when I saw *them*. Or rather, I stopped only when I saw *her*.

The image was an old Westclox ad from the 1920s. It must have been scanned from a magazine. Half the page was filled with text, waxing poetic about the product: a small, silver circle with a single bell on top. The numbers on the alarm clock were large enough to recognize, even though they'd been drawn or painted by hand.

Behind the clock were two women. One sat in a velvet chair, her long brown curls pulled back with an ornate clip. She wore a crisp shirt and pants. Her legs were crossed and she was leaning toward the blonde woman standing next to her. Even though the standing woman's short hair was covered by one of the funny-looking round hats of that time period, some golden strands still peeked through and warmed her face. The blonde was looking directly at the reader in a way that made me blush. She had freckles, bold green eyes, and endearingly crooked teeth.

She wore a sweet little pearl necklace and a matching bracelet. I followed her arm to her hand, which was playfully grasping the seated woman's. The artist made it look like they'd been caught doing something delightfully devious.

They're just friends, I told myself. You're always looking for something that isn't there.

Except this time, maybe my gut was right. When I clicked on the ad, it took me to an Instagram post from *@lgbt.archive.history*. The post featured a caption explaining the significance of monocles in the lesbian community back in the 1920s. I hadn't even noticed the seated woman wearing one. My eyes kept going back to the blonde. She looked to be my age but had the kind of confidence about her that always made me envious.

After I finished the caption about women loving women back in the age of flappers, I scrolled through the rest of the account's content. Drag queens from the eighties. Lesbians protesting in the nineties. A group of male soldiers with sparkles in their eyes and heels on their feet. Queerness captured throughout history, all new photos to me.

I scrolled until I came across a video compilation of people of all ages celebrating with their families and friends after coming out of the closet. One man gave a speech in his living room that was met with happy tears and a kiss from a drag queen. A person of androgynous sorts danced around in a crowd to "I'm Comin' Out." One young woman cut open a cake, revealing a rainbow sponge. Around her, parents and friends cheered. They didn't complain that *rainbows were for everyone,* draw up a petition to have the Pride parade shut down, or warn the woman that her public display of joy was an affront to the straight folks in the room. Everyone just cheered.

The video looped around and started again.

The music was happy, but a pit of sadness nudged the pit of grief in my gut. My whole being felt so heavy.

"Do you think anyone in Tombstone would bake me a cake for coming out, Potato?" I asked out of instinct. Silence. But even in life, Sweet Potato Grace had never answered when I mused about coming out of the closet, or moving to a new city, or looking for a new job. She never reassured me that these dreams of mine were sins in Mama's eyes only.

Call me crazier than an ice cube in hell, but seeing those people giving their speeches and eating their cakes gave me an idea. I had a speech to give the next day. It was one that, if written correctly, would elicit sympathy and kindness from all my loved ones: Mama, Nene, Ashley, Wanda, June, and Fanny. Sympathy gave way to grace, and grace was what I needed if I was to take a step out of the mother-in-law suite where I lived and . . . live. For myself. For once. At the end of my eulogy, I would come out of the closet.

This idea carried me off with it, and I never did buy that alarm clock. But if you ask anyone who knows the truth about the barefoot strangers, they'll tell you why I also wouldn't need one, not ever again.

TWO

Combination cat-eulogy-and-coming-out speeches sneak up on a person, so I suggest always keeping a pencil nearby. Laptops are too impersonal for this sort of task. The words on the digital page are distant, colder than an ice chest in the backseat of a pickup truck. Who wants to hear *clack-clack-clack* while trying to conjure up beloved memories of their ferocious feline companion? Laptops are for college essays. Words written by pencil are warmer and fluffier, like a cat that has not yet scampered over the rainbow bridge.

Write with a pen? No way. A pen leaves no room for mistakes. Besides, the ink of a pen will run the moment it finds a tear on which to hitch a ride. The pencil's rubber eraser is a steadfast ally, and for its sacrifice, I say, "Thank you." I was willing to go through all the pencils and erasers in Tombstone, Texas to get this speech right. I wanted it to be a life-changing feat of oration.

Now, I know what y'all have been thinking: don't you have a country to celebrate on the Fourth of July, Pinky Elizabeth? Won't the town notice that you and your kin are absent from the parade and following festivities? Won't a combination of Fourth of July Lethal Peppers BBQ and funeral foodstuffs create a party in the stomach that, like the Moscato- and Yellow Tail-fueled nights of your high school years, will result in indigestion and regret? I acknowledged those concerns, even if they were never spoken outside of my thick Texas head. But the Fourth was the only day I could reserve a pavilion that week. Everyone else in Tombstone would be marching in the parade. Or watching the parade and reminiscing on the times they'd marched in the parade. Respectfully, I was relieved to be setting up a funeral instead. I was not in the mood for parades.

Pencil in hand, I began my draft with a triumphant beginning that explained why the funeral was called the Goat Cheese Memorial in the first place.

Sweet Potato Grace loved goat cheese, as I know many of you do. No. Terrible start. Inaccurate. No one loved goat cheese like Sweet Potato Grace did. June always said Sweet Potato's palate made her bougie, but I'm not sure she was using that term right. In my opinion, Sweet Potato Grace was just a cat who knew what she liked.

Sweet Potato Grace loved goat cheese, just like she loved barbecue, fresh air, and me. No. Too boastful. Yes, in my heart of hearts, I believe that Sweet Potato Grace appreciated the warm bed I provided her and the three square meals a day I fed her. Her face, of course, couldn't tell you that. Her eyebrows arched like those of a housewife who'd made an enemy out of her Botox lady. And that's why I loved that cat so much.

I discovered Sweet Potato Grace's love for goat cheese one day as she tried to steal it off my plate. I chuckled writing this line, because Mama didn't like me having a cat for that very reason. "Those doo-doo paws better not stink up my freshly steamed carpets!" she would yell as she passed by the mother-in-law suite. No cats in the bed, no cats swiping at her plates. Those were the rules. But I had begged to keep Sweet Potato Grace when I found her, and Nene Miriam had cooed at the sight of the scruffy kitty. Nene Miriam hadn't displayed any maternal instincts since 1984, so Mama concluded Sweet Potato Grace's presence might do us some good after all. Didn't mean that her paws belonged near the dishes, though.

Oh, screw it. Sweet Potato Grace was dead and she wouldn't swipe her paws at the dishware anymore. I kept the third version of the opening line and continued with the damn speech.

I wrote and revised for hours. I envisioned all of my closest lady friends and family sitting attentively, shedding tears as I spoke about my snarling, scrappy kitty. Applause and comfort would follow. If I were to be shunned for being a homosexual, my poise and eloquence might overshadow the reputation I left behind.

How would Mama, Nene, my friends, and my neighbors react to me coming out? If I knew, I wouldn't have been fidgeting like a man waiting to share his opinion. My friends and family might react any which way. Fanny didn't blab or cause a fuss when she caught me watching *The L Word* five years ago, but her reaction was about more than acceptance. Fanny did not want to have to work full-time at Swear-It's, the family store. That was my fate. Running me out of Tombstone would mean she'd have to take over. She didn't want that, Mama didn't want that, and anyone who wanted exact change didn't want that. (Mama's words, not mine.)

Mama had prophesied my role in the family business ever since I asked to play cash register with Ashley during our first playdate. "You'll balance the books beautifully," she'd say, making it her mantra before I stopped sucking my thumbs. When Mama retired, the store could be run by me or by someone in Tombstone whose last name wasn't Swear. Option two didn't make sense. The store was called Swear-It's. A Swear had to be in charge.

Would Mama kick me out of her house for being gay? At best, she would shake her head like I'd said the sky was chartreuse. Mama didn't change her mind on things, you see. It's what made her a fierce business owner and a respectable figurehead in Tombstone. But that stubbornness had a downside, too. A lot of her opinions should have been left in prior decades.

But I couldn't let fear tighten the knots already in my chest. There was no more time for questioning. The death of Sweet Potato Grace was hitting like a hailstorm. Whatever happened after the eulogy was just another dent in the hood of the truck.

With the speech complete and delicately placed in a crisp black folder, I assessed myself in the mirror. My brown hair hung limply, brushed and adorned with a clean velvet headband. I had dug out an old black dress from my cousin's or Uncle Someone's funeral and slapped it on my bony little frame. Blush gave my cheeks some color and mascara opened my sad brown eyes. I never had the extra cash on hand to buy the waterproof mascara, but I wasn't worried about it on the morning of July Fourth, because mascara tear stains are glamorous.

If emotion overcame me during the speech or in its aftermath, at least I could look like those beautiful, elegant, distraught women in the black-and-white movies they showed at the Bloat Hill Cinema. Oh, they were fabulous. The women who could cry, scream, and make demands. Fall and be caught in the arms of an admirer before their curls hit the floor. Heck, if they wanted to, they could sport a monocle and pose for a picture holding hands with a beautiful blonde babe.

Those women said whatever the hell they wanted and lived wherever they damn well pleased. Champagne glasses were a natural extension of their pearl-encrusted wrists, and they traveled to New York and Paris and all over the world—only to end up in romantic entanglements that ended with mascara tear stains. How many of them would have been lesbians if they'd been given the chance? Was Katharine Hepburn actually queer? I'd heard a rumor that she was.

In a past life, Sweet Potato Grace might have *been* one of those fabulous women. After all, she had no fears about expressing who she was and what she wanted. I had never been one of those women, and I knew that. I had never been on a plane and never been in love. I couldn't shake the deep conviction that champagne glasses were a waste of money, as Mama once told Fanny and me. Nothing was worth celebrating with champagne toasts in the town of Tombstone, because nothing out of the ordinary ever happened there, and that was how I was supposed to like life. Generations of our family lived the same life, as God intended, and none of the women in our knobby family tree ever found it necessary to buy champagne glasses or move to Paris—the one in Texas or the one in France. Tombstone was enough. Tombstone provided the women in our family with a thriving business despite the husbands, boyfriends, or fathers who tried to take everything away from us. I was supposed to give thanks for Tombstone. I was supposed to give thanks for everything being the same.

In the isolation of the mother-in-law suite, I felt prepared, if not confident, regarding my grand proclamation of differentness. Walking into the Swear home proper, however, I felt a shift in the winds. I needed to talk to Fanny, alone.

Right on time, at the sound of the front door opening, Mama came down and gave me a sympathetic look.

"I'm so sorry, Pinky," she said softly.

"It's okay. Thank you for driving Nene to the funeral."

"I loved that cat."

Like hell she did.

"I know I gave you grief about the couch in the mother-in-law suite," Mama continued. "But I don't care that she tore up that $10 couch. The price of the couch wasn't the point. The point was that cats have a personal vendetta against your Mama."

"Yes, ma'am."

"The point was that Sweet Potato Grace was no different than any other cat."

"Well."

"The point was that . . ." Here was the moment. "The point was that when you get up and leave me one day because you've found a man you think is oh so charming, or you've found a town you think is better than the one I raised you and your sister in, with nothing but grit, Lord forbid, I'll be the one to pick up that couch and replace it. Oh, my back aches more than a call girl after she finishes a double shift. I don't mind it, though. I don't mind."

"Mama."

"You know, couches don't come cheap these days."

Mama only got the couch for $10 because Mayor Johnston took pity on her. Both women had been dumped, hustled, and swindled by the same man—my biological father, may his soul squirm six feet under—in the chaos of Y2K. Mayor Johnston, feeling connected to Mama by way of calamity, gave her a deep discount for the couch and refused to charge shipping. Darryl

Johnston, Mayor Johnston's husband, simply dropped it off in the mother-in-law suite in exchange for an Alexander Hamilton, a glass of sweet tea, and a morsel of town gossip.

The alarm for Nene's morning medication rang. Mama wrapped up her monologue as she always did: "There's no point in leaving, changing, or shaking things up." As Mama went to her duties, Fanny poked her head out of the bathroom. I put a finger to my lips and waved my younger sister onto the front porch. She rolled her eyes, put her makeup brush down, and followed me outside with only one set of lashes on. A good and loyal sister, indeed.

"Are you going to need the car after the funeral?" she asked, shutting the door behind her.

"No. I have a question for you. I was writing the eulogy, and—"

"Oh, Pinky, I know you're nervous. Trust me, it won't be like last time."

The last time I gave a public speech was in 2009 when I volunteered to emcee the Our Lady of the Obituary Youth Group Talent Show. Afterward, Sister Krista reminded me I was forgiven in the eyes of the Lord for boring the audience. "Besides," she had said, "most types of humor are sinful anyway."

"It's not that, Fanny," I said. "I think . . . I think I'm going to tell them."

"Tell who what?"

"Tell everyone . . . at the funeral . . . about myself."

Her eyes bulged, making the fake lashes on one side even more prominent. "Pinky."

"Fanny. It's time."

"Why now? Are you thinking about leaving Tombstone?"

"No."

"Well, you might want to consider it, if you're already being so bold."

"You really think I'll have to?"

"Why subject yourself to the judgments of the people in this town if you're not going to leave? Wait." She grabbed my wrist. "Are you dating someone?"

"No."

"Oh." She let my hand fall. "Boring."

"Thank you, sister," I said, reconsidering my plan. "I don't know what's been going through my head since Sweet Potato Grace died."

"And you haven't been seeing what they say on the news, either. Well, I'm here for you if you want to talk about things . . . outside of the homosexual experience. I've never had one of those."

"I'm well aware you are Tombstone's favorite heterosexual."

"And she is always going to be here for her sister."

"But don't *you* want to move?"

"Wouldn't that be grand?" Fanny got a glossy look in her eye whenever she talked about moving to California to become an influencer. But she only ever mentioned it to me. "But if we both leave," she said, "who is going to take care of Mama like Mama takes care of Nene?"

"Can we figure that out tomorrow?"

"Sure." She sighed. "If you're disowned, they probably won't let you near the doctor's office anyway."

"What would me being a lesbian have to do with the doctor's office?"

"Keep your voice down!" Fortunately, none of our neighbors

were out watering their grass. "We live in Texas, Pinky. I don't know. I don't pay attention to the laws. Just—"

A rap on the window interrupted her warning. Mama stood with her hands on her hips.

"Get your face on, Fanny!" Mama said. Her voice sounded like a scuba diver's, but the message was received. "A pageant queen looks symmetrical."

"You hear? I need time to look symmetrical!" she whined.

"I'll take my own car to go set up, Mama," I said. "Y'all can take your time." As Mama left the window, Fanny turned back to me.

"All you have in this world is women, Pinky," she whispered, echoing Mama's other favorite mantra. "But you also can't trust your lovers . . . so I'm not sure where that leaves you."

"I don't think Mama spoke those particular words with me in mind."

"Well, protect yourself, anyhow." She opened the screen door and left me to think.

Instead, I drove myself to the abandoned gas station at the edge of town, where I could bellow out a nice, hearty scream.

THREE

If you ever find yourself driving through the town of Tombstone, first of all, I'm sorry. Second, after you pick up some Lethal Peppers BBQ or roadside coffee and kolaches from Ms. Novak's, put aside time to pull into the abandoned Exhaust 'n' Rest. It's past Tickled Pink Drive, past Honeysuckle Street, and a quick right on Dusty Road. At first glance, the empty lot doesn't look like much, but in my humble and probably misinformed opinion, it's the best place to have a good scream of agony.

Inside one's car, of course. Screaming in public is unladylike, and the people of Tombstone could teach a college course on the art of gossip. Sure, the people of Tombstone also don't frequent abandoned gas stations, but I've never wanted to take my chances. I've never been one to gamble, and besides, casinos are illegal in the state of Texas.

So I don't scream out in the open where people can see me. I don't scream under the boarded-up windows, nor do I scream underneath the station's sign, which is a relic of a long-past administration and still advertises gas at $1.25 a gallon. (I can never remember who Mama or Mayor Johnston or the Swear-It's shoppers are currently blaming for the rise in gas prices. It seems to change every day.) Anyway, my preferred place to scream is inside my car, my 2005 Subaru Outback, in the last parking space, tucked away and out of sight. After a good scream, I typically turn the keys and drive back home, where I soothe my throat with hot tea. During the pandemic, when shops were closed, the gym was shuttered, and all people could do was look at the inside of their houses, everyone developed their little habits for coping with the calamity. Screaming at the Exhaust 'n' Rest was my habit. It stuck.

Was I ready to come out of the closet? Was I just drowning in an ocean of grief? Was my grief just a kiddie pool? Was I being dramatic about everything?

Grief and sadness and indecision and fear threatened to rip up my brain cells like shingles in a tornado. I sat in my car, closed my eyes, and let out a holler. My vocal cords rattled and my fingernails dug into my palms and I tried to keep my head on straight. The first time I screamed like this during COVID, I surprised myself with the voice that came out of me. By 2022, I was accustomed to the mature wail, a gift from generations past.

I kept my eyes shut for another inhale and exhale. My mind was clear. I was okay.

Then I opened my eyes and let out a yelp.

Parked directly across from my Subaru was an orange Volkswagen van. I blinked, feeling like my eyes were going to pop out of my head and bounce off the windshield. I swear on all Swears living and dead that when I'd closed my eyes to scream, that van hadn't been anywhere within my line of sight. I took another deep breath. How loud did I scream? How did I not hear this van chugging around the corner and into the Exhaust 'n' Rest parking lot?

I had never seen a van like this outside of old movies. And I had never seen people like the ones inside, either. A man sat in the driver's seat, wearing a goofy grin like the Cheshire cat. A plume of smoke and the tint of the windshield covered up the rest of his face. My eyes locked onto the woman's in the passenger seat and I almost yelped a second time. She was blonde, with big green eyes and a crooked, blushing smile. She had longer hair than the woman in the Westclox ad, but I immediately thought I was looking at the same person. I shook my head. This was 2022. That ad was from 1922. I was just seeing all blonde women the same. I wondered if face blindness was a symptom of grief. I wondered why a woman in an old alarm clock ad was still at the front of my mind.

Both the woman in the van and its driver looked eerily happy. I was offended, to be completely honest. I'd never known any decent folk to be entertained by the wails of a young gay woman in an abandoned gas station. If anything, my scream should have been a sign that danger was afoot. But they maintained calm, wide grins as I pinched myself back into reality and put my keys into the ignition.

Twenty minutes later, I tried to put the van out of my mind and focus on my posture as I prepared to give my eulogy. Shoulders back. Chin out. Mind sharp, but not looking anyone in the eye. Just like Mama taught me.

My gaze was drawn to one of the wooden beams that held up the accessible covered pavilion right next to the parking lot. If you squint and know where to look on the beam, you can see half a *W* where nine-year-old Wanda tried to carve her name before June admonished her for the vandalism. Under the pavilion were two wooden benches with more than enough room for Mama, Fanny, and Ashley to sit. Nene sat in her wheelchair, hands politely folded over the crocheted blanket that Fanny had oh-so-*beautifully* made two years ago. "Hasn't she done it again, Mom?" Mama had asked Nene when Fanny presented the blanket. "Fanny doesn't drop a stitch. What a little lady. A perfect child."

Mama, Fanny, Nene, and Ashley. Before I could ask myself where my other two best friends were, I made excuses for them. Wanda must have gone to the Fourth of July parade because her sister was in one of the floats. June must have gone because Michael wanted to go. Oh, well. Four people with kind hearts willing to attend a feline funeral was more than many people had in their lives. They'd all dug out black attire, even in the mugginess of July. I was a lucky person. *I should be grateful,* I told myself. *Maybe I shouldn't slobber on the hands that feed me.*

A dozen goat cheese and basil pesto sandwiches, which I had made in lieu of sleeping the night before, sat covered in plastic wrap on the bench for the mourners. Thank goodness I would have so many leftovers. I couldn't imagine I would have the energy to make anything besides a call to Epitaph Pizza after the memorial anyway. And if I was kicked out of town for loving women the way I did, the leftovers could fuel me on my drive out of Texas.

I cleared my throat to cut the hum of the July heat and began the eulogy: "I discovered Sweet Potato Grace's love for goat cheese one day as she tried to steal it off my plate." I spoke slowly and carefully. If I mucked up a single word, I would never be allowed to give another eulogy. It would be the Our Lady of the Obituary Youth Group Talent Show of 2009 all over again. That would be my legacy. *Remember that lesbian,*

Pinky Swear? The one who couldn't give a speech to save her soul? Devastating.

Do it for Sweet Potato, I reminded myself.

"I first found Miss Sweet Potato Grace on the side of the road right here in Tombstone. I could tell she was a native Texas gal because she was heading straight for the dumpster near the barbecue place." No one laughed. Geez Louise. Sister Krista had been right all along.

"When I approached her, I noticed that she was especially excited about the sweet potato fries. This little Potato needed a home, and I gave her one. She was resistant, of course. You could see it in her eyes. I always needed a second person to help clip her nails—thank you, Ashley. It took months for Sweet Potato to snuggle in my bed."

Mama cleared her throat with the heft of a smoker with a cedar allergy amid the Texas summer. I could hear her old protests: *The only animal that should lie beside you at night is the one that will eventually pay your child support.*

Mama's protests were of no use now. I continued my eulogy.

"She always had a grumpy look in her eye and she never came around to receiving any pets below her chin. But she showed love in other ways. I've never met a cat so diligent about greeting their person at the door. And after a while, she didn't squirm when I picked her up. But golly, that grumpy look in her eye never went away. My Sweet Potato Grace had a glare that won over the hearts of Tombstone."

Oh, I should have practiced. This wasn't the crescendo I had intended to write. Sweet Potato Grace deserved better. I was a sinner without a sense of humor.

"Everyone who ever saw a picture of Sweet Potato Grace

in my wallet or on my Instagram feed fell in love with her. For someone so angry, she brought a lot of joy into our lives. And for that, I have to say thank you to my gal, my friend, my fellow goat cheese fan, Sweet Potato Grace."

I took a deep breath to stall. The first part of my speech was over, and I had a choice to make. The speech could end right here and nothing would change. I had been in the closet my whole life and my eyes were adjusted to the darkness. Or, I could take a step outside and look at the vast, overwhelming sky of possibility. I took an exhale and squeezed the folder with my thumb.

It was time to step into the sunshine.

But then I saw the orange Volkswagen van turning into the park.

Was it following me?

As the van chugged its way into a parking spot just a few steps away from the pavilion, it parted the Red Sea of boring, sticky air that hung over Tombstone. It bopped along to the music that sang from its array of windows. Everyone turned their head to see who was making such a racket.

One by one, the passengers hopped out of the van. The driver stood by giving each of them a hand, so I had time to take in his groovy attire. His round yellow sunglasses took up the top half of his face and his scraggly beard covered the rest. He wore a denim bucket hat that had seen better days and his long, shiny hair brought shame upon my shoulder-length cut. He must have gotten those regular, healthy trims Mama was always bugging me to get.

A tie-dye shirt and baggy pants finished off the look, which reminded me of a "1970s Man" costume from Spirit Halloween.

He didn't wear anything on his feet. No socks, no shoes at all.

As he helped the other seven passengers out of the van, I noticed that none of them wore shoes either.

Most of them wore "1970s Man" attire too: bell-bottom jeans too hot for summer in Texas, brown vests with long fringe, headbands made out of ripped fabric. Had these people driven into town from a historical reenactment of Woodstock? Tombstone was only a few hours from Marfa, a West Texas town known for its art exhibits and droves of quirky musicians, but I didn't know of any festivals taking place in Marfa this time of year. It was too dang stifling. I looked at my phone, two benches over. It was on, in case June or Wanda called, but the phone never lit up.

"Are these friends of yours?" Fanny asked, taking in the group. The longer I looked at them, the more details I found that didn't add up. One fellow wore a tight T-shirt that said "I Heart New York" and mismatched, striped pants. Another had an ascot of pink satin. The blonde who looked too much like the woman from the ad sported a pink pearl necklace. I wracked my brain. Were the pearls in the ad pink? Memories of the day before sloshed around like suds in a bucket.

"I don't believe I've met them," I said. It caused Mama to scrunch her face at the approaching group. They didn't seem to take any notice of us. They were laughing and twirling. The only other woman besides the blonde had brought a hula hoop and a boombox, the likes of which I hadn't seen since I was walking by the Checkmate Pawn Shop on the way home from elementary school.

"You don't *believe* you have?" said Mama. "I think you'd know if you did." As the group came closer to the pavilion, she yelled: "Just what do you think you're doing here?"

"Folks around town say it's the Fourth of July!" the driver said through his cigarette. "We're fixing to set up one heck of a barbecue."

"Cookout, honey," another man said, putting his hands on the driver's shoulders. His dark, curly hair was tied up in a big bun on top of his head, with a few strands falling down like wind chimes to frame his tan face. He looked at Mama, who no doubt was scrunching her face harder, and dropped his hands.

"Cookout!" the driver repeated emphatically.

"Not right here, you're not," Mama growled. "We're having a dead cat's funeral." The group's faces fell as they took in the scene.

"I guess it would be more of a memorial service," I offered. "Her remains are still at the vet in Bloat Hill, and I'm just . . . I'm so sorry, I don't have enough sandwiches."

"Bread!" The driver snapped his fingers and looked at his friends, who all looked straight back. "Bread. *There is not a thing that is more positive than bread,* and yet we forgot it! Should have brought Dostoevsky along for the ride. Let's go find us some bread and butter before we get this thing started."

Everyone turned back toward the van at the second snap of his fingers. The driver stayed behind to look at us, finally taking the cigarette out of his mouth. "You know how food shopping is. We learned a long time ago that it's best we all go together." He looked to me with a sparkle in his eyes. "Do you mind showing me on our map how to get to the nearest grocery store?"

I worried this might be the final straw for Mama. We'd closed Swear-It's for the holiday, and she hated knowing that she was losing money. But she just sniffed, stood up, and plucked a sandwich from the pile.

Before I could follow the driver to his map, Ashley power walked toward me like she had weights on her wrists and a sweatband on her head. "Pinky," she said, looking at me with perfume-sweet sympathy. "This was very sweet. I am so sorry for your loss. It's about time for Baby McKinleigh to—"

"Thank you for coming, Ashley," I mumbled, distracted. She seemed relieved to be interrupted.

Ashley nodded. "Do you want me to go talk to those people with you?"

"No, I got it."

"Okay. Do you want me to talk to June and Wanda for you? They should have been here." She put a hand on my shoulder. "It's not right that they missed this for another look at the same parade we've been watching for twenty years."

"No. I can talk to them."

Ashley looked disappointed, which only added to the mess of feelings I would have to sort through later. "Mmhmm. Well. Guess I'll see you at the Sewing Circle." Before I could offer a sandwich to go, she snatched the handle of her baby carrier and was off. She raised an eyebrow as she assessed the folks parked next to her.

✿

In my folder, two pages of stark honesty remained unread. The time to flip the world upside down was out of reach now that the strangers had asked for directions. I couldn't be impolite. I closed my folder but kept it under my arm as I approached the van.

Trying not to squint, I searched for any sign that the driver was someone I knew from the grapevine. Wanda's ex-boyfriend, back from deployment to right his wrongs? No, the ex had a crew cut cleaner than the whistle he blew whenever he picked Wanda up from a night out with the girls. Joe Clark's no-good nephew? He was supposed to come to Tombstone for the Fourth of July festivities, but no one had mentioned he would bring a whole caravan of rag-tag friends. I was stumped.

"Hi," I said when I got to the van, readjusting my posture. "Normally I would recommend Swear-It's, but it's closed today. The Walmart is that way." I pointed beyond the park. "Take a right on Tickled Pink Drive and it's two streets from the first stoplight. I don't think you should need a map."

"Thank you, sister," the guy said.

I froze. Sister? Me? Was this a half-brother of mine? Had my biological father taken his misdeeds outside of Tombstone?

"Are you," I asked, "the son of a man named Jenson?"

The driver chuckled at the panic in my eyes. "No, my pop's a fellow named Timothy Brown, and I highly doubt you know him. I apologize for the disruption, ma'am. We're supposed to be in this town, but not right here, right now, I guess." Behind the driver, the passenger was looking at me with a gentle smile. Her freckles danced in the sunshine. I felt myself blushing as the driver handed me a little card.

"I'm Blaze," he said. "This must be for you."

The front of the card displayed a faded old picture of a maroon-and-yellow circus tent. On the back were eight words written in cursive:

Take off your shoes and join the circus.

"I'm Pinky," I said, shoving the card into my pocket. The

woman in the passenger seat was still smiling at me as the van pulled out of the lot.

"Sorry for your loss!" the driver yelled as they reversed and turned out of the park. Mama and Nene were already eating their second goat cheese sandwiches when I returned to the pavilion. Fanny's lips were puckered in worry.

"Who were they?" she whispered.

"Not a clue."

"Looked like a group straight out of a documentary on the dangers of marijuana."

"That's not nice, Fanny."

"It wasn't an insult. Are you . . . finished with your speech?"

The strangers had made such an impression that I'd almost forgotten about my big announcement. I took it as a sign from the universe. Maybe from Sweet Potato Grace herself.

"For today, yes, Fanny."

"Well, it was a wonderful speech."

"Thank you."

She turned me away from Mama and Nene. "But if you ever want to finish it . . ."

"Yes?"

"Run it by me first? Just in case. I got nervous. I'm sorry for your loss, Pinky."

"I understand."

It was time for a goat cheese sandwich.

FOUR

The next day at work, I stood behind the Swear-It's cash register contemplating the card with the circus tent on it. When no customers were looking, I twirled it around in my fingers. *Why are the barefoot people here? Where did they come from?*

The card offered no answer.

Strangers only come to Tombstone for two reasons: the land is cheap, and the government doesn't bug you. At least, that's what those California types say when they park their Teslas in front of City Hall, asking for the nearest business registry and car charging station. Sorry, Brent. Sorry, Bradley. No charging stations here. Austin is over a hundred miles away. Permit office is on the second floor.

I appreciate the business that these Patagonia-clad strangers bring to Tombstone, but it takes more than just one person to change a place where folks like everything to stay the same. Unless the call is coming from inside the house, the phone will keep on ringing.

When the experimental coffee shop came to town in 2002? They were roasted.

When the oxygen bar came to town in 2004? They were choked out.

When the yoga studio opened its doors in 2008? Tombstone was so bent out of shape that the studio closed before the year was done.

Every time a new business closes down, Mama chuckles and enjoys a celebratory whiskey neat. She likes knowing that Swear-It's will last longer than any stranger's nonsense. Also, any time men fail, Mama feels immense joy.

I keep Swear-It's listed as a flower shop on Google Maps as an ode to its humble beginnings. Nene was just a lady with floral dreams in a dusty town when she opened the place. Now, the flowers live in one small corner to make room for cans of foodstuffs, handmade candles, fancy root beer, one specific brand of olive oil, and other items that Tombstone's Gro-Sir-Ee used to stock during the twentieth century. When the big box stores squeezed the Gro-Sir-Ee out of business, Mama was left without her nightly "I Can't Believe This Was Made from a Tree" root beer. So she surveyed everyone in town, sent away for that and the other things that had gone missing from their routines, and stocked them at Swear-It's. Mama has since made lucrative opportunities out of the town's other failed businesses, and I can't help but admire her for it.

When Tombstone said "See you latte" to the experimental coffee shop, Mama got their espresso machine for cheap and started serving hot cups of Tombstone's favorite "Not Those Baked Beans" coffee.

When the yoga shop folded in half, Mama bought the yoga mats for cheap and crafted them into play mats for the town's toddlers.

Mama didn't do anything after the oxygen bar took its final breath, because the concept of an oxygen bar was the stupidest thing Mama had ever heard of.

"And trust me," Mama told Fanny and me as we dusted the counters, "the man who begat you said a *lot* of stupid things. He told me the earth was flat; to which I told him he could go fall off of it."

Everyone who visited Swear-It's on July 5 had three points of business: to pick up their groceries, offer me condolences, and ask who had crashed the Goat Cheese Memorial for Sweet Potato Grace.

"Terrible to hear about your puss, Pinky. Now, did you get the names of the folks who crashed the funeral?"

"I cannot imagine the sorry state you are in over Sweet Potato Grace. Did those strangers in the Volkswagen tell you what state they were driving in from?"

"My condolences on your kitty. Was there anyone in that van named Chip? I have some unfinished business with a man named Chip . . ."

On and on the questions went, and each time, I answered with everything I knew. Well, not everything. I didn't tell anyone about the "join us" business card, and I didn't tell anyone about the passenger who looked exactly like a lesbian from the 1920s.

Probably a dozen customers asked me about the funeral before Mama and Nene arrived to check on the store and drive me home. As the door opened and Mama wheeled Nene in, I could feel a change in the wind. It smelled like lilacs.

Lilacs are nice, but they're not native to Texas. When their perfumy smell travels on the wind, the people of Tombstone get antsy. New smells and new sounds are considered suspicious.

Nene Miriam's legs didn't work, but her nose sure did. Before I could say hello, she said, "Smell that, Pinky?"

"Smell what?" I asked.

"I don't like it."

"What's troubling you, Nene?"

Mama chimed in. "There hasn't been a change like this since those Mormons tried to set up a mission here in 2018. You didn't smell how sweet they smelt."

"Change is hard," I said, looking at the corner where we kept the potted plants. I once brought Sweet Potato Grace to Swear-It's, shortly after I adopted her, and she used a pothos for her litter box. It was her first and last time visiting.

"There's only one change that makes sense in this town," Mama said, putting her arm around me. She wasn't thinking about Sweet Potato Grace at all. "I think it's about time I handed the store down to you. I took over from your Nene when I was twenty-three, after all. You've got a few months left of your youth."

I looked up at Mama with a grimace. "Now, I know your pussy dying and all is tragic," Mama said, "but you need to learn the ropes here."

I didn't want to talk shop. Not on July 5.

But no tragedy or holiday could keep Mama from thinking about Swear-It's. She was so proud to take it over from Nene and keep it running, especially as a single mother. I knew I was lucky to have her as an example. But I wasn't as enthusiastic as she was about taking the torch. I wanted to stall.

"There's a lot to think about first," I said. "Like . . . what if I want to change the name of the store?"

I might as well have told them I was going to paint the walls the color of shit.

"I'm not letting you call it The Sweet Potato Grace Grocery," Mama said. "I don't plan on retiring until Christmas, anyhow. I just want to start some paperwork. Nothing to fuss over."

I shrugged, helpless.

Mama seemed to take this as agreement, because she moved on to the next bee in her bonnet: "Have you heard anything new about those folks in the van? Do you know if one of them was named Chip? Mr. Keen down the street wants to know. His brother told me he owes quite a bit of money to a man named Chip."

FIVE

Ashley, Wanda, and June had never been too helpful when it came to romantic advice or employment decisions, but when it came to gossip, I couldn't have asked for a better group of friends.

We've called our gatherings the "Sewing Circle" since tenth grade because "Prank-calling Oklahoma Pizza Shops after a Bottle of Wanda's Dad's Whiskey" doesn't roll off the tongue as easily. I can't sew. Ashley can't sew. Wanda is good at stealing clothes from department stores in Bloat Hill, but that doesn't count. June knows how to sew, but June knows how to do everything. At least, that's what she'll tell you after fifteen minutes of preamble. She gets to the point she's trying to make . . . eventually.

"And Michael was like, 'Why the heck do you need bananas anyway? You're making a cake,'" June was saying to Ashley when I arrived at June's house. "Men are so stupid. I told him, 'Michael, don't you know that you can replace eggs with bananas? All the recipe needs is a binding agent. Eggs and bananas are binding agents.' When we took home economics in high school, Michael was taking driver's ed. But Michael's sister is lactose intolerant this month, so he should know better. Why do we have to train our husbands?"

"I don't have a husband," Ashley said.

"Oh!" June said, playfully smacking her forehead with her diamond-encrusted left hand. "Why do I always forget? You have a baby, but not a husband."

"Hi, June," I said, sliding my voice into the conversation. June stood up and placed her hands on mine in an attempt to grab the bottle of "Pinot Evil Red Blend" I had brought from Swear-It's. June couldn't wrap her little hands around mine if she stretched them every day, but the effort was there. I handed her the bottle with a smile.

Everything about June was tiny: her mousy face, the low bun she'd worn since middle school, the slim frame that made every cheerleader at Tombstone High hate her. (Actually, they might have been more upset that she told the whole school about Gina Bailey's boob job, but June always preferred to believe they were jealous. Cheerleaders bullied the protagonists of high school movies. Her victimization made her a main character. "It was a rite of passage," she'd say whenever we cracked open one of our old yearbooks.)

"Pinky," June said, lowering her voice. "I was so sorry to hear about Sweet Potato Grace."

"Thank you."

She gestured to a bouquet of bright red roses in a vase on the table. (Also purchased from Swear-It's, on my day off.) "We got these for you. All of us. We feel terrible about your loss."

"I appreciate that."

I would have appreciated them showing up to eat the goat

cheese sandwiches more, but two weeks had already gone by and I had more important things to talk about.

"And thank you for the wine," June said. "Wanda would love some. Don't you look comfy, Wanda?" Wanda did look comfy lying on June's velvet couch, although her big hair and oversized cardigans gave her a cozy look wherever she went. Wanda's specialty had always been big hair, big sweaters, and a big personality. I tried to be like her all through high school, but all it got me was a bad perm and moths in my closet.

"Fill 'er up!" Wanda said, grabbing her empty glass and shaking out her curls. As she walked with me to the kitchen, she whispered, "I finished a whole glass listening to June's story about bananas. My gift to you is that I won't ask her to repeat it."

"I bet Sally Granger doesn't know that you can use a banana as a replacement for an egg," Ashley was saying when we returned to the couch. "She eats raw buffalo meat now. Posted about it on Instagram. Apparently, celebrities are doing it."

"I bet she's just too lazy to cook meat," Wanda said.

"Actually," June said, "she's probably eating the raw buffalo meat because it has a certain type of enzyme in it that cooked meat doesn't have. When you cook meat, a lot of things get burned off, and those health fanatics want to get as much as they can in their, like, two meals a day. Also, raw meat is easier to digest."

"I was being sarcastic, June."

"There is no way you're getting me to eat raw meat," Ashley said. "It'll go straight to my milk, probably hurt the baby. Sally Granger doesn't have any littles, does she? Oh, god. I don't want to intrude, but if she's putting them in harm's way . . ."

"Have you seen her abs?" Wanda asked. She had lain back

down on the couch and was applying a face mask. I took the spot next to her, slightly sunken in from where I'd sat in it over the years. "There's no way Sally has any children with those abs," Wanda continued. "Posted a photo of herself in a bikini about two weeks ago. I might start eating raw meat if it makes you look like that. Maybe I'll snag myself a boyfriend."

"If you had taken a moment away from thinking about your crow's feet and walked your human feet over to the park two weeks ago," Ashley said, "you might have feasted your eyes on the first eligible bachelors Tombstone has seen since that motorcycle broke down and the Iron Pigs stunk up the diner."

The wait was over. Pleasantries had finished. We could get down to business. "Have you heard anything more about them?" I asked, trying not to sound too eager. "About what they're doing in town? What their business is? A man drove the van, but a blonde woman was in the passenger seat . . ."

The corners of Ashley's mouth fell. I knew she'd been giving Wanda and June an opportunity to apologize for their absence at the funeral, but my disappointment wasn't as important as my curiosity. And I was tired of hearing people say they were sorry for my loss.

"I heard they're all barefoot," Wanda said. "Skip down at the gas station said the driver hopped out of the van with his piggies out. Then one of the passengers came into the store and bought some snacks. They were barefoot, too! Unsanitary."

"That could mean they're part of a religious movement," June said. "Maybe a cult. Or they're just a bit queer. But not in the homosexual sense."

"Possibly in the homosexual sense," Wanda said. "Who knows? Everyone at the parade heard their van drive by during the moment of silence for Tombstone's be-loved troops. Blasting 'Fortunate Son.'"

"What does that have to do with being gay?" I asked.

Wanda threw her hands up in defense. "That's just what I heard."

"Why are you so curious, Pinky?" Ashley said. "You're not usually one to gossip. I mean, I'm proud of you, but this isn't like you."

"I don't know," I said. "Just because they were at the memorial, is all."

"Are you sweet on the driver?" Wanda said. "Do you like guys with long hair? Makes sense why you don't have a boyfriend, if you like guys with long hair."

"A few guys at Blinn had long hair and she never said a word," June said, waving Wanda off. "That's not it. Why *are* you so curious, Pink?"

All their eyes were on me. I couldn't tell them that I was actually more curious about the *passenger* in the car. Coming out to my friends felt more daunting than coming out to Mama and Nene. I'd lied to them for years, talking up boys I would never date or only thought I was attracted to. I'd shared beds and snuggles with these girls since we were reading The Baby-Sitters Club. If I told them I was gay, would they go back through every slumber party, every compliment, every moment of our friendship and recoil? I harbored no secret romantic feelings for any of my best friends. But I had harbored a huge secret about who I was for close to ten years.

Fortunately, I didn't have to change that now. Because I had brought along something more exciting than a penchant for the fairer sex.

I reached into my pocket and showed them the business card. "The driver handed me this at the funeral. He said his name was Blaze. Possibly Blaze Brown, although I'm not sure. I don't know what it means."

Wanda sat up, grabbed the card, and held it to the light like a counterfeit bill. June took to her phone, presumably to look up Blaze Brown on Facebook or Instagram or whatever social media site she used for sleuthing. Ashley knitted her eyebrows at me, silently urging me to return to the subject of our friends' absence from the funeral, but I shook my head. It wasn't the time.

"Nothing on Facebook, Instagram, or Google," June said. "Shocking."

Next, they looked up the phrase on the card.

"Here's a banner with similar wording, but it's really old," June said.

"Well, that's obviously not theirs," Ashley said. "They looked like they were in their twenties. I wonder if they have children? A van is no place for children."

"From what I hear, they're probably more interested in marijuana than motherhood," Wanda said. "And apparently that Blaze guy still smokes cigarettes. Grow up! Get a vape."

For once, my friends were stumped. "Should I take this to my silks teacher in Bloat Hill?" Wanda asked. "She might know of circus performers in the area."

"I don't think there's any reason to take this past town limits," I said. "I was thinking maybe I could ask them myself."

"Do you hear that?" Ashley said, eyes wide. "Pinky wants to investigate! That could be so much better than Google!"

"I don't know," Wanda said. "I mean, I want to figure out who these people are and what they're up to. Who the heck comes to this town for just no reason? They don't look like they have any business starting a business. But we should be careful. I'm sure we can find something online if we keep trying. And if we can't, maybe we should steer clear. Who's not on the internet these days?"

"Serial killers," June said.

"I didn't get the sense that the folks in the van were serial killers," I ventured. "Blaze seemed real sweet, and the passenger in his van looked like she couldn't hurt a fly. Can't I just talk to them myself?"

"What if that lady passenger's been kidnapped by the rest of them?" Wanda asked in a low voice.

"Uh . . ."

"That's how they get you," Wanda said. Ashley and June nodded. "If they can't recruit you, they scoop you up like Patty Hearst."

"Just because they're barefoot doesn't make them a cult," I said.

My friends rolled their eyes in different directions.

"Have you been watching all those documentaries about the cults, Pinky?" Wanda asked. "They've all got something. The NXIVM people had those sashes. The Manson girls had those X's on their foreheads. The MLM people had their leggings."

"Wanda . . ." Ashley warned. She hadn't joined any MLMs during the pandemic, but her sister had joined just about all of them.

"Wanda's not far off, Ashley," June said. "Cults aren't just freak shows. All of the leaders are sweet as pie until they stick a brand on you. So maybe that woman in the van is a Mother God and the rest of those fellas are her fathers."

"What in the heck are you talking about?" I asked, a little too loudly.

"A *lot* of cult documentaries are streaming right now," Ashley said. "You should watch some. I didn't think there was anything left on Netflix a year into the pandemic, but I was wrong. Then I got into the podcasts, the news stories . . . I don't watch that stuff when the littles are up, I'm afraid they'll develop phobias. But when they nap, Mama's talking cults."

"I've seen *every* documentary about cults," June said. "It makes me so glad to live in Tombstone where I know and trust people. We know everything about everyone who's from here."

"We left Tombstone to go to college," I started.

"And look what good that did us," June said. "We ended up right back where we started."

June was hard to argue with. June also believed I was a straight woman, so I knew she was at least wrong about one thing. But the last time I tried to prove June wrong, she created a whole PowerPoint presentation about the subject we disagreed on to show her intellect. (We had a lot of free time during COVID.)

I considered creating a PowerPoint on the importance of showing up to your best friend's cat's funeral, but I knew I wouldn't have the time. I was going to find out who these barefoot strangers were, and I wasn't going to get kidnapped in the process.

SIX

What does one wear to infiltrate a group of barefoot strangers who have sent a whole town into whispers? Circus getup? Beads? I had given away most of my non-practical clothes during the pandemic, so I settled on jeans, a T-shirt, and sandals to expose the toes.

During the first month of the barefoot strangers' presence in town, two juicy morsels made their way from one side of Tombstone to the other. First: they'd moved into a house owned by a California landlord who came to Tombstone in 2019 and tried to open a climbing gym. At the crux of the pandemic, the man sent himself back home with nothing but a failed business to his name—and the deed to 101 Bluebonnet Drive. (Mama bought the leftover rope from the gym and sold it to Ashley's Aunt Brenda, who fashioned it into scratching posts for kitties at her animal rescue.) The house at Bluebonnet Drive had been empty since the California occupation, but in July 2022 it came to house six men, two women, and zero shoe racks.

Second: they liked to have cookouts at Peace Valley Park during the day. None of them had applied for employment or a business license, which raised eyebrows. Instead, from the moment they took up residence in Tombstone, these barefoot folk bought meat, smoked it, ate it, sang songs, played instruments, and went home at sunset. Not a bad routine, if you ask me. But no one asked me.

✿

I tried twice to join these cookouts, unsuccessfully. Each time I biked past the parking lot and laid eyes on the site of Sweet Potato's funeral, I found myself pedaling on until I reached the Exhaust 'n' Rest. Finally, on a day off, I decided to join the speed walkers, stroller-pushers, and bench-sitters and amble in on foot. Easy does it.

They were there—six of them. Blaze, the driver with the beard and the bucket hat, sat on the pavilion bench that my goat cheese sandwiches had occupied just a few weeks prior. His collared shirt blared a strange, swirly pattern of mustard, orange, and purple, and it flapped open as he took long swigs of his beer. Two men danced to music blasting out of the van. One wore a cowboy hat, the other a conductor's cap, but they skipped in unison on the concrete pavilion floor. A fourth man tended to the grill outside the pavilion. I couldn't see his front, but his tush was wiggling along to the beat as he flipped burgers, hot dogs, and a tofu-like slab of beige that must have been brought in from out of town.

Everyone was still barefoot.

I tried to remember the warning signs of cults that my friends had listed. Crosses on their foreheads? No, they didn't have those. Sashes? Didn't see any. The more I kept looking, the more I simply saw joy, bumping the stale sadness of the memorial out of the atmosphere. I couldn't remember the last time I felt as free-spirited as they looked.

I need to stop looking at their butts, I told myself. Maybe this is why no one ever questions which team I play for.

Paints, canvases, and art supplies were scattered about another table nearby. Two people, a man and a woman, fed each other hot dogs and giddily laughed at what was left behind on their lips. I squinted and saw the woman wasn't the passenger from the Volkswagen van. The freckled passenger wasn't there at all. Had she already high-tailed it out of Tombstone? I wouldn't blame her if she had.

Seeing that the blonde-haired, freckled woman was absent, I felt tempted to turn around or walk right past the group of barefoot strangers. What business did I have asking questions of a mostly bare-chested group of men anyway? I didn't need to stick my nose in. My friends were right. I wasn't one to gossip, even if that meant I had nothing to talk about with most of my neighbors. What was I doing here in the first place? Where was the passenger who rode alongside Blaze?

As I tried to justify backing out of my mission, Blaze took another swig of beer and caught my eye. With a satisfied sigh and a wave, he called me over to say hello. Fine. I would be polite. And I would investigate the barefoot strangers, even if it didn't involve seeing the freckled passenger. How would I know, I wondered, if they were involved with an MLM?

"Howdy-ho, friend!" Blaze yelled.

"Hi?" I ran through some small-talk options in my head. *The weather sure is nice. The town is gearing up for elections. Avocado prices have just soared, haven't they?*

"Hope you don't mind the music. We haven't had the chance

to listen to Talking Heads for quite some time. Their first album didn't come out until 1977!"

I blinked. "I don't mind at all. My math teacher used to play them in class all the time."

"Right on!" Blaze said. He lifted his glasses and gave me a wink. Light ricocheted off his twinkling eyes like kickballs off a metal pole and straight into my soul.

I could feel the tension in my shoulders. How long had they been scrunched up like that? I took a deep breath and let them down.

"Anyway, Pinky," he said. "Glad you're here. I'm Blaze."

"You remembered my name?" I remembered his, of course, but he seemed a lot more memorable than I was.

"Of course. But I've been wondering. Is Pinky your real name, or are you pulling my leg?"

"Is Blaze *your* real name?"

Blaze whipped out two finger guns. "Ha! You got me there. Let's just say that it is. Now, how about a beer?"

I had nowhere else to be. "Well, I'm not one to turn down a drink with a new neighbor."

"I like you already. Come meet the gang."

The barefoot folks kept on dancing, grilling, and feeding each other as Blaze walked me through the pavilion to the cooler. I tried my best to take mental notes. All their toes were intact. There was nothing nefarious in their paintings. Nothing that said *Father* or *God* anywhere.

"These two dancing fools are Jimmy and Charlie," Blaze said. "Charlie doesn't speak much English, on account of the fact we picked him up hitchhiking in Capilla del Monte, but who needs language when you've got a drink and a smile? Just give him a thumbs-up and you'll be fast friends in no time." He demonstrated, and the fellow in the conductor's hat grinned so wide he could lick Oklahoma. I recognized him as the one who wore the "I Heart New York" T-shirt on the day of Potato's funeral. Thumbs-Up Charlie. I could remember that.

"Back there are Tip and Dolly. They're married, but, you know, it's open."

"To what?"

"Not to me anymore, I'll tell you that. Jean-Luc is over there grilling some sweet, sweet sausages for the gang. Howdy-ho, Jean-Luc!"

The man at the grill turned around. He was still sporting a pink ascot and matching round sunglasses. With a wave of the spatula, he cooed, "How do you do?"

Ascot-Jean-Luc seemed friendly enough.

"Do you eat meat?" Blaze asked. "We've got extra!"

"Why wouldn't I eat meat? I live in a town called Tombstone, Texas."

Blaze threw his head back. By the grace of Jesus, his hat stayed on. His laughter soared to the roof of the pavilion and bounced like a pinball. "Pinky pinky," he sang at me. "You're alright. Now, can you juggle?" He held out two beers. At my look of horror, he laughed again and took a drink from one, offering me the other.

When was the last time I had Lone Star? June had a wine-only policy. And most of our social gatherings took place at her house, ever since Ashley's had been taken over by baby stuff.

The fizzy grains tasted like rebellion, and the beer paired perfectly with Ascot-Jean-Luc's sausages.

"What's the secret to your grilling, Jean-Luc?" I asked him.

"Curiosity and a brief stint in Kansas City," he said over his shoulder. His accent was European, but not like the Czech folks down in West Texas.

I already had more questions than I'd started with.

The bell of a tandem bike dinged before I could tell Ascot-Jean-Luc to keep his Kansas City answers to himself in the state of Texas. Riding in front was the man with shoulder-length, dark-brown curls, now stuffed under an old helmet. In the back was the freckled passenger. Her eyes, green as jade and soft as a meadow, were on me as she hopped off the back of the bike. I felt my shoulders relaxing further when I caught her gaze. I realized what I was doing, overcompensated, and sat up straighter than a polecat struck by lightning.

"Mars! Mika!" Blaze yelled. He stretched his arms out. The beer that surfed out of its bottle nearly splashed me.

"We're back, my wandering parakeets," the woman said with a half-smile. "Isn't this just the darndest little way to get around town?"

She sounded like Katharine Hepburn in an old-timey movie. If you closed your eyes, you would have thought she was one of those fabulous women with mascara stains. The accent didn't match her flowing peasant top, but I liked both equally. On her neck hung the pearls that looked just like the ones from the vintage ad—I had checked a few days before. I felt like I had conjured her.

Was she Mars? Was she Mika? I didn't want to make a wrong guess, not even in my head.

Despite all my years of watching Tombstone boys pick up my friends, and all my secret swipes on dating apps in college, I'd never learned how to talk to women myself. I just stared dumbly—politely, but dumbly—at Mars and Mika until someone else could introduce them to me.

The curly-haired fellow came to the rescue by sticking out his hand to me. "I call myself Mika," he said. "What universal hiccup brought you here?"

Curly-Haired Mika. So the freckled passenger's name was Mars.

Curly-Haired Mika spoke with a drawl, the kind Mama declared "close enough" when we watched old Westerns with Nene. With his sweet honey voice, he would fit into Tombstone just fine. As long as he buzzed his head and donated the leather fringe vest to a thrift store two towns over.

With every new voice that echoed in the pavilion, I became more confused about where this group came from and how they knew each other. I really wished I had brought a notebook with me.

"Pinky," I said, taking his extended hand. "And . . . uh . . ."

"We met Pinky the other day, toots," Mars said softly, resting her elbow on Mika's shoulder. Is something going on between them? I wondered.

Mars sat on the bench next to Blaze. "Pinky was the host of the funeral we so rudely interrupted. The pigeon we saw when we . . . well, when we got here." She winked at him and gave me a crooked smile.

"Oh," Mika said solemnly, but he quickly perked up. "We're here for you!"

"What do you mean?" I asked, adding so much sweetness that the words came out like a nervous Costco sheet cake.

Blaze ruffled Mika's hair and gave him a look I couldn't quite understand. "No, Pinky, what my hunky friend means is that . . .

well, we understand how tough it feels to go through what you're going through." He tripped over his words, as if he knew more about me than my having a dead cat but didn't want to let on. "We're here for anything you need."

The sincerity in his voice had me grasping for words of gratitude. Why did I feel like this meant more than Ashley's appearance at the memorial or June and Wanda's digital condolences? I had been holding back my grief and emptiness over the past few weeks. Blaze's softness unlocked the door and let me spill it into the pavilion.

"I'd really like to honor her somehow," I said. "Sweet Potato Grace, I mean. My cat. I feel like I haven't been able to. Not properly."

"I know how that feels," Mars said, grasping my free hand. My other hand squeezed my Lone Star so hard it almost popped out and hit the roof. "How perfectly dreadful, to lose a cat like that."

"She was like a friend," I said. "She just lived the way she wanted to and looked like a mean old bitch in the process."

Blaze threw his head back, cackling again. "You're a riot, Pinky."

"I don't know why I'm telling you this."

"Well," Blaze said, "maybe we *can* help you. We've got some arts and crafts here. Want to paint us a picture of this mean old bitch?"

I did.

I'm no artist. I can't paint a picture any better than I can tell jokes at a Youth Group Talent Show. But I had enough talent to paint a basic picture of Sweet Potato Grace. I knew her features from memory: the freckle on her lip, pink in her ears, the grey fur that covered one eye like she was the Phantom of the Opera.

I couldn't get her eyebrows just right, but I showed Blaze, Mars, and Mika enough photos of Sweet Potato Grace on my phone throughout the process that they got the picture. Figuratively and literally.

I recalled how I lured her back into the mother-in-law suite with goat cheese when she escaped. I described her favorite scratching post. People always avoid asking questions about the recently deceased, but Blaze, Mars, and Mika were so eager to hear about Sweet Potato Grace that I almost forgot why I'd come to the park that day.

The card Blaze had given me was lodged between a receipt for toenail clippers and a Ziploc bag of cat treats I kept for Tombstone strays. I dug it out and held it up like a priest holding the Eucharist. "I wanted to ask you about this," I said. "What does it mean?"

Mars smiled, revealing those white, crooked teeth. Mika snatched the card out of my hand and dangled it in front of Blaze. "What are you doing giving these out? I thought we weren't putting on any shows this time around." He chuckled. "Ha. Time. This time—"

"Mika, why don't you let me explain." Blaze ruffled Mika's hair and leaned in like he was going to give the man a kiss on the forehead . . . and then thought better of it, as two of Ashley's mom friends power walked past our little scene. They each gave us an eyebrow and continued talking about Channing Tatum.

"Pinky pinky, our group is a little strange, I'll admit. But that's what going on a journey like ours will do. See, we're a traveling circus."

"Is that why you've got the outfits on?"

"What's wrong with our outfits?" Mars said. I immediately

started to apologize, but she interrupted me with a hand on mine once again. That shut me up. "I'm just pulling your leg, toots. I'm not offended."

"I like the outfits!" I chirped. "And I like you, too. I haven't been able to speak much about Sweet Potato Grace. I apologize if your ears are ready to fall off."

"You're a breath of fresh air, sugar," Mars said.

Blaze stuck out his hand. "Friends?"

I took it. "Friends."

"Want to join the circus?"

"I can't tell if you're being serious or not."

"No one ever can."

"Are you here to stay?"

"For now."

That sounds a little contradictory, I thought. I realized I'd been talking quite a lot. Was I on my second beer? Third?

This was certainly not how a proper detective went about their investigations.

Fortunately, I wasn't a proper detective. I was Pinky Elizabeth Swear, and I enjoyed my time with the barefoot strangers until the sun went down. Their music choices were just as eclectic as they were: Talking Heads, Taylor Swift, and the occasional sea shanty that really excited Jean-Luc. We painted more pictures and exchanged more stories, and I asked myself if the strangers were a gift from Sweet Potato Grace herself. They might make life in Tombstone more bearable, if they stayed. And if they did that, I could live here and work in the store and stay in the comfort of my cozy closet.

"What's a bunch of chickens to do after dark in a town like Tombstone?" Blaze was asking.

"Uh . . ." There was only one thing I could think of, but it would require footwear. "Do y'all have . . . any shoes?"

Blaze pointed to a canvas bag sitting on top of the van. "Got all the sandals we need in case of an emergency. What are we talking? Rocky cliffs? Hot coals? Sticky floors?"

Definitely the latter. I was taking them two-stepping at Fun Earl's.

SEVEN

Fun Earl's two-step lessons don't accommodate beginners. Everyone in Tombstone learns the basics from Rip Ripple, June's uncle and Tombstone Middle School's P.E. teacher. Newcomers with dancing in their souls have to go to Bloat Hill for beginner lessons.

I can't recall my first two steps in Mr. Ripple's class, but I do remember my first time at Fun Earl's, clear as day. Nene was walking on two feet back then, yet I had to walk back and forth from her seat to the water jug in between her beers. My little seven-year-old hands couldn't fit around three plastic cups—one for her, one for Mama, and one for Fanny—so I cracked them and spilled water all over my new dress. June still belly laughs any time I go to the water jug at Earl's, even though she wasn't at the Easter egg hunt that year.

Admittedly, taking the barefoot strangers to Earl's was a risky idea. But in the blur of Lone Stars and grilled meats, I couldn't figure out what else there was to "do" on a Saturday night. Drive to the lake? Hope that Wanda was called in to sub at Applebee's trivia night?

Fun Earl's was our best option.

Three of the barefoot travelers stayed behind to do who-knows-what, but Mars, Blaze, Curly-Haired Mika, Ascot-Jean-Luc, and Thumbs-Up Charlie seemed happy enough to check out the bar. Jean-Luc offered to drive because he "couldn't be bothered with cheap beer." When I wrinkled my nose in response, Blaze assured me that Jean-Luc didn't drink, end of story. Jean-Luc and June might get along after all, if they laid down arms and agreed not to challenge each other to a judging contest.

That evening, June had plans to wash her hair. Wanda had a date in Bloat Hill. I didn't bother texting Ashley, as she didn't leave the house without her baby strapped to her, and Fun Earl's was no place for children past eight o'clock. It had especially been no place for Fanny, who as a young child shrieked at the animal pelts (eyes intact) and massive, framed, fading photo of the Twin Towers on the walls. The choices behind said decor were known only to Big Chuck, owner and manager of the establishment (and Wanda's granddaddy).

Big Chuck spoke mostly in approving grunts, for little happened at Earl's that Big Chuck didn't condone. (*Freedom* was the only word I had ever heard him enunciate.) He wasn't a big fan of a screaming child, however, and last I heard, Fanny was still boycotting the place.

Big Chuck was lumbering up the stairs to his apartment next to Earl's when we arrived that night. I contemplated calling him back and introducing him to Charlie. They would get along just fine, wouldn't they? The barefoot people already had so much in common with Tombstonians!

I was getting excited to report back to the Sewing Circle.

At nine on the dot, the country-western elevator music faded out and Rip Ripple clopped onstage sounding like a horse on its second-to-last ride of the day. "Uh . . . er . . ." he mumbled. The lesson had begun.

There was no spotlight at Fun Earl's, but I could have sworn one was shining on my new friends. In a world of light browns, beiges, and worn leather, Blaze's paisley shirt and Jean-Luc's soft pink ascot opened new possibilities. The air around them had the freshness of new flowers in an attic that hadn't been opened in years. Even though my new friends had come to town in a Volkswagen van, it was becoming clear that they were more peony than patchouli.

At Mr. Ripple's mumbles, the crowd quickly parted, leaving Mika, Mars, Blaze, Jean-Luc, and Charlie in the center of the dance floor. They hadn't gotten the memo about boys on one side, girls on the other. A beat passed as Charlie looked left and right, then begrudgingly sat down in a nearby booth. When I reached out for him to come back, Mars grabbed my hand and whispered, "He's not a fan of the jitterbug." I brushed down the hairs that stood up on my arms and nodded.

Mars took a dainty step toward me and the Tombstone women, shooing the boys to the other side. Silence hung in the air, broken only by Belinda, Nene's old friend who could still kick a two-step. She coughed in disapproval. Mr. Ripple grunted in response. Unlike when he taught fourth period, he wasn't battling the bell. He could wait all evening for the crowd to get situated. Time is always on your side at Earl's—the sign in the women's bathroom says so.

Once the boys stepped to their side, Mr. Ripple said, "Pair up."

The usual shuffling of feet and noodling of guitar strings commenced. Barry Jenkins, a quiet former classmate of mine who frequented Earl's, made eye contact with me from the back of the crowd and walked in my direction. It had been a few years since I last saw Barry—Earl's was a hotbed of germs and mask-stomping during the pandemic—but he looked the same as I remembered. Tall, lanky, and stooped over, as if he wanted to hide the strong core and fierce discipline that you needed to two-step as often as he did. His untamed hair puffed out limply, as it had back when we attended prom. No, not together, although I remember dancing next to him during "Chattahoochee." Wanda always thought we'd end up dating each other, on account of the fact that we never tried dating anyone in high school. "There's still time," she would whisper to me every time we saw him after graduation.

I waited for Barry. Mika, Blaze, and Jean-Luc formed a huddle of sorts. Next to me, Mars watched, chewing her lip and shaking out her hands.

"Howdy, Pinky," Barry said quietly. "I see you've brought some new friends with you. Are these folks you met at Blinn?"

Mars stepped up to introduce herself before I could. "I'm Mars."

Barry looked down at his shoes and tried to hide a wince. "You might want to be careful on the dance floor with your toes out."

"Oh, we've got sandals if we get too hot to trot. Plus, Pinky will be gentle with my feet, won't you, doll?" She held her hand out to me, palm soft and small. I wanted to take it, but I didn't know how.

My sentence got mixed up in my mouth and three different words came dancing out at once. "Oh, ah, no, excuse me. I don't lead, Mars. Barry, why don't you dance with my new friend? You know what you're doing. I trust you'll take care to be gentle with her feet."

Mars shrugged at me. "Next time," she said gleefully.

I nodded quickly, turned to the huddle, and grabbed Jean-Luc's hand. Two down. But as I looked around for spare females to pair with Blaze and Mika, I watched them lace their hands together and stand at the ready for some two-stepping.

My stammers were interrupted by more mumbles from Rip. He rattled off a combination of steps so complicated it sent Blaze into little giggles behind me.

"Don't worry," Jean-Luc whispered in my ear. "Mika taught me how to dance and he's been working on Blaze. Turns out it's helpful to have a southern fella in your little group of travelers." He turned to face me, extended his hand, and sent me twirling. The house band's familiar cover of Alan Jackson's "Little Bitty" put a smile on every two-stepper's face.

Two-stepping requires little from a follower besides knowing how to slow-slow-quick-quick, keep the tension, and trust your partner. Jean-Luc quickly earned my trust. In fifth grade, June had told Mama that I'd trust the Devil so long as he told me his horns were a Halloween costume, and Mama has repeated that joke twice a year since. But Jean-Luc wasn't the Devil and I had proof that he knew how to dance. We blended into the crowd as best we could, although Jean-Luc's big, round sunglasses (perched atop his head) drew some eyes. So did his bare feet. So did Blaze's bucket hat.

Everyone was watching us.

With my hands and feet occupied and my eyes looking anywhere but at my fellow dancers, I let my mind wander. "Next time." That's what Mars had told me, with such confidence I had to believe she meant it. Was she just being polite? Why should she? No one expected her to want to dance with me, least of all me.

It was already jarring to see new friends—heck, new people—in a place that had been a constant in my life since I was drinking from a very different bottle. I wasn't sure I liked it, to be completely honest. If Mars hadn't been the hand shaking my maracas, I don't think I'd have had the courage to embrace such an interruption to my routine at all.

I watched Barry twirl Mars around as the song changed to "Suds in a Bucket." I trusted Barry with two-stepping more than I trusted the sun to rise—which might not be saying all that much. But he held Mars carefully, politely, reassuring her with nods that her stumbling feet were no problem at all. I felt myself wanting to do the same. Let her know she was in good hands. A good hand in hers, another good hand on her waist. I wanted to let her know she was making the opposite of a fool of herself. If there was a next time, in an empty Earl's with nothing more than songs playing from a speaker, maybe I could hold her that way, too.

I felt foolish—what must Jean-Luc be thinking when my eyes darted for a glimpse of Mars at every turn?—but I couldn't help it. I wanted to know she was still there, as if she might disappear.

Why was I so afraid? No one had disappeared from my life, besides Roger and Sweet Potato Grace. Everyone in Tombstone, besides my new friends, had been in my life since I could remember. No leaving, no changing, no shaking things up.

Fun Earl's had seen my laughter, my tears, my hideous homecoming dresses. Those memories never disappeared. I wanted Mars to know it all, see it all, and come to Earl's for many years. I wanted to show her everything. I wanted her to show me everything. I didn't want her to disappear like Sweet Potato Grace. The thought of it made me want to cry.

After "Wagon Wheel" wrapped up, the lesson ended and Mars caught her breath enough to say, "I'm so happy I could cry." I found myself wanting to see all the places she had laughed and cried, and all the places she would in the future.

Now, I'd had a few Lone Stars back to back before, but I'll admit I was out of practice that night, which may have contributed to the melodrama. The house band took their leave, the speakers started playing Reba, and most dancers left the floor. My feet stopped spinning around but my head had not gotten the memo. As I waited for Brenda (Ashley's aunt, the founder of Tombstone Animal Rescue, and Fun Earl's best bartender), I tried to blink myself back into where I was at that moment. I'd let my dreaming take me too far into the future and lost track of time.

"Miss Swear," Brenda said, drying off a glass. "Glass of white?"

"Not today, ma'am," I said. "Two Lone Stars."

"Where's June?"

"Had to wash her hair. Hey, do you need me at the shelter tomorrow?"

"Oh, Pinky," she said, putting down the glass and turning to open the Lone-Star-filled fridge behind her. She had the strongest hands in Tombstone, Mama had told me, and that's why she was single. "You don't need to do all that. I know you've been having a tough time after Sweet Potato Grace and all."

"I want to stop by. Honest."

She squinted at me before setting the beers down on the bar. "Are you okay? You can tell me. You don't look so good."

"I'm fine. Just a little lightheaded from dancing. Seeing the kitties will do me good."

"You're twenty-two years old. You don't know what does you good." She chuckled as she opened the beers and slid them to me. "On the house. Don't drive home. Have some water before you go to bed."

I nodded and made my way to the booth at the back of the bar where Jean-Luc and Mars sat watching Blaze and Mika play pool. Jean-Luc offered his seat to me and went to check on Charlie, who smiled as he counted the panels on the wall.

"Thanks for the introduction, pickle," Mars said.

As I tried to respond, I realized my mouth was dry. "Barry's a good dancer, isn't he?" I croaked out.

"He is. But come on. Haven't you ever thought about leading?"

"Lead? No, I . . ." I shrugged in front of the Twin Towers picture, under the disco ball, next to the pool table which had been added before my Mama could reach the felt. "There's no reason for me to do that."

Mars chuckled. "2002, ain't it?"

"2022," I mumbled. The stains on the carpet might have been relics from 2002, but I kept that thought to myself.

Mars shrugged. I looked over at Brenda and wondered why I hadn't asked for some ice cubes. I needed my stomach to be replaced by a fresher, younger stomach. Even though I was sitting down, sitting next to Mars had my head spinning faster, and I felt my cheeks warm at the idea of turning to meet her green eyes.

I didn't know what to say. I heard myself start with, "I can see myself crying." How those words got fast-tracked from the folds of my brain to my vocal cords, I'm not sure, but my hand was too late. It covered my mouth halfway through the sentence. The tightness in my chest told me the damage was done.

"What?" Mars asked sweetly.

Well, I wasn't going to tell her I could see myself crying and laughing and dancing with her as we grew taller and older and wider, until one of us joined Sweet Potato Grace in the Great Beyond.

"There's no reason for you to do that," Mars said.

"It's just . . . my cat. You know."

Mars looked down. My cover had worked. "Oh, that's right. Your sweet puss," she said.

I cleared my throat. "I've just been a little down since she passed away. I don't feel like I've found a good way to honor her yet. The paintings were great, but I just feel like I need something . . . bigger."

"Grief is an absolute rat. You really loved Sweet Potato Grace, didn't you?"

I launched into it all again: how I loved the way Sweet Potato Grace took no crap and lived the way she wanted to, how she wasn't afraid to look a little angry, how she valued adventure and independence. I must have sounded crazy. But hopefully less crazy than a woman who was ready to cry over a woman she had met a month prior.

"Sounds like a real role model of a puss," Mars said.

I wished she would stop saying that word in Fun Earl's. I nodded and gulped. "Anyway. Sorry to duck out early, but I think my sister's here to pick me up. Blaze can have my beer." I pushed it across the table to her and stumbled to the front entrance, shooting Fanny a text.

As I clambered into Fanny's car a few minutes later, I caught sight of Mars and Blaze opening the door to Fun Earl's. Mars wiggled her fingers at me with the same devious expression as the woman in the alarm clock ad. I gulped, shut the door on myself, and slid down in the passenger seat, telling Fanny to hurry up and take me back to my closet-sized mother-in-law suite.

EIGHT

Beyond nights with the Sewing Circle and long-forgotten college parties, I hadn't had much practice reaching for a second or third glass of alcohol in one night. The morning after my rendezvous at Fun Earl's was, unfortunately, anything *but* fun. It was a "rise and dim." Acid swished around my stomach and my brain felt like someone was squeezing it from the inside.

I replayed everything I'd done and said the night before. I brought a bunch of barefoot strangers to a place that required shoes and a little subtlety. To make things worse, I left them there, alone, after rambling about my cat. Again.

The only coherent thought I could string together was that I should say sorry. To someone.

I don't have many talents, but I can grovel and plead like nobody's business. One has to be humble if they're going to live in a town like Tombstone, where burnt bridges send you plunging into the river to drown.

Take tenth grade. The Sewing Circle and I polished off a bottle of Pinnacle Whipped and stayed up all night giggling and prank-calling pizza places until it came time to talk Spin the Bottle. I wanted my spins to land on Elizabeth Stewart, but I couldn't say that, so instead I blurted out Aaron Stewart, Elizabeth's older brother. Ashley had already laid claim to Aaron Stewart. I had to apologize that night, the morning after, and throughout the week until she believed I *actually* wanted to play Spin the Bottle with Joe Clark's nephew (the one who was the decorated archer and marksman, not the no-good one.)

Or take prom night. Wanda's date from Bloat Hill sat next to me at the afterparty and offered me a glimpse of his new camera, as I had been exploring an interest in photography. I had to apologize to Wanda for her date's and my mutual interest. Later, when I was taking photography classes at Blinn, I never even told her about it.

Take our first week at Blinn, a blur of adjusting to new schedules and signing up for info sessions about organizations I wouldn't end up joining. My schedule was so full that I didn't see June for a whole twenty-four hours and didn't update our roommate calendar. I then set out on an apology tour. "Why do you need all these extracurricular commitments when you have lifelong friends?" June asked.

The familiar feeling of dread, of needing to apologize, shivered through my insides as Sweet Potato Grace's abandoned feeder rang out its morning reveille.

"Where do I start, Sweet Potato Grace?" I asked my empty room. My head pounded something extra. I decided to prepare an apology to Fanny first.

Sorry I made you drive me home. Sorry I giggled too loud when we walked through the door and you had to shush me lest Nene wake from her slumber. Sorry, sorry, sorry. I had plenty else to apologize for, as all sisters do, but I figured I would stick to what I was sorry for in terms of the previous night.

When I crossed the yard to enter the main house, Fanny was already sitting in her proper place: on the couch, drinking a coffee, watching her soaps. Hollywood was Fanny's moon and the soaps were her stars. She believed that if she wasn't any good at writing Instagram captions or roping a videographer for a boyfriend, at least she had the face for daytime television. Soap operas were timeless, were they not? They might even outlive Instagram.

Fanny wasn't expecting an apology. She called out, "Say hi to Brenda for me!"

It was only when I didn't answer that she looked up. Steam from the coffee mug in her hands framed her face like a ring light as her eyes met mine and blinked with innocence.

"Do you need something, Little Lone Star?" she asked.

"Fanny," I said, pushing out a deep breath, "I'm sorry."

"For what?"

"I'm sorry you had to take care of me last night. I'm sorry . . ."

She raised a finger. "I drove you home and took a slice of cold pizza out of the fridge. I hardly call that caring."

"It's just . . . I'm your older sister. I should be the one taking care of *you*. You should be out having fun and calling me to pick you up."

Fanny muted her soap. On screen, an older woman scolded her daughter mid-bikini-wax.

"You're grieving," Fanny said, setting down her coffee. "Sweet Potato Grace was your best friend and she's dead now. I don't mind throwing you a slice of cold pizza during this time."

"My friends should be doing that. June's my best friend."

Fanny crinkled her nose. "May I be frank?"

"I prefer you to be Fanny," I said—the response our mother always gave to this question.

"June didn't even show up at the funeral for Sweet Potato Grace," Fanny said gently. "But you know who did?"

"Ashley?"

"And those folks in the van. The barefoot strangers."

"They didn't come there for me." *Or did they?*

Fanny shrugged. "You seem to really like them."

"What makes you say that?"

"When you got in the car, you were all blush and fluster. As you yammered on, I realized I haven't seen you that happy since Mama said you could keep Miss Sweet Potato Grace." She shuffled her whole body to fully face me. Behind her, the soap continued, the freshly waxed daughter now scolding her mother.

"You're under a lot of stress, Pink," Fanny said. "I know you don't realize it, but you're in the throes of grief, and you've got to take over Swear-It's, and Nene has been skating on a rusty blade for years. On my shows, stress like this sends a woman into a conniption. You've got to get it together so you can get on with your forbidden romance."

"I'm not in a . . ."

Fanny lowered her voice and looked around for signs of the matriarchs. "Don't pretend you weren't blushing, Pink. I saw how your tongue hung out over that blonde girl with all the toe rings in front of Earl's. If you want my honest opinion, I'm not sure you're her type, but what do I know about lesbians?"

"Thank you?"

"You're welcome."

"Well, I'm sorry again."

I stood there in silence. Fanny slurped another sip of coffee. On screen, another daughter, marked by mascara tear stains, removed herself from the clutches of a smarmy-looking man.

She looked around at the family Christmas party and took off running into the night, discarding her heels. As she kept running, her smile grew wider.

When the commercial break started, Fanny offered some parting words: "I'm happy as a pig in the mud watching soaps and tidying the house and waiting for a lazy man to scoop me off my feet and into his dirty, dusty house. But I'm not you, Pinky."

"I guess I'd rather be happy around a lot of smelly kitties."

"Is that what they call themselves?"

"You know what I mean, Fanny."

"Have fun at the animal rescue. Tell Brenda and the barefoot people I say hi."

Tombstone Animal Rescue, or TAR for short, is a pet name for Ashley's Aunt Brenda's house. Caring for animals is her day job. Her bartending gig at Fun Earl's is just for that. Fun.

If you drive up Hillbilly Road to TAR, you'll hear the hounds before you see the rest of the dogs, kitties, and bravest little guinea pigs who run freely in Brenda's massive, fenced-in yard. Brenda's never had a child and never had a partner, as far as anyone knows, but no one can say she's lonely. Animals can save a person that way.

Gossipy moms occasionally try to ignite a rumor that Brenda is a hoarder, a lesbian, or a Wiccan, but every time someone decides to investigate, they end up going home with a one-eyed chihuahua or a sweet senior pit bull. Brenda sees them off with a bag of pet food and a holler heard all over town: "Stay outta my business and I'll stay outta yours!"

That dries up the grapevine for a few months at a time.

Brenda's third bedroom is reserved for kitties with health problems and character flaws. Max, my favorite at the time, lived in his own separate cat condo, which was painted bright colors and had held the saddest of cases throughout the years. Max had a laundry list of reasons to be euthanized at a traditional shelter: feline leukemia, ringworm, and an abscess on his jaw that was barely healing. At TAR, he was placed on a waiting list to go to Austin. Austin had animal shelters with open arms for sick kitty snuggles. It was the only place left in the world for him.

Max had been through the wringer, but that didn't bother him at the age of four months. String toys made his pus-smeared little face light up. His butt wiggled as he jumped for his toys or ate his food. Yes, I needed to wash my hands three times before I could think about petting any other kitty, but the joy in Max's eyes was worth the extra steps.

Brenda let me in after I texted my arrival (the doorbell set every dog and their mother off) and fetched a glass of sweet tea as I walked straight to Max's condo. My heart ached thinking of him with nowhere to run, only the same bed and the same litter box in the same small space. I could imagine that would make a cat go crazy after a while.

"If I didn't want this little guy to go to Austin so bad, I'd bring him home with me," I told Brenda, waving a string in Max's face.

"Pinky," Brenda said firmly.

"Oh, I know. He's better off leaving."

"We don't have the resources for ringworm kitties, much less ringworm kitties with all of Max's other maladies. Man, your Mama must have had to tell you no more times than she told Greg Beales to go screw himself." (Greg Beales had been the captain of the chess team when Brenda and Mama were students at Tombstone High. Mama only liked bad boys at the time, and look what good that did her.) "I've finished up my afternoon tasks," Brenda said. "Come sit and have a drink when you're done playing. I'm surprised you came in today! I told you to take all the time you needed to grieve."

Brenda was a patient woman. We shot the shit and she watched me play with Max for close to thirty minutes. (Ten of that was washing my hands.) As I passed his condo one last time, I saw him rolling around a catnip-filled avocado plushie.

"I'm sorry I can't help you, Max," I whispered. He kept rolling around, bumping into his bowl of water and splashing himself in the tail.

"I just can't help it, ma'am," I told Brenda, sanitizing my hands before taking a sip of sweet tea. "I can't bear to see all these sweethearts sleeping alone at night. They need homes."

"Pinky, I sleep alone every night. I've chosen to do that for more than forty-five years. I love it. I'm sure at least one of these prickly kitties feels the same."

"Maybe I should . . ."

"I'm not sure you should anything right now." Brenda was Ashley's aunt, but she was an aunt to all of us. In all the squabbles and tiffs between June, Wanda, Ashley, and me, Brenda spoke as the voice of reason. No one acted up for long if Brenda had any say about it. Even Mama agreed that Brenda had a good head on her shoulders.

Not two sips into Brenda's stevia-sweetened tea, which I never once complained about, I found myself putting my head in my hands and wiping away tears.

"You did the best you could, Pinky," Brenda said, putting a hand on my shoulder.

"It doesn't feel like it."

"I know. Hearing it from me once isn't going to help, but

I want my message to keep ringing. You did the best you could with Miss Sweet Potato Grace. That's all we can do. You gave her the most comfortable last chapter. You care so much about everyone else. You didn't have to come here today, remember? I know your Mama doesn't believe in taking sick days, but I do. And if I had to go out of town, I would have figured something out. Don't you worry about me. I want you to stay healthy just like I want all these rascals to stay healthy."

"I'm not sick."

"Sick with grief! Sweet Potato Grace meant the world to you, Pinky. And even if she was still around, the whole world is grieving. Heck, we're barely two years out from the start of the pandemic. Over a million folks die, and we're just going back to normal? Taking on *more* than what we were taking on in 2019? I swear, Ashley's talking about going back to work, and she's got a little one to take care of. I can't imagine. People do too much."

"It doesn't feel like people have much of a choice. Ashley needs her job."

"I'm just saying, don't overwhelm yourself. Take a step away sometimes. I know coming home wasn't easy for you."

I sniffled into my tea, failing to meet Brenda's eyes. Was it known all around town that I was an anti-Tombstone sourpuss? What else did people know about me that I thought I was keeping secret?

"Brenda," I said quietly, "do you ever wish you had a partner?"

"Why do you ask that?"

"I don't know. Ashley's got a man. June's got a man . . ."

"Women don't need a man to be happy."

"Now you sound like my mother." I looked up and chuckled.

I could tell Brenda was waiting for me to say more. The

moment was accompanied by the quiet, twinkling music that kept the kitties calm. And also . . . jazz? A *je-ne-sais-quoi* within the drawn-out bubbles of smooth, brassy moans twinkled in the air and tickled me pink.

"Ma'am, I might have dove off the deep end of insanity," I said, putting my tea down on a coaster, "but do you have new music playing back by the dog kennels?"

The corners of Brenda's mouth crept up. "I was hoping you would ask that," she said coyly. "Guess who's responsible for those little lullabies?"

She winked. Who would warrant a wink?

"Uh . . . someone donated a record player?"

"Guess again."

"Ashley picked up her saxophone from high school and decided to re-enter the marching band?" (June had guilted Ashley out of donning those old feathery hats and stiff uniforms long ago, saying, "Band is for women who can't get boyfriends.")

"Pinky, come on, now," Brenda said. "It's Blaze."

"Blaze? Barefoot Blaze?" I lowered my voice. "The one that everyone in town's talking about?"

Brenda let out a bellowing laugh and clapped my shoulder. "You know it! This town's sure got a stick up its ass, doesn't it? Seems like these newcomers are rubbing splinters into everyone. Barefoot or wearing spurs, that Blaze is a hoot, isn't he?"

"I do like him, I suppose."

"I do, too. Saw you with the barefoot folks at Earl's last night, didn't I? Did you know they stayed till last call? I haven't laughed like that in years."

"What's Blaze doing in your kennels today?"

"Why don't you go ask him? I've got to get ready for my

bartending shift anyhow. You go on back there and tell him hello for me. He's quite the fellow. So is that celestial lady. What's her name?"

"Mars," I croaked.

Brenda winked. "Yeah, Mars. She seems quite nice, too."

Stay outta Brenda's business . . .

After collecting my glass, Brenda shooed me out the door.

Animal shelters are not always the most relaxing environments, I'll admit. First of all, there's a mess of smells—wet dog and dry dog and wet food and dry food, freshly hosed concrete and slobber. And the noises—barks and howls and paws hitting fences, dogs pleading to go for a walk or run free or have a little treat. There's a lot of chaos hitting your senses, usually.

As the Texas sun sank over that evening, though, I had to ask myself if all the dogs had packed up and left. Even the most sensitive ears and nostrils could enjoy peace walking through Brenda's backyard kennel. The smell was almost sweet—like lilacs. No dogs jumped or panted. They only listened to the tender sounds of Blaze's saxophone. Belle the beagle snored gently. Shiner the Sheltie twitched a gallop in his sleep, no doubt dreaming of fields of chewable sticks and quick-but-not-quick-enough squirrels. Binx, the prize-winning Loudest Hound in Tombstone, kept her howls to herself, displaying her belly to the world.

At the end of the outdoor walkway was the source of all this tranquility. A barstool from Brenda's office held an incense burner, and smoke lazily rose into the great Texas sky. Blaze stood by the stool, sunglasses on, swaying with his instrument. Then he took the sax out of his mouth and started humming a song I didn't know.

I looked around, wondering when the dogs were going to disturb his peace. But they didn't.

He fluttered his eyes open after a minute, looked into mine, and said, "Sweet things, these critters. I gotta think they stick around. Maybe one day you'll be able to see your Sweet Potato Grace again."

I'd been all ready to apologize for interrupting his meditation or saxophone practice or whatever, but I changed my response to, "What?"

"I was realizing that I haven't properly expressed my condolences. Maybe it's better if I just say I'm sorry for your loss."

"Thank you," I mumbled. "I know I've been a bit of a downer, yammering about her up and down the whole town. I should probably apologize for that."

"Apologize for having feelings?"

"Well—no, I mean, apologize for . . ."

"You know what I have to say to that?" Blaze asked. He honked his saxophone. "Never apologize for your feelings, Pinky pinky. Don't feel sorry for feeling sorry."

For a moment, I couldn't think of anything to say.

"Where are my manners?" Blaze said. "Please. Take a seat." He moved the incense burner to the ground and gestured to the stool.

"I see you met Brenda last night at Earl's?" I said, taking a seat.

"Yes, indeed. Mama Brenda and I crossed paths late in the night, after your departure. The gang and I were hashing out our old argument about whether cherries belong in Manhattans."

"Doesn't just about everything belong in Manhattan? I've

never been to New York, but I've been told they have everything. And a lot of extra stuff that no human needs to see or experience."

Blaze blew a happy honk into his saxophone. "Pinky, you spin me around! I'm talking about the drink. Charlie believes a Manhattan makes for the best nightcap. I think. He's never said as much, but actions speak louder than words."

I was still unsure what he meant.

"You've never had a Manhattan? It's almost as timeless as bare feet. Very trendy in 2035."

"How would you know that?"

"What?"

"2035 hasn't happened yet."

"Is that right?" *Honk.* "Now, don't ask Mika for his opinion on how to make a Manhattan, because he's a grump and thinks that cherries only go in an Old Fashioned. He's incorrect, and he'll be incorrect for the rest of his stubborn days. A Taurus! A Manhattan needs its cherry. A good cocktail is all in the fruits. It's *all* in the fruits."

"All in the fruits," I repeated. I couldn't help but laugh. My laugh made Blaze laugh, and if dogs could laugh, they would have laughed too, but most of them were enjoying the best nap of their lives.

"All in the fruits, and so are we!" Blaze proclaimed. *Honk.* "Speaking of which. Mars!"

"Mars?" I tried to loosen my posture, knowing that the mention of her name made me stand stiff as a board. I almost stumbled over myself.

"Mars!"

"What about Mars?"

"She's nice, isn't she?"

"She is."

"She's one of my best friends in this whole world. I want you to know that, Pinky. We're not lovers. Never have been, never will be. No interest. She's a single woman."

"Okay."

"All I have to say is she's a great dancer, a loyal human, and one of the smartest space cadets out there. But she is a space cadet. Her mind is playing smooth jazz sometimes, just like this here saxophone. She won't remember your birthday, but if she's sweet on you, she'll make a grand gesture if she's given proper warning." *Honk.*

"My birthday's coming up, actually," I said.

"Thank goodness I'm here, Pinky! What day is it?"

"September 3."

Blaze played another sweet lick that startled Binx out of her sleep, but after a quick look around, she went back to her dreams of fuzzy rodents. Blaze lowered his voice and leaned in. "*Mars is a Capricorn, Pinky.*"

"Okay?"

"I don't know what that all means. But she tells me ladies like her know all about it. She's got only good things to say about Virgos. Early September." He perked up with an idea. "Say, why don't you come over to the house next Saturday night? We're throwing a party. A real disco of a boogie. Or is it a boogie of a disco?"

"That sounds great. You think you can wrangle up enough people for a party? Tombstone's a pretty sleepy town."

"Oh, we've noticed that. Fortunately, we have a lot of experience drawing a crowd. So bring your dancing shoes! Or don't. We love walking around barefoot."

"Why is that?" I hadn't thought to bring a notebook to TAR for writing down clues.

"Why not? Haven't you ever walked around barefoot? The feeling of your piggy toes on the grass reminds you that the earth is always underneath you. It's the only thing we can be sure of. Walking around barefoot is timeless, in the sense that everyone thinks you're strange for doing it no matter what's in style. Besides, shoes are expensive!" *Honk.*

I wasn't sure if that answer would satisfy my friends, but I'd give it the old college try.

"Now, do you know how to get to the house on Bluebonnet Drive?" Blaze asked.

"I could tell you how to get to every registered address in this town plus a few that have avoided the strictures of bureaucracy. What should I bring?"

"Don't bring anything, unless you're allergic to cheap beer or fresh juice. We'll take care of it. And come whenever your Tombstone heart pleases."

That answer was not specific enough. After a beat of silence, Blaze suggested ten o'clock.

"Ten it is," I said. "Need a ride home in the meantime?"

"No, Pinky," Blaze said. "The dogs want an encore. I can feel it in my bones." He sat down, put his sunglasses back on, and played a score for the daydreams that followed as I walked to my car planning my outfit for the party.

NINE

The front yard at 101 Bluebonnet Drive is massive, big enough to hold firefly-catching contests and all the ATVs that once belonged to the Beans boys. Before the California landlord scooped up the real estate, the Beans family had occupied the house with their car dealership money. I hadn't seen or heard of a Beans in over ten years (they moved their business out of Tombstone, and Mama hasn't spoken their name since), but the sight of the front yard felt like the beginning of a favorite movie.

By ten o'clock, the party was in full swing. There were two huge, crackling bonfires in the front yard. Two women, Tombstone High alumnae a little older than myself, walked in front of me up the long driveway.

"Do you think any of them are single?" one asked the other.

"Maybe the one who rides around on that tandem bike. He's so cute."

"I heard last week that he got so drunk he said it was 2032."

"Boys will be boys. Do you think he really met Andy Warhol?"

"He said *Andy Warren,* the bartender from Bloat Hill."

"I swear he said Andy Warhol."

"You were just distracted by his twinkly eyes."

"No, that was the other guy who had the twinkly eyes."

Were they talking about Mika? Were they talking about the twinkle I saw in Blaze's eyes? Everyone seemed as drawn to the barefoot strangers as I was. I'd have to use a year's worth of charm to get an audience with any of them at a party like this. After the mishap at Fun Earl's, I might as well have been last week's newspaper. I listened for any gossip about the blonde woman, but the girls in front of me were not interested in talking about her.

At the front gate, to the side of the driveway, Blaze sat in a dilapidated office chair with a pink robe draped over his skinny shoulders. A bathrobe. I made a mental note to look for more of them around the house. Blaze greeted the women in front of me with a toothy grin and a spin of his chair.

Underneath my arm was a picnic basket lined with my best red-and-white-striped linen and filled with six heavy cans from Tombstone's short-lived Dead Again Brewery. The brewery had shown promise, especially after they planted a story in the gossip circles claiming that "the liberals" were trying to cancel them for their name. In response to the accusation of political incorrectness, Tombstone folk bought beers by the dozens. When it was revealed that the outrage was manufactured, Dead Again Brewery went the same way as the rest of Tombstone's business ventures. Mama used the beer barrels as planters in our backyard. On account of June's rules, the beers themselves sat in my fridge—until they hitched a ride with me to this party.

"Pinky pinky," Blaze said, spinning himself around. "How are things in your universe?"

"Oh, same old," I said, trying not to scan the party for any freckled women in particular. "Here to sign up for the circus."

"You are welcome to join! Tightrope Walker or Magician's Assistant?"

"Who's the magician?"

Blaze laughed. "I see what you're getting at, Pinky. Mars is in the kitchen, and so is the fridge. Thank you for the beer, the kindness is greatly appreciated."

How did he know I was looking for Mars? I wouldn't be surprised if the man could read minds. I thought this loudly while scanning Blaze's face for any sign that he knew I was onto his telepathy. He just chuckled and continued drinking his Lone Star.

The living room of 101 Bluebonnet Drive was filled with decorations, permanent and temporary. No framed pictures of eight pasty Beans like in the old days. Streamers hung in all different colors; posters and records filled the walls. I imagined how long it must have taken for Mars and Dolly to put these up. At least, I assumed it was them. Mama had a saying: "If your man wants to do the decorating, check his browser history with caution." Then again, the barefoot strangers didn't seem to pay much heed to proverbs. I shook the words out of my head and headed toward the kitchen.

If there was a theme to the decor, it was nostalgia. The tenants of this home had memorabilia that referenced every decade in the twentieth century. A Talking Heads ticket. An Elvis record. Posters for bands I didn't recognize, from times farther away. There were a few pieces of clearly thrifted furniture—a worn leather couch, a tattered fabric chair, an end table that had once belonged to Wanda—pushed against the walls to make room for dancing. The rug's original design was unrecognizable, but it did its job of protecting the hardwood floors from the dancing shoes of at least a dozen guests. People had wasted no time getting to the dancing, as if they only had one evening to use their shoes. ABBA played from big, dusty speakers hooked up to . . . an iPod mini? I hadn't seen one of those since I got my braces off.

Although Hannah-Ann Beans was closest to me in age of all the Beans, I'd never liked her much. A decade ago she'd had her twelfth birthday party in this room, and Mama said it would be impolite for me not to attend. During the festivities she made fun of my thrift store shoes and I cried all the way home. This incident was what really started the Beans–Swear cold war, years before the Beans turned traitor and left Tombstone.

Mama had busted into the Beans house the morning after Hannah-Ann's party to give the girl's father a piece of her mind. As I begged her not to make a scene, she stormed past Mrs. Beans and almost flipped her ironing board over. A verbal smackdown of "uppity" this, and "you think you're too good for secondhand clothes" that, ensued. Mr. Beans tried to settle Mama down with talk of business collaboration, but Mama huffed and puffed and flourished her finger, then took my hand as we stomped out of the house and down the driveway. Hannah-Ann never said a word to me after that.

The kitchen still looked exactly as it had on Hannah-Ann's birthday: the same white tile floor, blue tile backsplash, and yellow tile all around the doors. I felt like a child again. I felt lost in time and had to blink the room into focus. I took stock of the few additions, or rather subtractions, since the days of the Beans. Appliances were sparse now: besides a fridge, oven, and sink, only Tuscany-orange tile countertops offered to help prepare food. No dishwasher, no microwave, just counter space and Jesus Christ.

Mars was wiping down the counters and singing along to the

music, twirling around and leaving crumbs behind. An oversized blue sweatshirt with "Idaho Darlings" embroidered across the front hid her shorts, revealing nothing but tan legs and bare feet, toes painted pink and adorned with rings. They tapped to the beat as she jumped back and forth, her hair swinging with her.

I had rehearsed for this: a flirty tap on the shoulder, my hand brushing against hers. I had even rehearsed a wink in the mirror. My wooing eyes were rusty, but I had to use them at some point if I didn't want to die alone.

Beers in basket, I was stepping forward to stay hi when Mika appeared in front of me.

"Pinky! Blaze told me you just arrived. Would you like a tour of the place?"

With his sunglasses off, I could see Mika's brown eyes, so kind they offered you sweet tea and biscuits. I couldn't let on that I would rather see Mars.

"Sure, Mika. Show me around."

"Gee whiz! Let me put those beers in the fridge for you and I'll give you the best dang tour of your life!"

"That sounds lovely, Mika."

Carrying my basket like a gentleman from an old movie, Mika escorted me out of the kitchen. When I looked behind me, Mars had moved on to cleaning some dishes.

"Well, you've seen the kitchen, dance floor, and front yard already," he shouted over the music, "but let me take you to the crafting cafe!"

Behind the living room was a sitting room where young folks, including Joe Clark's nephew (the one who was the valedictorian at Tombstone High *and* Blinn, not the no-good one) sat on the floor around a table covered in magazines and newspapers.

This was my first time in the sitting room, as Mrs. Beans was what Mama called a "clean woman" and rarely let children sit on her good furniture. Mrs. Beans would have been horrified at the beers sitting on the table without coasters, the scraps of paper flying as people crafted, and the occasional bare foot.

I recognized Ascot-Jean-Luc by his ascot, which matched a bright pink shirt that was halfway open. His drink was pink, too, and he sipped casually as he presided over the crafters. When Mika caught his eye, he waved coyly.

"Jean-Luc is the most artistically gifted among us," Mika said. "And the best on the grill."

"A man of many talents," I said.

"Just don't ask him to throw you something. We thought we could teach him to juggle, but he's better at catering."

Jean-Luc excused himself from the couch and made his way to us, not spilling a drop of his pink drink. He patted Mika's shoulder delicately.

"Look at you, friend of Dorothy," he said, gesturing to the basket. "Have you come to craft?" He spoke smoothly, like a knife spreading caviar over crostini. (I'd never had caviar, but I'd seen it in movies.)

"No sir-ee," Mika said, "just giving Miss Pinky the tour." Jean-Luc eyed me with a glance I would've been tempted to describe as *queer* if I was in the habit of making assumptions.

"Remind me where you got that name, Pinky?" Jean-Luc asked.

"Well, when I slipped out of my Mama, Dr. Nuri said I looked like a pink piglet from the way I was squealing. It took a week for Mama to realize she had named me Pinky Swear, like the promise. She says that's what happens when you get an epidural."

"Is that what happens when you get an epidural?" Mika asked with wide eyes and genuine fascination.

"I don't know, I've never had children."

"Well, aren't you a regular Dorothy Parker?" Jean-Luc took a dainty sip from his glass. Friend of Dorothy. Dorothy Parker. I had heard someone mention these allusive Dorothys once before, but only later did I remember where and when.

"Okay now," Mika said, putting his hand on Jean-Luc's, "we have a lot more house to tour."

"If you see Charlie, can you tell him I'd like another mocktail?"

"I'll try my best." Mika led me out of the crafting cafe, pointing out a bathroom as we walked through a laundry room and into the backyard.

"Now, if you consider mural painting a craft, you can consider this the back patio to the crafting cafe," Mika said.

The Beans' tall wooden fence ran beyond where the porch lights could reach, but the handful of partygoers with brushes and paints hadn't gotten to the shadows quite yet. Music played here, too—Carly Rae Jepsen. What kind of playlist had they put together?

"Y'all are really into the arts," I said.

"It's the only thing that will last after the apocalypse."

Mika waved to get the attention of Thumbs-Up Charlie. When he had it, he made a wild gesture as if he were drinking from a gallon jug and pointed to an imaginary ascot around his neck. "Charlie makes a virgin Cosmopolitan just the way Jean-Luc likes it," Mika said.

I wondered if it had cherries in it.

Mika excused himself to clarify his order with Thumbs-Up Charlie, leaving me to watch the party as if it were a snow globe.

Pristine. Months before Hannah-Ann had made fun of my shoes, she'd sat me down and lectured me on what it was like to be an adult. Parties. Boys. Beer. Boobs. Babies. I'd nodded along, dreaming up a world based on rom-coms and Disney shows. Hannah-Ann had failed to mention crafting rooms, mocktails, or conflicted sexuality, but for a moment I felt like the party I had dreamed up as a child was happening in front of my eyes.

"Hey! Do you live around here?" The snow globe was shattered by a young man passing slowly through my line of vision. He wore an oversized tan hoodie and his facial hair spiked out in patches. He looked like a porcupine with a skin condition. I looked down at his feet; he wasn't barefoot. Then I realized what I must look like, giving him the up-and-down, and tried to divert my eyes to the right and left. I don't think I recovered gracefully.

"In Tombstone? I do," I said. "Pinky Swear. My Mama owns Swear-It's. Irene Swear. Are you, uh, new in town?"

The young man guffawed and flailed, looking behind him too fast and almost knocking himself to the ground. "Timmy!" he yelled, waving over a man who stood closer to the murals. The man approached, squinting his eyes at me with a look of caution and disbelief. He also wore shoes. I wondered if this was how Sweet Potato Grace felt when I first found her behind Lethal Peppers BBQ.

"Timmy, look. It's Piggy Swear," said the porcupine.

The second young man, dressed in a polo shirt and pastel shorts, looked mortified—and familiar. *Timmy Beans*. I might not have put it together so fast if this party were being held at any other address. And if Timmy was in the polo, then the porcupine was . . .

"Tommy Beans?" I whispered. I could see now what remained in his face from boyhood: those bulging eyes, the general egg shape of his head. His lips were still in need of balm, and every word that came out of them was just as cracked. Cruelty was Tommy Beans's game, and years of it had made it his teeth jagged like rocks in a cave. They weren't endearingly crooked. Not like Mars's. For the first time that night, I was thankful Mars hadn't joined Mika and me on the tour. I wanted to face the Beans boys alone.

Tommy had always been the less promising of the Beans boys. Timmy dabbled in trouble, but he always knew where the line was—and where the line *really* was. Tommy ran past both lines like a horse with a cruel jockey. On an ATV, he dug up the grass past those lines, too.

"*Pinky* Swear, Tom," Timmy said, putting his hand on his brother's shoulder. His class ring ballooned off of his finger. A&M. Of coursc.

"Tommy? Timmy?" I said, trying to feign excitement. "What brings you back to Tombstone?"

"Someone told us this is the *party house* now," Tommy said. He covered one of his nostrils with his fingers and snorted so loud you could hear it in France.

"That's *not* why we're here," Timmy scolded. He looked at me, exhausted. "Hi, Pinky. Nice to see you. We were visiting some old friends outside of Bloat Hill and they invited us to this party. Apparently that Blaze guy has made an impression. Our friends couldn't stop talking about how charismatic he is."

"They're not wrong," I said. "How is it being back in your old house?"

"It's still *our house,*" Tommy said, bobbing his head like a turkey. He was drunker than a goldfish in mouthwash. The type of drunk you didn't laugh about the next morning.

"Tommy, relax," Timmy said. "How are you doing, Pinky Swear? How's your Mama? She still got that store?"

"She found a boyfriend yet?" Tommy slurred. "Daddy always said she needed just a good . . ."

Timmy let out a sharp, "Thomas!" to shut his brother up. Apparently, this wasn't how you spoke to people at the country club wherever he was living now. I wanted to tell Tommy off, but the look on Timmy's face was so tired. I had heard rumors of Tommy's troubles. Drug addiction. Running away from home. Just not being able to hold it together enough to uphold the squeaky-clean image of Mr. Beans, his clean wife, and their clean family. Christmas cards never turned out quite right when Tommy was in the picture.

I could hear Mama's voice in my head: "That's what happens when you leave Tombstone. Every road out of here only leads to trouble."

I sensed Mika behind me, hesitating to join the conversation. So I wrapped things up. "Well, it was nice to see you," I said quickly, turning my back to the Beans boys. I looped my arm around Mika and we moved to another part of the backyard.

"Who are those fellas?" Mika asked, peering back at Timmy, who was trying his best to scold his brother with a straight face.

"Guys from school." I wanted to change the subject. "Are we ready to dance?"

I actually wasn't, as I don't think I had been at a party with freestyle dancing since freshman year at Blinn. But I didn't want to talk to or run into anyone else. I followed Mika into the living room and let the dance floor separate us.

Fortunately, my old, rusty joints managed to loosen up to the ever-changing playlist. Louis Armstrong. Madonna. The Talking Heads, once again. The lights were low, but everyone's smiles brightened up the living room. People came and went. I waved to acquaintances and shared a dance move with anyone who passed by. I looked for Mars, who finally did make her way in to dance with just about everyone. Did she *know* everyone? Or was she just that free?

It must have been in between a Charli XCX and a Chuck Berry song that I checked my watch and saw it was two in the morning. Hours had gone by in a state of bliss, and I must have hit some milestone in terms of steps. I found myself thinking how happy I truly was in that moment—until I remembered *why* I hadn't been so high in the clouds for the past few weeks. Sweet Potato Grace. My kitty, whom I'd failed.

Grief hides like that, doesn't it? In between songs or song lyrics. I didn't know how to feel both happiness and grief at once, and the static of the beers I had consumed made things even more top-heavy, so I allowed myself a break.

I took a seat on the front porch of the house and looked out at the front yard and the dying bonfires, getting wrapped up like leftovers with a tinfoil sky of stars.

Stars are always moving. Hour by hour, mile by mile, everyone is looking at stars in a different position. Yet from day to day on Earth, very little changes. In the weeks since Sweet Potato Grace's departure, people had picked up their usual orders from Swear-It's, worn their usual clothes, and gone about their usual days. Meanwhile, I was adjusting to a different world, one without anyone to greet me at the door or wake me up in the morning.

"Did you ever use the stars to roam, Sweet Potato Grace?"

I whispered into the front yard. I'd like to believe that in her days as a stray she used them as guideposts, like sailors and travelers did in the days before Google. How did she account for the movement of the stars throughout the night, as she scavenged for barbecue?

A tap on the shoulder took me out of my thoughts. I turned to see Mars. Dangling from her thumb and pointer finger was an open bottle of beer, a pale ale like the ones she had been drinking all night.

"Saw you were empty."

"Oh, are you sure?" I asked.

"Just pour a little out for Sweet Potato Grace. It's only polite. Come sit with me."

Foaming beer blessed the grass in Sweet Potato's name as Mars and I moved to a porch swing and watched the partygoers dance or huddle up by the fires on the lawn. The porch was its own little world and the entertainment wasn't half-bad.

"You came to Tombstone at the wrong time," I said. "I'm never this down in the dumps."

"What if I were to tell you we came into Tombstone *because* this was the right time?"

"Well, then I'd ask you what the heck you know that I don't."

"I know a lot of things that you don't," Mars said, smiling. "But you probably know a lot of things that I don't, either. I don't know who the heck Lady Gaga is."

"What do you mean?" I said. "She's one of the biggest pop stars in the world."

"That's good to know." She took a sip of her beer. "Let me change the subject. I'll just embarrass myself with how little

I know about pop culture. What do you think happens after you die?"

She seemed to take joy in my surprise, and I felt my gaze turn up to the stars. I heard Blaze's voice in my head: *Maybe you'll be able to see your Sweet Potato Grace again.* "Why are you asking me that?"

"Oh, I don't know. I just want to get acquainted. Is that a crime?" She elbowed me and sent a shiver up my arm.

"Uh. I guess not."

"So tell me! What happens? What happens, in the mind of Pinky? What are you planning for?"

"I—don't know, I suppose. No one's ever asked. I grew up in the church, so it's easy to imagine an all-white dominion of fluffy clouds and harps that greet the kindest folks. The more I sit with that, the more I find it kind of childish. But I guess I was a child when I conjured up the image, wasn't I?"

"What about the down belows, toots?"

I closed my eyes. "Fire. Just all fire. Clouds are red." When I opened them, Mars had her chin in her hands, just watching me. "What does the Devil look like?" she asked dreamily.

I cackled. "Exactly like the old cartoons. You tell me now. What do you think happens?"

"I don't know, and I'm fine with that." She said it so confidently, as if uncertainty about the afterlife wasn't hanging over everyone's heads and pressing on their shoulders every day.

"That's not fair!" I said. I tried to keep my eyes on Mars's eyes or the porch, away from her hip creases or the rings on her fingers. I put my beer down to stall. "Don't you *want* to know what happens?"

"Oh, sure, pickle. It's the world's greatest mystery, isn't it?

But I'm happy not knowing. I thought for a while that I might know. Or that I might have figured it out by now. No human will ever figure it out, though. No one will know until they *know*, and by that point, they can't tell anyone."

"And until then?"

"Until then, it's just a choice of how you want to spend your time at the party."

"I'd hardly call Earth a party. I *wish* every night was like this."

"Every night *is* like this. Not always with speakers and boozing and mayhem, but every night living with these crazy people is a party."

"Don't y'all ever disagree?"

"About?"

"I don't know . . . the state of the world?"

"Sure. Who doesn't?"

"Do you get to hide things from them?" At that moment, I admit, I was thinking about June's lectures on cults.

"Like what?"

"Oh . . . nothing. Secrets, I guess. Do you hide secrets from each other?"

"I guess so. But I don't have to hide the important stuff. I get to be myself with Blaze and Mika and the rest of these guys."

Life was just a breeze for a barefoot stranger, wasn't it? I changed the subject. "What animal would you want to be in your next life?"

"I used to say I'd like to be a little ladybug who looks at a blade of grass and thinks, 'Gee! I'm just a little gal in a big, big world.' I've changed my mind, though."

"Oh, yeah?"

"I'd like to live as a stray cat eating barbecue until a very pretty lady picks me up."

My foot popped and kicked over the beer, spilling it all over the patio. Mars looked around for something to sop it up. Amid the calamity, I thought I saw some red in her cheeks. Was she blushing? Was it just a symptom of pale ales and a hot summer night? Before I could take a second look, she ran into the house and came back with an old bath towel.

"Don't you worry about it, Pinky," she said, wiping up the spill.

I stood up, leaning from foot to foot. Then, I just blurted it out. "It's probably a sign. I should head out. This was a wonderful party, Mars."

Before she could protest or give me a second glimpse of the blush on her cheeks, I marched out the gate and hopped on my bike to go home.

TEN

The morning after the party, the gears of Potato's feeder sang their tune. I went through my to-do list over an instant coffee.

Dump the uneaten food from Sweet Potato Grace's feeder into the food bag. Donate the food bag to Tombstone Animal Rescue. Cancel the flea medication shipments. Disassemble the cat tree. Sell the cat tree, so I had no reasons left to stay in Tombstone. My list was stretching longer than a grocery list after a month in the desert. It was easier to ignore the list entirely and replay the memories my mind held onto from the night before. As I stirred the contents of my mug with more gusto to unstick the dandruffy coffee flakes, I thought about Mars's hip crease, the blush, the hand held out to me at Fun Earl's.

I needed to edit my to-do list.

Find somewhere to stow the cat tree. Give my new friends a tour of Tombstone. Give my new friends a tour of Swear-It's. Ask them where they moved from, so I could relay it to the town grapevine. Figure out Mars's view of death after all. Introduce my new friends to June, Wanda, and Ashley. Bring them all together as one big, happy friend group. Think about what it meant to take over Swear-It's from Mama. (That one, I was dreading.)

One day, when that was all settled, I could revisit the unspoken addendum to my eulogy. Maybe I could even buy that alarm clock.

I still wasn't sure how long it would take me to make it to the bottom of the list.

Once again, three beers had left me more hungover than a gambler who won enough chips to build a house, and I should have known by that point in my life that instant coffee would be no cure. Diet Coke was much better. Ever since I was a girl sneaking shots of Jim Beam from Wanda's dad, Diet Coke had smacked a kiss on my forehead when it was rattling of a hangover.

With not a drop of aspartame to be found on our property, I took my bike to the Bloat Hill Cinema. Only then would I be able to think straight and figure out the rest of my not-so-straight life.

Bloat Hill was the next town over, established on a hill that, to some pioneer without the gift of the gab, had resembled the bloat of a well-fed man lying on his back. No one had argued with the pioneer when the name was made official, because that pioneer was also the patriarch of the entire population. Tombstone ain't perfect, but at least I wasn't born in a town called Bloat Hill. For that, I am thankful.

Bloat Hill Cinema has one very strict rule: no noise. No talking, no cell phones, and no potato chips. No exceptions. I don't mind the rule. I wish more places were silent and had bottomless fountain Diet Coke. And Bloat Hill Cinema has the best Diet Coke I've ever tasted. The chemical interactions between the soda, the ice machine, and the plastic ripple cup in which the Diet Coke is poured create a reaction more tender than a baby's first word or a kitten's first blink. Is it actually Diet Pepsi?

I'll never know, because I stopped drinking Diet Coke anywhere else. Only in the silent Bloat Hill Cinema.

The film playing that morning was *Sweet Charity,* a musical that played every year when the theater's owner, Edna Price, took her annual cruise out of Galveston with her women's business group. *Sweet Charity* would have never made it onto the marquee otherwise. The screening was kept secret from Edna, who preferred her Shirley MacLaine movies *without* musical numbers or allusions to sex work; however, Edna's daughter Marge preferred movies with both.

"She leaves Tombstone with big Miss Texas dreams and look what happened to her," Mama told us while preaching about Marge's misdeeds. "This is why I never put you in pageants. Who goes out of their way to be *judged* by *men?* Sick people, that's who. Scrambles your brain. No wonder she wanted to move to *New York.*"

On the drive over to the theater, I repeated my sacred mantra and hummed the tunes I knew from *Sweet Charity*. Diet Coke and a dark room. "Big Spender." Diet Coke and a dark room. "The Rhythm of Life." Yet memories of the night before kept breaking through. The blush on Mars's face. Her calling me a "pretty lady." The winks from Blaze and Mika when they mentioned her name. Talking about Sweet Potato Grace.

Sweet Potato Grace would never have been allowed at the Bloat Hill Cinema. She meowed too often.

The frame of the chair in Theater 3 stuck out to poke my shoulder blades, making me feel bad for my fellow moviegoers. I was the only person in the theater under the age of 76, and the only patron who wasn't a member of the Bloat Hill Women's Club.

I never would be admitted into that club, either. The Swear women were permanently banned after Nene's removal. Someone in the club had been peddling certain stimulants—they were in demand amongst the women whose husbands were still around—and Nene was a born entrepreneur, so all arthritic fingers pointed at her. And there are no fair trials in the Bloat Hill Women's Club.

The club didn't see me, since they took up the front two rows of the theater. Sweet as sugar. I didn't need anyone to perceive my sorry self as I watched the film. I sat further back, thinking no one would join me.

But after previews for *The Aristocats* and *A Clockwork Orange* had played, my new barefoot friends walked into the theater.

Five people, ten feet. A blur of patterned vests, furry coats, and funky sunglasses, shuffling in with big tubs of popcorn and extra-large sodas. I sank into my chair, hoping the size of my soda would shield me from socializing. Hangovers are for being in the presence of junk food and Jesus Christ alone. Vain as it might be, I will admit I also didn't want Mars to see my bees' nest of hair, even if it was in the dark.

The other three barefoot strangers arrived halfway into the musical's first song. It was the same three who'd declined my invitation to Fun Earl's, so I fear that my judgment of them is colored by the bitterness of rejection. But they were noisy as they scuttled in, whispering excitedly about Bob Fosse and pointing out the rest of their friends, who up to that point were sitting quietly. I shrank into my seat. I didn't want anyone to tip off the Women's Club that the traitor's granddaughter was in their midst. I just wanted to sip my Diet Coke and watch the musical.

Sweet Charity is known for several big songs, but my personal favorite has always been "Big Spender," a bawdy number featuring a gaggle of women who gush over men with money in their pockets. I don't think I have to go into the details of Mama's complaints when the girls' choir of Expiration Middle School performed the number in our winter jamboree.

I covered my mouth with my hands when I heard an off-key version of the song ring out through the movie theater, thinking for a second, Is that me? But no, I hadn't lost my mind in some Pavlovian response to the song's introduction. Behind me, people were singing out loud.

I tried to turn slowly and catch a glimpse of who was singing. I'll admit, I wasn't surprised when it was Jimmy, Tip, and Dolly. They were standing up, unapologetically trying to harmonize as Blaze, Mars, and the rest of them tugged on their jackets to get them to take a seat.

The singers were not entirely disrespectful. They sang at a volume that let the performers on screen sing along. But that didn't matter to the Bloat Hill Women's Club, who began to throw popcorn toward the back row. Their throws were weak, so none of them hit anything beyond me. The short-range hailstorm did not deter the singing barefoot folks, who seemed to misinterpret the violence as celebration.

All I had to hide my identity was a pair of modest sunglasses. I put them on. The president of the Women's Club scootered out to speak to a manager before the song had reached its first chorus, which was a shame, because the three singers harmonized beautifully.

The manager—my hairdresser's son, whose name escapes me—walked up the aisle not even two choruses in. He couldn't have been more than fifteen years old. I hunched over, staring daggers at the sticky floor. I was like a turtle without a shell, squeezing my muscles as tight as I could.

Despite the high tension whipped up by the Women's Club, the barefoot folk didn't seem to mind being chastised. Giggles preceded their walk down the aisle and out of the theater. One man, possibly Jimmy, whispered to the employee, "Hey, buddy, this ain't Buckingham Palace. Feel the rhythm, man."

"Demons!" I heard one of the older women yell, followed by a smattering of agreement from her fellow club members. I peeked up just in time to see a piece of popcorn hit Jimmy in the face. He stopped short, forcing Tip to bump into him from behind. Tip patted him on the butt like a baseball player at the end of an inning. Jimmy opened his mouth wide and stuck his tongue out, asking for another piece.

I prayed that this particular group of Women's Club members had driven in from the memory care facility. Because if there's one thing that Bloat Hill and Tombstone have in common, it's that once someone causes a public disturbance, no one ever forgets.

ELEVEN

Tombstone's local newspaper, *The Epitaph,* had gone out of business before I was born. No journalist could write down a story faster than Tombstonians could send it through the grapevine. Before I could tie my apron strings at Swear-It's the week after my friends' "performance," Mama had prepared a sermon on the *Sweet Charity* showing. Turns out, the secretary of the Women's Club had a mighty sharp memory and knew how to use a cell phone. Bless her heart.

As a child, I dreaded gossip because I dreaded Mama's sermons. They were worse than actual church services. When June had clarinet lessons, Ashley was at church camp, or Wanda was on road trips with her family, I would sit on the floor of Swear-It's with Fanny until it was time to mop and listen to Mama's sermons. Each one centered on whatever scandal was floating through the grapevine that week: a divorce; a teenage pregnancy; someone moving away from town. If the town at large behaved itself, the sermons honed in on a lone, unlucky male: an old classmate of Mama's, an old lover, or even Fanny's and my sperm donor.

"The men of Tombstone, Texas, have no motivation to look

like they should," Mama might start, pointing her spray bottle of cleaning liquid at a Ken doll. "Maybe it's the dip, or the booze, or the lack of self-respect that keeps them from picking up the chisel of fitness." Mama would warn about men who drive cars, men who wear hats, or men who went to all-boys schools as Fanny and I clacked our dolls' heels on the ground and sent our brains to outer space. The message was always the same in the end, anyhow: Don't trust 'em. Don't believe 'em. And don't leave your Mama all alone in the town of Tombstone with 'em.

If Mama's sermons had a "Top Hits" album, the following tracks might make the final cut:

"A donkey could drive better than him."

"Tie together three pumpkins with a string and I would have had a better prom date."

"What was that rectal thermometer doing in his kitchen in the first place?"

The incident at the movie theater became the latest addition to her repertoire. "Do they have the slightest idea what they've done?" Mama said. She was shelving cereal boxes with the kind of fervor that only came from a fresh sermon bubbling in her breast.

"They didn't break any laws," I said, though I knew it was useless to reason with a sermon.

"Not yet. But I've heard this story before. Watched it on a documentary. Bunch of retired folks, living peacefully, and all of a sudden some yoga clowns get bussed in, build a commune, and poison the water supply."

Did everyone in town have a cult-themed movie night without me? "Mama, they're harmless. I promise."

"I heard they're wearing robes," Nene mused.

"What?"

"Remember that moronic boutique hotel that shut down last month?" Mama asked. "Apparently those barefoot people bought up all the robes the hotel left behind. Mayor Johnston saw them all waving from their patio like fluffy pink lilies of the valley. What are all those men doing living together in robes?"

"Not all men. There's two women."

"Not anymore."

I almost sprayed disinfectant in my coffee. "What?"

"I heard there was a big old argument between the Jesus-looking one and the three who are always holding hands. No one around town has seen the three since."

"Those little piggies went to market," Nene declared.

I let out the breath I'd been holding. Mars was still in Tombstone. "Mama," I said, "I'm sure those three were just rogue troublemakers. The rest of the barefoot people are alright. I'm sure they won't cause any more trouble."

"You better not have sung along with them," Mama said, pointing a box of Texas-O cereal at me. (You can only fit one or two Texas-O pieces on a normal spoon. But for Tombstone families with lots of children—and Texas-sized bowls and Texas-sized spoons—it's a delicious way to start the day.)

"What's wrong with singing, Mama?"

"What's wrong with singing is that it's not for the movie theater. What kind of ignoramus doesn't know that? The people of Bloat Hill can go bloat on a hill, but at least they follow the basic rules of civility. And they're absolutely going to rub it in our faces that Tombstone folk caused a ruckus. They're going to send the worst of their own here for revenge."

"Isn't Bloat Hill mostly a retirement community? What are they going to do, shave their bunions in the town square?"

Mama shot a glance at Nene Miriam. "Don't you get any ideas."

Nene Miriam bobbed her head in compliance. She couldn't afford to engage in any rebellion or ruckus, what with her already tainted reputation.

Stale air hung in Swear-It's as I searched for a different topic of conversation. Mama had no interest in Mars's hips or the rings on her fingers, but that was all I had on my mind. What if I just came out right then and there? For a moment, I pictured it: *Mama, who cares about a little singing in a movie theater? I'm gay as the day is long.*

There's a version of Pinky out there who would do it. She could rip a bandage off and walk a tightrope without breaking a sweat. But I was no circus performer. I was the heiress to Swear-It's of Tombstone, Texas. Arguing with Mama was useless and surprising her was dangerous, especially when she was in the middle of a sermon.

Instead, I clung to the fact that she'd called my new friends "Tombstone folk." That was a win. They were Tombstone folk now, and we took care of Tombstone folk. Perhaps time and circumstance could heal the scrapes that my new friends had made on the knees of the townsfolk.

"Well, Pinky," Mama finally said. "That's done, for now. The store is yours. I'm taking Nene to pinochle."

"Mmhmm."

"One day, I won't have to tell you that. The store will just be yours all the time."

"Mmhmm."

"It's coming soon." Her eyes shone as she gripped the handles of Nene's wheelchair. "I'm proud of you, Pinky. You've got big things in store for you."

"Mmhmm."

"Get it? Store? We're in a store."

"That's funny, Mama."

"I trust everything will go like it does every Monday, but call me if you need me."

It did not.

TWELVE

No one was supposed to come into the store for another five minutes (you can set your clock by the townsfolk of Tombstone) when the bell announced Mars's arrival. I looked up from the espresso machine to the sight of her blonde hair and the sound of her smacking on a hard cinnamon candy, and it just about ruined the work I had done tamping down a little puck of coffee.

"Look who it is," she cooed, her fingers dancing around a stack of postcards advertising Texas's best features. I could feel my brain trying to flick itself awake, but without coffee in my system it was like a stovetop with no gas. Time to improvise.

"It's me," I said. Improvisation is not a strength of mine.

"Pinky pinky," Mars said, smiling. "I'm glad you came to the party last week. Took me a few days to recover from drinking all that giggle water. Blaze told me he was talking me up." She turned to look at me, her face now bare of mascara, blush, or any of the fixings. A party of freckles danced on her rosy cheeks, feigning innocence as to the secrets behind her eyes.

"He said you were single," I blundered.

"Well, I am."

"Okay." I knew what I wanted to believe about that, but

I couldn't entertain the fantasy. More likely Mars would ask me to set her up with a man in Tombstone. What good would that do? All the single young men in Tombstone were cheaters, liars, con artists, or fools, as Mama's sermons demonstrated. I didn't want to set Mars up with any of them.

But if the Sewing Circle believed I was helping Mars look for a man, maybe they wouldn't notice how closely I was looking at her?

Mars laughed. "You're something."

"So are y'all." Did she know I knew about the movie theater incident? I figured I might as well apologize, just in case. "Listen, I wish I had said something at the movie theater."

"Wait, you were there?"

Damn. "I was. It all happened so fast, I didn't realize you were getting kicked out. If it were up to me, I would have given y'all a microphone. You had quite the harmonies going! And you knew every word. But those old ladies . . ."

"Why didn't you come and sit with us?" She spoke so plainly, so optimistically, without any layer of judgment or bite on her words. This woman did not come from the American South.

"I . . . I don't know. I was there before you, and then . . ."

"Next time, Pinky! We'll host a movie night in our backyard—I don't think we're allowed back in the cinema. I do want to apologize about the behavior of my three friends."

"I hear they've left town."

"Left 2022 entirely." She arched an eyebrow at me and laughed. The stovetop of my brain was still flickering with no flame.

"I don't follow."

"I'm just joking!" Mars said, waving her hands in the air. Then she smacked them lightly down on the counter. "*Or am I?*"

"I'm not awake enough to guess."

"Good, good." She giggled. "Can I tell you a secret?"

I nodded, keeping an eye on the cup of coffee that I now desperately needed.

Mars lowered her voice to a whisper. "I didn't like them that much anyway."

"Why were you traveling with them?" I asked, whispering too.

Mars rapped the counter with her knuckles. "They're Blaze's old friends from when he lived on the compound. They've traveled together for ages. But they're a little restless. They want to draw attention to us. Blaze, Mika, Jean-Luc, Charlie, myself... we would rather not."

"If you want me to explain what happened to the movie theater manager, I can. He's my hairdresser's son. He's harmless, really."

Mars waved me off with one hand. "Oh, applesauce. Don't bother with all that. We're not big movie people anyway. We were just driving by and saw the marquee. I mean, who doesn't love *Sweet Charity?*"

Plenty of people our age have never even heard of the masterpiece that is *Sweet Charity.* I appreciated Mars's love for musicals. What was her favorite? *Jesus Christ Superstar? Evita? Hair?* Oh, it was definitely *Hair.* She could have walked straight in or out of a production of *Hair.*

"What do you like to do, then? I'd be more than happy to give you any sort of tour around Tombstone. What brought you here, anyway? I still have no idea."

Mars drummed her fingers on her cheek. I tried not to watch as her pinky ring, adorned in gold, swept over her lips. "What brought *you* here?" she asked.

"Consummation of my Mama and her sperm donor."

She laughed again. "Pinky, you're a breath of fresh air in this town, you know that?"

"Oh, I don't know. I wouldn't say I'm all that."

"Well, I will. A breath of fresh air and a sigh of relief." She inhaled and exhaled for effect, throwing me a whiff of cinnamon candy. "People in small towns can be wary of strangers," she said, "but you know there's no need for it. Everyone's just a bunch of limbs and fears."

"We're all 90 percent water."

"Are we?"

"Like a cucumber. That's what my friend June says."

"Or like a pickle?"

That stumped me for a second. "I guess?"

"Well," Mars said, standing up straighter, "this little cucumber's got to get back to the boy cucumbers so we can discuss life on the vegetable farm. See you around, pickle."

I don't know if I *was* a sigh of relief, but I certainly gave one. The movie theater incident had not derailed our acquaintance. Everything was going to go well for me, my new friends, and the town of Tombstone from now on.

As Mars was leaving the store, Former Mayor Joe Clark walked in. Face to face with her, he stopped for a minute.

"Veronica?" he whispered.

"Must have me confused with another dame!" Mars said quickly, running off so fast that the door would have hit Joe Clark where the good Lord split him, if the door weren't as old as Nene.

I went back to my hockey puck of coffee.

Former Mayor Joe Clark's routine was this: Saturdays were for cleaning the birdcage, even though Mr. Hooplah the parakeet had flown the coop five years prior. Sundays were for afternoon walks with his daughter, Tina. Mondays were for errands, kicked off with a trip to Swear-It's. One bag of pasta, one jar of sauce, one block of cheese. The same ingredients, the same conversation with me, every time. A few years ago, Tina had tried preparing a more elaborate pasta dish for her father, but the bread wasn't always in stock and the vegetables gave him gas, so it caused entirely too much turmoil and the notion was abandoned.

As Former Mayor Clark's wires started to tangle, Tina discovered how routine helped him hold on to memories: his wife's name, Tina's name, the criminal record of his no-good nephew. But I didn't know that when he entered the store that day. I hadn't heard many updates on Joe's condition through the grapevine. Joe was a proud man, being the former mayor and all. He didn't know he was losing his marbles. That was supposed to be between Tina, Dr. Withers, and Jesus.

So how was I supposed to know his routine was so important? Everyone in Tombstone had a routine. A dozen people came in on Mondays, bought the same dozen or so items, exchanged similar pleasantries with me, and went on their way. Working at Swear-It's was a rhythm that played automatically, one I'd stopped paying attention to until Mars came in with a blaring saxophone solo of a smile that stopped my heart and rattled Joe Clark's marbles.

By the time the blush had receded from my cheeks, Joe was absolutely discombobulated. I was, by my own humble guess, no more than two minutes late for our chat in the dry goods aisle, but by then it was too late.

"Former Mayor Clark," I hollered, rushing over. "How are you doing today?"

"You know how I'm doing. You and your little friend Veronica know exactly how I'm doing."

This was far from Joe's usual saccharine answer, "Just preparing for the day the Lord has made." His mutters coated the dry goods in a glazy layer of spit and disapproval.

"Excuse me, sir?" He wouldn't look at me, but I saw his hands fidgeting in a way that was unfamiliar.

"The government's put cameras in the streetlights. Papa's going to come home and give us the belt."

"The—do you mean traffic cameras, sir? They've got them in other parts of Texas, but I don't think they're in Tombstone yet."

"They're watching us," he seethed, gripping a packet of spaghetti so tightly the strands began to snap. Something was wrong. "Laughing at their Capitol Hill jobs as they poison our water!" His voice brightened like a tea kettle reaching the boiling point. He raised one finger in the air, almost knocking his World War II Veteran hat off his head.

"Sir, the sauce is—"

"The water is turning the boys into girls and the girls into boys, Esther! Didn't Veronica tell you that at the farm? She was just here!"

My name has never been Esther. Esther was the name of Joe Clark's first wife, who ran off with Joe's former political rival. Mama was not going to be pleased if she learned the name had echoed through the dry goods aisle.

Former Mayor Joe Clark was an old man. He'd once tutored Nene in math, but frontal lobes melt with old age, and I now realized that Joe Clark's was hanging on by a thread. Still, his comments stirred something heavy in my gut.

"Sir," I said gently, "let me call your daughter. In the meantime, I can put your groceries together?"

"They're poisoning us!" he started yelling. I looked up at the clock. 9:32. In five minutes, Janelle Watkins would come in for her post-run iced coffee. If I held her up, I would then hold up Andrew, who came to the store for Marlboro Reds. I needed to act fast. Cell phone usage on the clock is a sign of poor management and work ethic, but I needed to reach Tina. Fortunately, Tina was also Ashley's cousin.

"Ashley?" I said when she picked up, walking as far away as I could while keeping the man in sight. "Former Mayor Clark is having, uh, a tough time right now. At Swear-It's. Where's Tina? Can she come pick him up? I don't think he'll be able to find his way home."

"What happened?" Ashley asked. "He never gets upset on Mondays. Mondays are for errands."

"I . . . I don't know. It happened so fast. I went to see how he was doing in the store and he just started screaming about poisoning."

"Oh god. He's on that again. Listen, I'm about to put the baby down for a nap. I'll ring Tina. Can you hold him at the store until she gets there? It won't be more than fifteen minutes."

Janelle. Andrew. God, *Scooter* would come in before Tina could arrive, and all of them would see the mayor's debacle. "I think so."

"Great. Whatever you do, don't stress him out. Don't talk about Hillary Clinton, okay?"

"Why would I talk about Hillary Clinton?"

"Shh! Pinky. Keep your voice down."

I switched to whispering. "Okay. I'll put him in the back room."

I managed to put together Joe's order before Janelle Watkins came into the store, but when I tried to wrangle him into the back room with it, he just followed me back out onto the floor. Janelle went to her usual aisle, looking for the organic, gluten-free skincare that Mama got shipped from Dallas. On the way, she ran into Joe. His eyes were vacant and his muttering smelled of tobacco and conspiracy. I braced myself for confrontation.

Instead, affirmative grumblings soon filled the store. Apparently, Janelle Watkins was also a listener of whatever AM radio station first "reported" on this poisoning that was making the good people of Texas question their gender identities. I don't know how spy cameras or Esther's friend Veronica fit into things, but Janelle seemed to speak his language. More and more of my pity turned to anger.

Before I could bring some sanity to the discussion, the bell tinkled and Tina's sour face entered the store.

"Hi, Pinky," she said flatly. Her seat on the school board was up for grabs soon, and the stress of it showed under her eyes.

"Tina, hi. I'm glad Ashley could get a hold of you."

The pleasantries were not reciprocated. "What happened? He usually does great here."

"I don't know, I . . ."

"Did you change the layout of the store?"

"No."

"And the pasta, the sauce, and the cheese are all in the same place?"

"Yes, ma'am."

"What got him out of his routine? He's not doing too good

these days, okay? He needs his routine. One ounce of change throws him off. He gets on these crazy Alex Jones tangents that I can't get him out of for hours. If I block his Facebook, he gets all loony. It's awful. And that one"—she glared at Janelle—"only encourages him every chance she gets."

"I don't exactly know what set him off, Tina. I'm so sorry."

"You can't get him out of his routine. You can't get anyone in this damn town out of their routines. People stay here for a reason. They like what they like, and Tombstone doesn't change like the rest of the world does."

I nodded.

"So what happened?"

"I don't know. He saw that girl? Mars? And then . . ."

"He saw *who*? Is she one of those freaks who caused that scene at the movie theater?"

This was not going well. "I don't think I would call them freaks."

"What's their deal? Do they get a kick out of rattling up old folks? Haven't our country's seniors been through enough?"

"Mars didn't have any intention of confusing your father, honest. Even I didn't know he was this sensitive to changes."

"Sensitive?"

"I can't apologize any harder, Tina. I truly am sorry."

"You keep those shaggy-haired, barefoot buffoons away from my father in the future."

"I will."

Tina took one last nasty look at Janelle before switching into a candy-striper voice and escorting Joe Clark out of the shop.

I walked behind the counter. Janelle still had items to pay for. She kept to her routine, too; I've only ever known her with the same Kate Gosselin haircut and dye job, done by a revolving door of hairdressing students.

"I don't understand what Tina's problem is," Janelle said, putting her items on the counter. Three organic face masks, one iced coffee, and a specific brand of bottled water that Mama only stocks for her.

"Tina's always hated me," Janelle continued as I rang her up. "You're probably too young to remember mixtapes, but back in the eighties, I made a mixtape for a boy she liked. Gerald Schuster. Oh, Tina was so mad when he broke up with her. She's had it out for me ever since."

"I think she was just upset that her father was stressed." My mouth was a can opener, only compatible with cans of worms.

"Well, and he should be!" Janelle said emphatically. "He's got a screw loose, but the whole government is crooked. Evil. Tina wants to live in this made-up sham of a world where the government takes care of its people, but let me tell you something about the people in office. They don't have your best interest at heart and they don't have our children's best interest at heart, neither."

I didn't have any children.

"Former Mayor Clark may be older than electricity, but he's not wrong. The government is full of snakes. Politicians have different DNA. Have you read the research on the poison in the water?" She picked up her bottled water and shook it at me. "It's why I drink this. The things in our water, Pinky. You wouldn't believe it."

I gave a slow nod and watched the charms on Janelle's silver bracelet bounce against her tanned wrist. Her French tips squeezed the water bottle as she and her haircut left the store. Not a minute later, Andrew walked through the door.

Monday was back to normal.

THIRTEEN

Former Mayor Joe Clark fell back into his routine quickly, but the grapevine was still fruiting when June called an "emergency Sewing Circle" two weeks after his incident. I had yet to invite my friends to a party at 101 Bluebonnet Drive or an afternoon with the barefoot strangers at Peace Valley Park. My investigation into my new friends' backstories always seemed to get derailed by arts and crafts, keg stands, or a look from Mars that made my cheeks turn the color of a fire hydrant.

"Don't worry, Pinky, I've filled them in," Ashley said, grabbing the bottle of wine and bag of snacks out of my hands. I shut the door behind me. Everyone had already taken their places on June's furniture.

"What was that hippie woman doing disturbing Joe Clark, anyway?" Wanda asked.

"She wasn't disturbing Joe Clark," I said, taking my place on June's couch. "Is that what you told them, Ashley?"

"That's what everyone's been saying, haven't they?" Ashley said. "The week after they went and ruined *Sweet Charity* for the Women's Club, one of them went and lit a sparkler under Joe Clark's ass."

June gasped before Ashley could clarify that she was not being literal.

"Mars said nothing to Joe Clark," I said. "She came into the store to check out a local business. If anything, it was my fault. I should have gotten to helping Joe find his stuff quicker."

"Don't try to cover up for them, Pinky," June said. "They're terrorizing our seniors. Everyone's saying it."

"Couldn't you see this coming?" Ashley said. "We sent you out there to investigate those barefoot folk, and you made it seem like they were harmless."

"I told her she should have put together a more thorough dossier so we could have a discerning look at it," June said.

"Why aren't you furious about this too, Pinky?" Wanda chimed in. "It could have been your Nene in that movie theater. They came into Swear-It's and made a disturbance. They crashed your cat's funeral! All in the span of what? A month? Month and a half?" Wanda had been extra grumpy since she decided to quit vaping. She shoved her lollipop back in her mouth and I could hear sugary spit wash around like waves in a storm.

"Why are they doing this?" Ashley said quietly. "Is it because you're trying to take a peek into their business?"

"They're not doing anything. The funeral was an accident. The *Sweet Charity* thing was a misunderstanding. No one bothered asking them to stop singing before they got kicked out. Mars didn't say two words to Joe Clark, and she was in the store before him."

"Did they see Nene at your funeral?" Wanda asked. "That's what ties it all together, isn't it? The old folks. Baby boomers. Is this some kind of revenge against senior citizens?"

"Why would they seek revenge against a bunch of old folks they don't even know?" I asked.

All eyes turned to June, who adjusted her posture in preparation for a lecture. "Haven't you heard what people are saying about baby boomers on TikTok? They blame them for everything. Gas prices, racism . . . not that we have any of those problems here in Tombstone. I don't even know what-all they complain about. But there are people out to get the seniors."

We had all agreed after the 2016 election to avoid the news, after we all shed different types of tears. Our friendship had always been more important to us than what was going on in the world outside of Tombstone. As political talk threatened, Ashley, Wanda, and I squirmed in our indented spots on the couch.

"I wouldn't know, I'm not on anti-senior TikTok," I told June. "My feed is just cat gadgets and food recipes. But Joe Clark was the one causing a fuss in the store. You should've heard him. He was talking a bunch of awful nonsense about poisoned water and transgender people."

"He's from a different time, Pinky," June snapped. "He's not used to all these new terms. He's confused."

"His memory has been going for years," Ashley said. "I wouldn't fault him for that."

"All I'm saying is, Joe Clark was the one complaining. Not Mars. Not her friends."

"Are any of her friends transgender, is that why you're so offended?" Wanda asked.

"No. I mean, I don't know. Who cares?"

Wanda shrugged. "I was just asking. You're the one supposed

to be getting all their backstories. Sniff out whether they're here to cause trouble."

"They're not! They just like to dance and make art. That's about it. They're circus people, and I guess that is a little bizarre, but they're not out to hurt anyone."

"What kind of art do they make?" Wanda asked. "Penis sculptures?"

"Why would they do that?"

Wanda shrugged.

"I painted a picture of Sweet Potato Grace when I hung out with them. They've really been helping me get through my grief. They're always happy to hear about her. Blaze said I might see her again one day. Wasn't that nice?"

I shouldn't have said that. Ashley told me later about a new Netflix docuseries they'd all watched, about a woman lured into a cult of one by a man who claimed he could make her dog live forever. But I hadn't watched that, because I had better things to do.

"Pinky, I don't think these people are good for you to be around," June said.

"They're good people! Sally Granger's older brother was at their party the other night. I haven't seen him that happy since the football team beat Bloat Hill High in 2013."

"You went to a party at their house?" June said. She gripped the arms of her chair as she leaned forward. "When were you going to tell us this?"

"I didn't think you'd be able to come. I'm sure they'll have more parties. I'll invite you next time."

"That's not what June meant," Wanda said. "It just seems very unlike you to go to one of their wackadoodle drug parties."

"Drug parties?"

"That's what I've heard. People are saying they set up shop in Tombstone to run drugs through it. You've got to be on drugs to start talking about immortal cats."

"That's quite the busy schedule they've got, running drugs through town and terrorizing seniors," I said. "What are they going to do next? Work as paid actors at a protest for gun control?"

"That's not funny, Pinky," Ashley said. "What do you think they're doing here? Haven't you asked, since you're best friends with them now?"

"I knew we shouldn't have let her take on this investigation," June muttered. "She's too trusting."

"Did you get high at that party?" Wanda asked.

"I didn't get high," I said.

"Were people doing drugs? Hard drugs, like meth?"

"I didn't see anyone doing meth."

"They might have all been high the whole time. Oh, Pinky. We're going to go with you to the next one."

"Why? So you can interrogate them about how they're terrorizing the seniors?"

"We love you, but can I be honest, Pinky?" Ashley asked. "You see the best in everyone."

"What's wrong with that?"

"Remember when Ashley's sister joined that MLM and you bought stuff from her?" June asked.

I knew it was an MLM when I bought those leggings. I just felt bad for Ashley's sister. The Sewing Circle has not been able to let it go ever since. Before I could protest, Wanda took the baton from June and ran with it.

"You want to believe that everyone has good intentions. A lot of people do, especially people that live in Tombstone. I mean, just look at all the people who buy from Swear-It's and defend your Nene after she was accused of pushing pills to the husbands of the Women's Club. What we're saying is, you might have missed the signs of meth use when you were at that house."

"What signs of meth use?"

"Exactly!" Wanda said.

"We just want you to be careful," June said. "We care about you. And if you're spending too much time or putting too much of your trust in these barefoot people, you might get roped in with them."

"Nene never actually sold Viagra to the Women's Club," I said, in one final attempt to hang on to my dignity. "They found out who did it."

"Was she kicked out too?" Ashley asked.

"She was already dead."

FOURTEEN

I couldn't tell if it was the heat of late August or the dread of replaying the conversation with the Sewing Circle that was making me sweaty, but I found myself starting all my shifts at Swear-It's by checking myself in the mirror for flushed cheeks or tired eyes. I continued to spend time with the barefoot strangers when I could, though no one in town listened when I said they weren't nefarious. The stress was taking a toll on my posture. Fanny was the first to notice.

Thursday mornings were the only time Fanny ran the store. Mama didn't like it—she didn't trust her youngest daughter with basic math—but the delivery man dropped off inventory on Thursday mornings and Mama didn't like his manhandling of packages. Fortunately, what Fanny lacked in computation she made up for in the ability to sweet-talk a man into using his biceps for good. No more cracked eggs or broken vases.

Fanny was sitting pretty when I arrived, waiting for me to relieve her so she could go on a date or to acting class, or just to look pretty somewhere else.

"You're free to go, sister," I said, but she didn't move.

"You're free to go," I repeated. "Do you need new batteries or something? Your shift is over."

"What's with your posture?"

"My what?"

"Something's dragging your shoulders down into the depths of hell. Are you planning on telling Mama or not?" With a wiggle to readjust herself on the stool behind the counter, she clarified: "Is that what it is? You want to tell Mama what you were going to tell her at the funeral?

"I'll tell her eventually."

"When?"

"The moment passed, Fanny."

"Just because a bunch of barefoot strangers drove to the park and interrupted your eulogy doesn't mean you have to stay in the closet for another . . . what? Thirty years?"

"I'm twenty-two, Fanny."

"Same thing."

"What does it matter to you whether I come out or not?"

"I'm just curious."

"Well, be curious about something else. Figure out what you're going to do before you move to Los Angeles." I tried to walk around where Fanny sat to prepare the espresso machine, but she stood up and blocked my way. Did she think she could intimidate me? She looked like a kewpie doll.

"Can you tell her before I go to college? So I know you'll be okay?"

"Asking me like that doesn't reassure me that I will be."

Fanny shrugged. "From the mother-in-law suite you can't hear what they say on the news, Pinky. I can. If Nene or Mama believe a quarter of that stuff they watch, I do worry for you."

"All the more reason for me to put off telling them. Now can you let me make the dang coffee? Lord knows you haven't made a decent espresso in your life."

"Yes, I have."

"You left the grounds in the cup for Mayor Johnston."

"It was Turkish."

"That's not how you make Turkish coffee, Fanny."

"I have other things to worry about than how to make coffee. Like whether my sister is going to live a sad life in the closet, manning this store, or whether she's going to tell the truth about herself. Don't you want June to know? Ashley? Wanda? You want to rewatch episodes of *The L Word* alone in the dark for the rest of your life?"

"Why would I be in the dark?"

"You know what I mean. Do you even plan on telling your friends?"

I hoped the answer would magically appear behind Fanny's ear. It didn't.

"Pinky, you've got to tell someone."

Fanny's pity made me feel like a wilted bluebonnet. I turned back to face her. "I tried to tell the Sewing Circle about the Joe Clark nonsense and they just waved it off like he was a confused old man."

"He *is* a confused old man. He's also a racist, bigoted ass."

"Everyone just seems to excuse that second part."

"Yeah, because most people in Tombstone are okay with bigoted asses. Why the heck do you think I'm getting out of here?"

"Because you want to be an influencer?"

"Ha! I mean, sure, that would be nice. No, I want to get the heck out of Texas because it's a gross place to be. Try as people might, they're never going to put a Beto in the governor's seat."

"Does Mama know you feel like this?"

"As if she'd empathize, Pinky. I'm telling you. Ever since you went to college . . . you can't imagine how bad it's gotten. The crap they play on the TV. I used to drive some of the women from the Women's Club around before Nene got accused of pushing Viagra, and the things they would say would make you think it was 1823."

"Why don't they talk like that in front of me?"

"They think you're a sensitive, naive, bleeding-heart liberal wooed by the promises of academia."

"I went to Blinn."

"I'm applying to Stanford, but don't tell Mama that. I was so jealous you got out, and I was so heartbroken when you were sucked back in during the pandemic. I was glad when Nene stopped hanging around the Women's Club because none of them have a vaccine." A rapping on the front door brought my sister and me out of the bubble of our conversation. Mayor Johnston was here for her coffee.

"Shoot, Fanny, I'm going to hold people up again. What's going to happen this time? Sally Granger's going to start yelling about lizard people?"

"I would pay good money to watch her try and convince anyone of anything." Fanny grabbed her purse and started for the door when I grabbed her arm.

"Hey, Fanny?"

"Yes?"

"Are you going to the football game tomorrow?"

"You know damn well I have no interest in watching high schoolers play sports now that I've graduated. Why do you ask?"

"I was going to invite my new friends to come watch the game."

Fanny's right eyebrow shot up to her hairline. "Yeah, that'll keep 'em in Tombstone. See ya, Pinky!" She wriggled out of my grasp and opened the door for Mayor Johnston.

"Ma'am, it'll just be a few minutes," I called, rushing to find the coffee grinder. As the mayor walked into Swear-It's, Fanny gave her a wink and added, "If you'd like to share any conspiracy theories rattling around your noggin, now is the perfect time." I could see her smirk through the Swear-It's window as she left the building.

"Ma'am, I am very sorry about that," I started, but Mayor Johnston held up a hand.

"Please, Pinky," she said. "I wanted to talk to you."

"Okay."

"I've heard you've come in close contact with the new residents of 101 Bluebonnet Drive."

"I have."

"Now, we are a *very* welcoming group of people here in Tombstone."

"Mmhmm."

"We believe that all lives matter and we're all the same deep down."

"Okay . . ."

"And we believe in protecting the most vulnerable. Our seniors."

"Ah."

"You're a nice young woman, Pinky. We were all very proud to have you, Wanda Gleen, June Ripple, and Ashley Novak representing our town at Blinn. You can provide a good example of what it means to be a Tombstonian for the new folks in town."

"I mean, I know they've been at the center of some misunderstandings, but they're quite kind at heart. I like them."

"*You* have a kind heart, Pinky. That's why you're maybe the best person I can think of to help them adjust. Have you ever seen those signs that say, 'No shirt, no shoes, no service'?"

"I believe I saw some at Port A, but we haven't been down to the beach since I snuck a hermit crab back in my suitcase."

"Well, maybe you could put up a sign like that here at Swear-It's. Just offer a little guidance, hmm? We wear shoes in respectable public establishments here in Tombstone. And we worship God. Not a cat. Can you tell your new friends that?"

I blinked. I had no idea what she was talking about.

"Great. You're a doll."

Her coffee was ready. I swiped her credit card. She turned on her heel, sipping. The jingle of the bell above the exit rang sharply in my ears.

FIFTEEN

"What . . . what is it?" Jean-Luc asked. He was trying to stay neutral but couldn't twist his face out of its horrified expression. It was clear he had never seen Frito chili before, and the first impression was not spectacular.

"Someone's not from Texas," Wanda said, grabbing the single-serving bag of Fritos, opened on the long side for easy access. Janelle Watkins and her Kate Gosselin haircut may have some problematic views, but the woman makes the best Frito chili in all of Tombstone and shows up ritualistically to every high school football game to sell it. Are her conspiracy theories and her attitude toward the LGBTQ community worth overlooking for the perfect mixture of Fritos, chili, and delicious chemicals? Ask any homosexual holding a bag of Chick-fil-A nuggets. I can't give an opinion with my mouth so full of chili.

"Actually, Wanda," June said, "Frito chili can be found throughout the Southwest, although Texas did make it popular."

Blaze, Mika, Mars, Jean-Luc, and Charlie nodded in unison. Ashley and Wanda examined their nail beds.

"Thanks, Wikipedia," Wanda said.

"Wikipedia," Blaze said, perking up beneath his bucket hat. "That's a beautiful name."

The initial meeting of the Sewing Circle and my new barefoot friends was stilted. The boys came in hot to the tailgate, laughing a little too loud at the idea that our whole town showed up for a high school football game. When I tried to assure them that this *was* the season opener, and things would calm down throughout the regular season, June and Wanda interrupted with scoffs.

"What's wrong with tailgating a high school game?" June had asked. "We're a strong community."

Wanda played Switzerland and excused herself to buy Frito chilis for the group.

In the end everyone ate the Frito chili, except for Jean-Luc, so Charlie ate double. But besides the bagged meat, beans, and corn chips, it was quickly very clear that my two groups of friends had little in common. Crickets had more to say than these folks, and the disconnect made June, Ashley, and Wanda's mouths twitch at the corners. The barefoot folk didn't seem to mind the silence. They just stared wide-eyed at the scene, like grade-school girls at their first petting zoo.

"So," June said. "Where are you all from?"

She was met with four answers spoken at the same time, and a shrug from Charlie.

"New York," said Mars.

"Virginia," said Mika.

"Grew up on a weird compound but never did find out *where* it was," said Blaze.

"I believe it's called Vienna now," said Jean-Luc. "And Charlie's from Capilla del Monte. It's true what they say. About the UFOs."

June sighed. When she didn't get the answer she wanted, she tended to wiggle her shoulders like a woman wearing fringe. Her eyes zeroed in on Mika's curly hair. When June wanted to be subtle in gossiping about someone's background, she might ask the Sewing Circle, "What bubble do they fill in on a census?" I sent up a silent prayer that she'd save her questions for a more private conversation.

"What matters is that we're all here now," Mika said, looking much too content for the Sewing Circle's approval. He giggled at their obvious dissatisfaction and took another bite of chili.

"Well," Ashley attempted, "how are you liking Tombstone?"

Blaze smiled. "Perfect place for a bunch of freak shows like us to enjoy our vacation."

"Fix your face, friend," I told Ashley, whose eyebrows threatened to fly off her head. "Blaze and these folks were performing in the circus before they came to Tombstone."

Ashley's face remained unfixed. "Our town wasn't built for freak shows."

"What do you mean by that?" I asked.

"The people of Tombstone are all getting a little tired of your—oh no, Charlie! Are you okay?"

Charlie blinked rapidly, looking to Jean-Luc for help.

"Oh no," Jean-Luc said, turning slowly toward the group. "Is there meat in that chili?"

"Is there chili without meat?" Wanda asked. She took another bite.

Jean-Luc took a slow breath in. "Charlie's a vegetarian. His stomach gets a little rumbly when he has meat. We have to go." He went to reach an arm around Charlie's shoulders, but with a look at June's squinted eyes, he decided on a nice pat on the elbow instead. Neither gesture seemed to soothe the terror of a man whose stomach was preparing for battle.

"It was a real pleasure mingling with you ladies and taking in the local color," Jean-Luc said. "We are truly appreciative."

Charlie nodded his head. His cheeks bulged.

"Don't worry," Jean-Luc reassured us. "Charlie will feel a lot better once this chili is out of his body." They scurried off to find a restroom or pair of bushes far away from the tailgating families of Tombstone.

Ashley and Wanda twiddled their thumbs as I ran through a mental Rolodex of conversation starters. Frankly, I couldn't blame Mika or Blaze when they decided to join Jean-Luc and Charlie. They tipped their hats in farewell and thanked June for the lesson she'd been giving them in Tombstone history. Before June could mention that she hadn't yet begun to tell the story of Tombstone High's famous state championship win, all of the barefoot folk except Mars were gone.

"Well," Ashley said. "Just us women. I'm sure it's nice to have a break from those boys."

"Oh, I don't mind them," Mars said, peeking into the remaining packs of chili in search of extra bites. "As long as we grill the tofu before the burgers, Charlie is lovely company to have around. He doesn't talk much, but Jean-Luc talks enough for twelve. Once you get him going on Leopold I or Faye Dunaway, he doesn't stop."

"I wish my husband would tell me about his day once in a while," June sighed.

"How the hell can a person go to work in the morning, then come home in the evening, and have nothing to say?" Wanda said, half-singing the lyrics.

"Exactly, Wanda," June said, not picking up on the John Prine reference. "Michael is a better listener than most men, but I'll ask him, 'How are you doing?' and he'll shrug, and I'll say, 'Oh, you have to have some stories from the day. I stayed at home cleaning and shopping for couches and I have plenty of stories that I can tell you.' He shrugs again, so I end up just telling him about *my* day until I've exhausted myself of talking."

"I didn't think that was possible," Wanda said.

Mars stifled a laugh.

"What she means is that men just keep so much inside," Ashley said. "That's just who they are. All they want to do is wrestle in the mud and watch fights on TV. Women are better at talking. It's the mothers in us, always wanting to share the world with our littles. Do you have children, Mars?"

Mars looked at the empty space where her roommates had stood. "Those are my children."

Ashley cackled a high cackle, putting a hand on Mars's and squeezing the empty bag of Frito chili in it. "Oh, that's *hilarious*, Mars. Men really are like a second set of children, aren't they? That's what I always tell Pinky. She is so scared of having a boyfriend, and I say, 'Oh, don't be *scared*, Pinky. They're harmless. It's like having a child: you keep them fed and remind them to wear clean socks, and in return you have a best friend.' Other than us, of course."

"I'm not scared to have a boyfriend," I said. "I just haven't met anyone who I'd like as . . . a boyfriend."

June spoke at Mars as if I weren't standing right next to her. "Pinky's Mama and Nene are strong, independent women. Back when, they were the only business owners in Tombstone who couldn't have credit cards. There's nothing wrong with that type of feminism, and the Swears have been able to support themselves with their family store for four generations in Tombstone. It's impressive! But they raised Pinky and Fanny to believe that all men were terrible. You just have to be careful when you tell a young girl that men are useless."

"If they're so useful, why do they need reminders to wear clean socks?" I muttered.

"Alright, ladies, time out," Wanda said. "The game's about to start. Let's clean up and go to the stadium."

High school football games smelled like home. For as long as I could remember, fall Friday nights had been for grabbing a bag of salt and meat and corn chips, scarfing it down, and feeling too full for popcorn as I passed by Mrs. Bailey at the concession stand. But darn if that popcorn didn't always smell delicious. Every Friday, I would enter the stadium, take a deep breath in to smell the popcorn I had no room for, and listen to the Tombstone High marching band. I never told anyone how I felt about this tradition. It was one of the many things I kept to myself. But it was a tradition I never failed to practice, including when I walked into the stadium next to Mars. She caught wind, followed suit with a big inhale, and flashed me a big, crooked smile.

"Smells delicious," she said.

It smelled like home.

Tombstone High was not known for its athletics, but we did win the state championship back in 1954. My smile gave my sore ears a nudge as I listened, again, to Wanda telling the story of Darrell "Scooter" Jacobs's 52-yard pass that secured the historic win against the Odessa High Boll Weevils. June gently corrected her, saying it was a 45-yard pass, but Wanda held firm. Scooter had dated her grandmother, and her grandmother had the memory of a monk. Wanda could point out Scooter today, she told Mars. There he stood, leaning over his walker next to the team's mascot, where he stood during the singing of our national anthem at every game. Talk about resilience. Talk about fitness.

"And so the local college lets you use their stadium?" Mars asked as we walked to our seats.

"Local college? If we had one of those, Pinky would have never stepped across Tombstone's borders!" Wanda said.

"That's not true," I said, deflated. Was there a way I could nudge the Sewing Circle to present me a little better *without* giving away how Mars made my cheeks flush? "But this is the high school stadium. It's just for the high school."

Mars took this in. "Why is your mascot a ghost?" she asked, her mouth sticky with cotton candy from the concession stand.

"Ghost? No," June said. "That's a tombstone."

"Duh!" I said, poking Mars on the nose. Mars squinted at the tombstone costume as Ashley squinted at me, and the discussion was over.

Ashley clicked up the bleachers in her heels, and Mars squealed with glee. "It spins me around to see you wear heels to these games," she said. "And with a baby in a sling the whole time! Me, I wobble like a newborn fawn just trying to walk in wedges."

"Wedges are pretty easy to walk in," June said matter-of-factly.

"I can never keep up with what shoes are fashionable, anyway," Mars said, ignoring June's tone. "Way I see it, barefoot has been in style since humans stood up straight and started looking over the horizon. Barefoot, denim, and pearls. Timeless."

"I'm sure denim will go out of style eventually," June stated.

Mars looked at me, then out at the football field. "It won't. I know that for a fact. So this is the big spot for young people to boogie on a Friday night? Where do you go afterward?"

"Applebee's," said June.

"Chili's," said Wanda.

"Home," said Ashley.

"Ashley has the baby," June clarified. Ashley confirmed by smacking said baby on the rump.

"What about Fun Earl's?" I offered. "We had a great time there the other night."

June scrunched her nose. "Too noisy. Mars, have you heard the story of Pinky spilling the water at Fun Earl's in her Easter dress?"

The first half of the game was predictable. Chet Bailey's arm was as unstoppable as ever; Wanda hogged the tumblers. Sally Granger walked past with Ashley's ex-boyfriend and we all diverted our eyes. Only after she was out of earshot and we'd checked for family members in the bleachers behind us did we comment on her haircut, which June called "an attempted bob."

After Ashley and Wanda returned from the restroom at halftime, the polite fun we'd managed to have that evening got sucked into a bummer tornado. The two of them elbowed each other like little kids encouraging each other to talk first as they sat down on either side of Mars.

Ashley caved first. "Mars. How long do you and your friends plan on staying in Tombstone?"

"We've got no end date as of now. We tend to sink our teeth deep into a town until it's time for us to let go and move on."

"Sounds violent," Wanda said.

"It was a metaphor. A bad one, I guess. If you want the honest truth in this beautiful moment, we have plans to stay indefinitely." The air simmered until Mars followed up: "Why do you ask?"

Ashley looked around as she sank into a whirlpool of cringe. "We were just curious."

"Some people were creeped out by you guys moving in here unannounced," Wanda blurted out.

"*Creeped out* may be too strong," said Ashley. "But we just encountered a barrage of questions while waiting for the ladies' room. Folks are curious."

"About what?" I asked.

"Well, there was the disturbance at the funeral," Ashley said, "which—that was unintentional, sure. But then there was the movie theater incident in Bloat Hill. And word has gotten round that you host parties at all hours of the night, and none of y'all seem to have an uncle or a parent or a good pal who currently lives in Tombstone. People are just . . . wondering why. What brought you here. What you're up to."

"Can we stop talking about the funeral?" I groaned. "That was *my* cat's funeral. Them stopping by didn't bother me one bit. Why can't this town get over it?"

"Scandal travels faster than forgiveness," June said.

"Lovely, June, thank you," I said. "So what, people are just asking *why?* Okay, then. Why here, Mars? Why did you decide to move to Tombstone? Why don't you tell us all of your business right now?"

Mars looked like a deer cornered by hunters. "We always trust that we'll come to the right place at the right time. We go where we're needed. I don't know if that's going to be good enough for whoever's asking, but that's the truth."

June looked like she had sucked on a lemon. "And what does Tombstone need from you?" she asked.

"Don't people have a right to move where they want?" I asked. "Isn't that what Texas is all about? Freedom?"

"Of course they do," June said. "It's just that no one has ever moved to Tombstone and started causing trouble without causing a whole lot more trouble later." Her expression was rehearsed: no teeth showing in her smile; rapid, creepy blinks. Mars wouldn't catch the insincerity behind it, but I did.

"Mars is a friend of mine now, and I hope she can be friends with y'all, too," I said. "She didn't have to stay for the game, but she did, right?"

"Why wouldn't she have stayed for the game?" Wanda asked.

"Her friends didn't stay for the game," June muttered.

"Enough." I looked at Mars's hands and squeezed my own against the edge of the bleachers.

Mars gathered herself inside the fuzzy vest she wore. "Maybe I ought to go," she said. "Keep the boys from getting into trouble. It was enchanting spending time with you ladies."

Great. My friends had done it—just pushed her out of the way. And for a second, I was going to let them.

I stood up. "See you next Saturday? For the party?"

Mars nodded. She opened her mouth but nothing came out.

"That's what you're doing on your birthday weekend, Pinky?" Wanda said.

"Yes," I said quietly. When Mars had told me about the party a few days prior, I'd neglected to mention I was celebrating my twenty-third birthday the day before. At the mention of my birthday, Mars turned back around.

"You're all invited too," she said sweetly. "You can join our little utopia on Bluebonnet Drive anytime you want."

The sound of Mars walking down the bleachers was drowned out by cheers, the announcer calling a touchdown, and the cheerleaders hollering on the field. My friends raised eyebrows and avoided eye contact with me as they mouthed the word *utopia* among themselves.

All surrounding popcorn bags had been reduced to kernels. As I tried to center myself with a deep inhale, all I could smell was the fading tendrils of Wanda's vape pen. She never did well with conflict.

I stood up again.

"Bathroom?" June asked.

"Nope. I'm going to head out, too."

"Wait, you're not coming to Applebee's with us?" Wanda asked.

"You know what, Wanda? I hate Applebee's. I really, truly don't like it."

Ashley dropped her jaw and scoffed at my incredible statement. June was in rare form: speechless. Wanda shrugged and kept her smile to herself. Secretly, I know she agreed.

Before anyone could defend the integrity of corporate spinach and artichoke dip, I took my leave.

SIXTEEN

My heart was beating fast as I walked out. I don't really hate Applebee's. I should have just said, "I've got to wash my hair," or, "Having lady troubles," or whatever people say to excuse themselves from events that make them want to walk on coals and forget where they're going. But my friends had been rude to Mars, and I couldn't let her walk through the parking lot feeling like she didn't belong. I felt like that too often to let another person suffer through it.

Amid the sea of moms taking slow sips from thermoses and dads lassoing children into cars, Mars stood alone, shaking.

Not trembling. More like . . . flailing?

The sight of it stopped me in my tracks. Mars was shaking her arms like she was drying them off at a truck-stop bathroom. The movement wasn't violent, just jerky, like someone trying to dance who'd only read about it in books. Or a doll, controlled by a puppeteer who was shaking out the knots in her strings before the show began.

I could hear Nene Miriam in my ears as I watched. "It's never polite to stare, unless you're on the side of the road and no fine gentleman has come to your rescue. Then you stare down every son of an unhelpful gun and you wave them down with your pretty, muddy-brown, desperate eyes." Practical advice; but seeing how I was not in the particular scenario Nene had described, I snapped myself out of my slack-jawed pause and walked up to Mars.

"You okay?" I asked, interrupting her trance.

She stopped, blinked, and gave an embarrassed smile. "Yes, pickle, I am. Actually, why don't you join me?"

"What do you mean?"

"Give me a shake. Loosen up!" She lifted her arms once more, leading with her elbows. As her knobby joints caught sight of her ears, she started shaking her arms around. No one in the parking lot noticed; I imagined they might call a medic if they did. Mars kept inviting me to mirror her.

What was the worst that could happen? Certainly, the *worst* thing would be a stray bullet going through my elbow precisely as I lifted it toward the sky. I was in Texas, after all. Emotions run high after football games. But no, no, that wouldn't happen.

The worst that could happen would be onlookers seeing the bizarre dance between Mars and me and calling attention to us. Everyone in the parking lot, including Ashley's sister's family, a regular customer from Swear-It's, and Mama's old neighbor from when she briefly lived with my sperm donor, would see me raising bare arms in Texas without having arms to bear, next to a woman who was already causing suspicion around town. This was a gamble, and no headway had been made in giving Texas a casino. But Mars had her eyes dead set on mine and I didn't want to look away.

I lifted my arms and jiggled them around. It felt as bizarre as I imagined, which made Mars throw her head back and laugh. Her hair danced and her smile shone.

"I'm not quite sure what this is for," I admitted, wiggling just my left arm.

"Exactly! Keep going until you do. It's just to loosen up." She flicked her hands back and forth. "To the misunderstood!"

I lamely followed suit.

She flicked them again. "To the freak show!"

"Maybe this is better suited for the privacy of one's home?" I said.

"To Sweet Potato Grace!" She closed her eyes and danced in circles, so I tried the same. And you know what? Tombstone disappeared. Texas disappeared. The particles of stress that were battering my brain rushed up through my arms and shot from my fingertips, out of my life. Goodbye to Joe Clark's rants and June's judgments. Sayonara to sixty more years of working at Swear-It's. Worries flew off my fingertips and I lost track of time. Quite possibly, I lost track of my mind, but I felt silly and I liked it.

I kept dancing and shaking until my laughter became entangled with Mars's and we both ran out of breath. Eyes open, spinning toward each other, we put our hands on our knees and came back to ourselves.

"What did we do that for?" I asked again.

"Pinky," she said through little bursts of giggles, "I'm not going to say anything about energy or good vibrations or any of that wacky stuff. I just felt stale in there. Have you ever felt stale?"

"What do you mean?"

"You feel it in your heart or your veins or the layer in your head between your brain and your scalp. Like a neglected cracker, stiff and out of place. A shake of the limbs un-stales me." She stood up and gave one final shake. I followed.

"Like you've got a dry mouth?" I asked. "And your ribs are shaking and every single day is just a Groundhog Day of the same crap over and over, but no one else thinks it's awful except you, so maybe you're the problem? And you've set yourself up for this life that's just Groundhog Day forever, but you didn't realize you were doing it because there was a global pandemic on? And you just wanted to survive and for your Nene to survive? And now, with vaccines, which not everyone has gotten because it's Texas, you feel like you're just realizing what you got yourself into? And you just want to get out because if you have to live like this in the closet, I mean the shadows, you're going to descend into madness? And also your cat just died?"

"Yes," Mars said. "Yes, pickle, you've got it. Don't you see why we're here?"

I didn't, but I was too excited to care. I lifted my hand to Mars as if I wanted her to kiss it. I did want her to kiss it, and maybe she knew that, too. I held her gaze. But when she started leaning her head forward, I started shaking my wrist around limply. My fingers bobbed and bounced and a smirk grew on my face. Mars reached out her arm to follow me and we shook our arms and shook our hips and shook our legs and started jumping around the parking lot, whooping and hollering until I was sure someone *did* see us. No music played, but it could have started and we would have been on beat.

"Can I drive you home?" I asked, wheezing between syllables.

"Pinky pinky, that sounds delicious. Do you want to hang out at the house?"

"I can't. I'm sorry. My shift at the store tomorrow starts early."

"Well, Pinky, a drive is nice, too. Any time spent with Pinky Swear is heaven on Earth."

We hopped in the car and drove to her house, not looking back.

"I apologize for June," I said. "At first, I assumed she asked why you were staying in town because . . . well, you give off the impression that you're a bit nomadic. The traveling type. I mean, you are part of a circus."

"It's okay. Wouldn't be the first time that we showed up somewhere and made people scratch their heads."

"What type of circus artist do you think I could be?" I asked.

"It's not up to me to say. What type of circus artist do you want to be?"

I had decided months ago, after playing it out in my daydreams between customers at Swear-It's. Down to the sequined straps. I had my whole character figured out. "Maybe a tightrope walker? I climbed once or twice in a real climbing gym that we had here before it went out of business. Being up high like that is such a thrill. Do you climb?"

Mars shrugged. "We had to scramble up a mountain once, and it did feel good to escape those tigers."

"What?"

"If you were a tightrope walker, what color eyeshadow would you wear?"

"Why do you ask that?"

Mars leaned back in the passenger seat, arms hugging the headrest, legs stretched out. Her toe rings kissed the glove compartment. I wiggled my cheeks to prevent blushing. "The picture in my head isn't fully formed yet, toots. I can see you up high, smiling as the crowd cheers, unfazed by the ringmaster and the lions below. But I can't see the details. Are you holding a baton? I think some dames do that."

Baton twirling was not a part of my backstory, but could it be? Would it be? I hadn't thought about eyeshadow or mascara. Maybe my mascara was running.

"Do you think it's silly to entertain this?" I asked. "I'm never . . . I'm not going to be a tightrope walker."

"You could."

"No, I couldn't."

"Why not?"

"It's . . . it's silly." I wanted to say, *Imagine me trying to tell June or Wanda or Ashley that I wanted to be a tightrope walker.* I could hear Ashley's laugh and June's explanation as to why tightrope walking was not a sustainable life goal. Wanda might support me, but she'd never let me live it down.

"Silly? So what, Pinky? You know what else is silly? Flailing your arms around in a high school parking lot to deal with your stress. So is being at a high school football game as a young adult with no children! So is football! So is high school! So is time and space, and questioning what the heck it all means. You've lived here all your life, but you have to admit." She lowered her voice to a whisper. "Texas, Pinky, is a very silly place."

"Silly is one word you could use."

Mars sprang up, emboldened and inspired. "And you know where else is silly? Brazil. Saskatoon. Czechoslovakia. Zaire. Every place has the same greedy humans and the same kinds of conflicts. People wind each other up until they're too tense to dream. But boy, life is better spent when you're free enough to dream."

"Isn't calling it Czechoslovakia a little . . . unwoke?"

"Hmm?"

"It's not Czechoslovakia anymore, right? It's the Czech Republic. Texas has a large Czech population. We had a whole unit about it in third grade."

"Oh," Mars said, tapping her finger on her chin. "Guess I was too busy dreaming to consult my map. When did that change?"

"Before we were born, Mars."

"We?"

"What year were you born?"

"Beginning of the century."

Okay, so she *was* my age.

"I can't believe you didn't tell me your birthday was next week," Mars said. "It's actually beautiful timing."

"Why's that?"

"We have a big surprise for you. We're putting the finishing touches on it tomorrow. You'll see it at the party."

I was glad the sun had set and I could hide the blush on my cheeks.

"Pinky, pinky," Mars said. "Do you think you'll ever leave Tombstone?"

"Why do you say that?"

"We've met a lot of people on our travels who need to get up and leave where they're living. They remind us a lot of you."

I stumbled over my answer. "No—well, not anymore, not after I've just made new friends! And it's not something I can just do whenever I want. Mama's been hoping that I will take over Swear-It's and become the Tombstone staple that she's always been. That my Nene was. And then I'll care for Mama just like she's caring for Nene. And so on and so on . . ."

"And you'll have a daughter that will care for you one day? She'll have a daughter that cares for her?" She shrugged and looked out the window. "I can see beauty in that."

"I don't know. Even if I stay in Tombstone, I don't think there's any hope of me starting a family." There it was. The point of no return. It was so close I could grasp it, exactly like I wanted to grasp my words and shove them back in my mouth.

"Why's that?" Mars asked.

I took a breath like I was diving into a pool. Mars was the one who'd grabbed my hand. *She* was the one who'd grabbed *my* hand. Plus, didn't I need practice with this whole thing? As selfish as it might have been at the time, I told myself that even if Mars spilled the beans on my sexuality, most people in Tombstone wouldn't believe her anyway.

"Well," I said flatly, "I'm gay. And there aren't many folks in Tombstone who embrace that sort of thing."

Coming out of the closet while in a motor vehicle is highly ill-advised. I remembered a movie where a woman told her daddy she was gay and he drove off the road in shock.

I thanked the idea of Jesus that I was in the driver's seat and kept my eyes on the road, even when I felt the warmth of Mars's smile hit my cheek. I exhaled slowly.

"Ha!" she said, throwing her hands up in the air. I had seen videos of parents who treated their children coming out like a birthday party, but I didn't think that happened in Texas. "Yee-haw! Do people say that here? Now? Yee-haw! Dang, that's the bee's knees. And you know, it's possible to have children. The developments coming our way in science . . . Oh, I was hoping I wouldn't be the only full-on dyke in this city."

I gasped, but my offense didn't seem to bother Mars. "Oh,

shoot," she giggled. "Is that not the word for it anymore? Has it gone the way of Czechoslovakia?"

"It's not really nice, is it? I don't know what people say where you're from, but . . ."

"Where I'm from, it's only not-nice if it offends you. Nothing pierces me! Except for the guy who put a little charm in my belly button." She lifted her shirt and showed off a dangling gem that *might* have sent me off the road if I hadn't already seen it peeking out when we were standing around at the tailgate.

"I wanted my belly button pierced so badly when I was younger," I said.

"What happened?"

"My Mama told me that belly button piercings were for women who ran off with married men. Nene confirmed it and said belly buttons were the Devil's territory. Of course, they didn't say that when Fanny decided to get hers pierced when she was sixteen."

Mars sat back in her seat, stunned. Then, she perked up. "Pinky, I was hoping that you were gay from the moment I saw you. I said to myself, 'That woman looks like the sweetest thing. I hope she's a flaming homosexual. I hope we can paint our nails and talk about women and go out on the town.' Women do that out and about, right?"

"Somewhere like Austin, sure. But in Tombstone?"

"In Tombstone . . . ?"

"There's not a gay bar for hours, much less a lesbian bar. I couldn't go with anyone, anyway. I'm the only gay person here, I think. And no one knows I'm gay besides my sister."

Mars sighed. "Ah, Sisters. I loved that club. Hey, you're only alone on the drive *to* the gay bar, Pinky. Once you're there, you're family."

"I think that's the Olive Garden."

"What a beautiful name for a gay bar."

Before I could tell her about unlimited breadsticks, we pulled into the driveway and waved to Blaze and Mika sitting in the front yard. The melodies coming from their guitars sounded like what Mama calls "California music"—The Mamas and the Papas or Peter, Paul, and Mary. Songs about road trips and sunshine. I sniffed around for the smell of fresh flower crowns. Maybe I'd make a crown for myself and Mars. Maybe one day we could sing together.

"Are you sure you don't want to stick around?" Mars asked as she got out of the car.

"I have a shift tomorrow morning, remember? In twelve hours!"

"Time isn't real. Time is fake! You can bend it, if you believe!" She threw up her hands and spun around three times, prompting cheers from the boys in the front yard. They repeated her chants:

Time isn't real!

Time is fake!

You can bend it, if you believe!

"The early-morning customers at Swear-It's will disagree, Mars. See you next week at the party?"

Mars kissed the tips of her two fingers and threw me a peace sign. "I'll see you whenever you'd like."

SEVENTEEN

11:20 p.m. was the time displayed on the home screen of my phone. The wallpaper behind it was a drawing of Sweet Potato Grace, one Wanda had made during the pandemic when there was nothing else to do besides take up a hobby. In the drawing, Potato's jaw hung open, revealing her sharp little teeth. She looked up with pleading eyes. I wish I had given her more treats when she looked at me like that.

11:21 p.m. Above the time, my phone displayed the date: September 2. My birthday was in thirty-nine minutes. As a birthday gift to myself, I forgave myself for the late-night indecision I was experiencing. Should I call Mars? Should I not?

Mars deserved a call. Spoken word was her preferred way to spread the news about a party or a cookout at Peace Valley Park or whatever they planned to do that day. But I couldn't bring myself to pick up the phone just to ask her such an embarrassing question.

Can we keep what I told you last week a secret?

All week, I'd felt the sticky sort of guilt and confusion and shame that had always kept me from coming out of the closet, seeing the light, facing the pitchforks. Yet I felt guilt and confusion for hiding, too. Every free moment when I wasn't working at Swear-It's, I was picking up the phone and putting it back down. Every time I put it down, I picked it back up again. Then I put it down. Telling Mars I was queer had felt like a peek into the outside world, but I didn't feel ready to swing open the door and blind myself with ridicule, or freedom, or both.

I had planned to come out to Mama first, then my friends, after college graduation. Really, I had. I never expected COVID to send me back home or Mama to throw me into a full-time job at Swear-It's before the rest of the world opened back up. Life moved so fast and so slow during COVID that no plan seemed right. I couldn't see a scenario where I could be myself and work at Swear-It's and keep Mama happy *and* look for other places to live. It just wasn't possible.

It was so easy for everyone online. "Mom, I'm gay." "Dad, I like girls." "I have something to tell you . . . I'm trans." Hugs and happy tears follow. No clicking tongues or wringing hands or weights chained to the ankle of your reputation. Weights that follow you like they followed Roger.

I wish I could have called Roger at that moment.

Roger Lindsay was Tombstone's resident handyman, caretaker, and homosexual. His mother had been my health teacher; her motto for all things, including contraceptives, was: "Plastic wrap will do just fine." His father had also been a handyman, but he'd died of a heart attack while Roger was traveling the world. Oh, the tales Roger told us about boat rides and backpacks and bright stars. He was the Big Dipper, and I was the little one. Roger had been living elsewhere—first abroad, then in Austin, Mama told us—until he hit fifty, when he came back to Tombstone to care for his ailing mother. For that, if only that, Mama respected him. And for his precision when taking on repair jobs. On the rare occasions when Mama couldn't fix a broken who-knows-what in the house or the shop, she would call Roger.

"He's a fruit who has chosen a life of depravity," Mama once told us with flared nostrils, "but he knows a hell of a lot about plumbing."

"I thought euphemisms weren't allowed in this house," Nene Miriam replied as she scooted past us.

"The point is, Roger's decent because he keeps all that stuff private. He doesn't flaunt it here in Tombstone. If he hadn't been photographed for *The Texas Tribune* at one of those rainbow sin marches, no one would even know he was living that way." She shook her head. "Disgusts me, but having to call a plumber in Bloat Hill disgusts me more."

Before I knew anything about the birds and the bees, I was sure fatherhood was just about being nearby. When I asked Mama if Roger was my real dad, she laughed all the way to the bank and back. Then she saw my disappointment and launched into her first sermon about how straight men are deadbeats.

I was wrong about the biology of it all, but I don't think my instincts were incorrect.

Fanny was disappointed when Roger turned out to have inadequate advice on walking in heels. I, however, found Roger's breadth of knowledge fascinating. Every time he laid a pipe or tamed a screw—don't tell Nene Miriam he did *any* of this—I was by his side. My little legs would dangle off the counter, safe in the cosmic knowledge that Roger's and my souls were compatible in a way no one around us could claim. I miss the candy bars we would split and the stories he would share.

I had to beg Roger once to let me watch him fix a leak. I must have been around twelve years old. The day before, I'd borrowed a documentary about Pride from the public library and snuck it into my room. The sight of Marsha P. Johnson and Sylvia Rivera set alight a curiosity and a feeling of kinship I couldn't quite explain. I *had* to know what they had done to get on the cover of a DVD. Roger would know. He knew everything.

Roger was under the sink when I asked him about it. "Roger? Who is Marsha P. Johnson?"

"We don't all know each other," he said, quick as a whip. He didn't pause or look away from what he was doing. He just kept on wrenching.

"What?"

"Oh, I'm just being silly. Where did you learn about Miss Marsha?"

"She was on the cover of a DVD. It had one of those big rainbows like you've got on the inside of your toolbox."

Roger stopped what he was doing and slid out from underneath the sink. If I ever get the chance, I would love to ask him what was going through his mind.

"Hmm," he finally said. "Did they show this at school? What grade are you in now?"

"Seventh. Mrs. Novak is my teacher, but she didn't show it."

"Ha! Like heck she did!" Roger said, throwing a bolt into a bucket. "Cassidy hasn't looked my way in ten years, not since I got back from living in Austin." He sat up, leaning my way and lowering his voice. "Do you want to hear a piece of teacher gossip?"

"Yes!"

"Cassidy Parker, before she went off and married that oil man, was my senior prom date."

My squished face sent Roger into a howling laugh.

"Oh, I knew I was a friend of Dorothy, Pinky. I had known for a long time! But Cassidy would have thought I was talking about Dorothy Braun in the year above us. Oh, what a hoot. I was the only man at Tombstone High that year who bothered to match his date's corsage to her dress. Lime green. I still shudder to think of it."

"Who's Dorothy?"

"Some people will tell you Dorothy Parker, but don't let those uppity queens fool you. 'Friend of Dorothy' started with *The Wizard of Oz* and those beautiful red shoes."

Roger enjoyed watching me climb through his lingo like it was a jungle gym.

"It means I'm gay, Pinky."

(It had taken me over a week of wracking my brain to connect this memory with Jean-Luc's Dorothy reference at the party.)

"Is that why you went to Austin?" I asked Roger. "Because . . . you know Dorothy?"

"That's why I went everywhere else. Travel is like a mirror. Tombstone is like an ID card with a picture you don't remember taking and personal information that someone else wrote." He held my gaze with a paternal sternness I recognized from movies. "There's family in Austin," he told me clearly, "but Texas is Texas, okay? Remember that, and be careful."

"Mama says there isn't any need to travel, because we have everything we need in Tombstone."

Roger's face fell. "Everything but a good place to get Indian food, and—" He stopped himself. "No, Tombstone is a nice place, I suppose." He went back to work.

Roger never said a bad thing about Tombstone, not really.

He never said a bad thing about anyone his whole life. People never offered him the same courtesy. Especially not Mama. The day after I asked him about Marsha P. Johnson, Mama found the DVD in my backpack and called Roger on the phone. She shook the whole house with her shouts and spitting rage. I cried into my pillow that night, unsure how to defend myself without confronting an unfamiliar feeling of shame.

But I've never cried harder than after Roger passed away. Tommy Beans broke the news when I was thirteen. "Did you hear that old fag died?" he told people on the playground. I heard him from across the blacktop.

"Don't say that!" I said, stomping over to him.

"He died last week," Tommy told me, looking me straight in the eye. "No one knew because he lived alone. His cats were eating his face."

"Stop it!"

"My daddy said that's what happens to old fags. They die alone. No one loves them."

I ran to the nurse's office, not sure if I was short of breath because I didn't like to run or because I was crying too hard for air to get in.

Roger had died of a heart attack, one year after his mama's death. Neighbors found out because they saw his indoor cat roaming the streets. I overheard Brenda talking to Mama one day about it at Swear-It's. At the mention of Roger, Brenda shook her head and looked to the floor.

"Caring for a parent is difficult, Irene. Maybe he died of a broken heart."

Mama shot back, "His mother certainly did, seeing who he turned out to be."

I may have been raised to believe that men were terrible, but that wasn't true of Roger. He was the closest thing I had to a father, and that's why I wished he was still around so I could ask him what he thought about my new friends. What did he think about what Mars had told me that night? And what I told her? And how I felt?

How could I explain it? I know my body's filled with organs and blood and cells, but with Mars, I just felt every hollow space filled with the desire to close the distance between us. I felt that way whether we were half a town away or sitting right next to each other. What was that, Roger? Was it what I thought it was?

In the weeks after Sweet Potato Grace's death, my deceased cat had begun to show up in my dreams. I don't know what happens when people die, but I hoped that Roger could show up in the same way. I decided to sleep on my question to Mars.

"You would have loved Roger, Sweet Potato Grace," I said to my phone screen. Those angry eyes. She always looked impatient, no matter what time was displayed on the screen.

11:25 p.m.

EIGHTEEN

Sweet Potato's feeder offered its birthday morning greeting after a night of nothing. No conversations with Roger. No snuggles with my deceased kitty. If my unconscious mind had gotten a chance to pet Sweet Potato Grace, I didn't remember it. I wished I'd had a more fitful night of sleep—being yanked out of your dreams at least allows you to remember them.

Sunshine greeted me through the mother-in-law suite's one window as I walked to the counter for a birthday coffee. This birthday coffee was different from a regular coffee only in that I drank it sitting down, to calm my restlessness. (I had been busying myself with chores while drinking my coffee since early summer, on account of how I used to enjoy it on the couch with a little reality television and the ever-judgmental Sweet Potato Grace, who I always thought looked shockingly similar to Lisa Vanderpump.)

Mama had given me the day off for my birthday. All I had on the calendar was an afternoon with the Sewing Circle. My gift was the choice of activity: would we tan ourselves at the watering hole? Picnic at Peace Valley? This was the one day where the decision was up to me. My gift to myself was that I wasn't going to make it until I arrived at June's.

Two sips into my birthday caffeination, I stopped. "Why do I feel so tense?" I said out loud. Stale, crusty air glided into the mother-in-law suite from the house across the yard. My skin itched. "Catitude" mug in hand, I left the suite and followed the sounds of an argument between Mama and Fanny.

By the time I opened the screen door, all that was left of the conversation was a sticky air of disagreement. Mama was facing toward Fanny, away from the stove, leaving my birthday casserole to burn. Fanny was seated at the table with her hands balled up into fists. Once she saw me, she loosened them.

"Happy birthday, Pinky," she said quietly.

"Happy birthday, darling," Mama said. At the sight of my face, her eyes bulged. She remembered the casserole and took it out of the oven. I'd saved Birthday Breakfast, even if it was a shade browner than usual.

"Thank you," I said. "Is everything okay?"

"Nothing could be better! My eldest daughter is a growing young woman and she's well on her way to claiming her rightful place as the head of—"

"Your friends made a flag and the town is upset about it," Fanny interrupted. She knitted her eyebrows as she turned back to Mama. "She's going to find out about it. They did it for her. Obviously."

"What are you talking about?" I asked. "What flag? Who?"

Mama sighed and rubbed her temples. "I did not want to get into this on such a special morning. But since the chicken has hatched, it's time to fry it up." She cleared her throat and looked at me. "Those barefoot *freaks* have erected some offensive flags.

One of which is at your expense." She stabbed the casserole with her spatula. "It's a strange way to be a friend, if you ask me. I don't know what you see in those dirty little—"

"Mama, stop it," Fanny said. "I'm sure there's a misunderstanding. I was planning on dropping Pinky off at June Ripple's house today; maybe we can stop by there beforehand and get to the bottom of this."

"I don't want you around those queer little troublemakers anymore," Mama said, her spatula now pointing at me. "You think they're cool because they've got shaggy hair and bare feet, but they're dangerous. Hear 'em out, sure, but we've done that. And this town has heard enough of them."

Queer. "What are you talking about, Mama?" I asked.

"How about we just go see for ourselves," Fanny said. "No more barefoot talk at Birthday Breakfast."

I protested, but Fanny's eyes shot me a warning: Mama's incoming sermon wasn't going to have me jumping out of my seat shouting *amen*. We scarfed down our casserole in silence, Mama only prodding the tension by saying, "Don't you want to open your present, Pinky Elizabeth?" I looked at Fanny, who smiled with the trepidation of a dormouse. I nodded and waited as Mama waddled into the living room to grab the same pink bag she put my gifts in every year.

Last year, the gift had been a collection of cat toys. "Now that the store's opening up again, you're going to be away from that snappy kitty," Mama had said. "Most cats hate their owners, but you've got a weird one, I guess."

No cat toys this year.

I reached my hand into the bag and felt a familiar fabric. Canvas. I pulled out an apron just like the one I wore to Swear-It's every day. Only when I unfolded it did I see it was brand new. Right smack in the middle of the chest, "Pinky Elizabeth" was embroidered in pink, curly lettering.

I tried to summon all the enthusiasm I would have given this five, ten, or fifteen years ago, but I was scraping the bottom of the barrel as I gave Mama a weak smile.

"Thank you. It's lovely," I said.

"Isn't it? I figured, considering you'll be taking over and all, that you would want to have an apron all your own." Technically, I already did have an apron all my own, since Mama wore Nene's old apron and Fanny didn't wear one. (Canvas didn't show off the shape the good Lord had given her.) But this was a gesture of kindness. My insides sank with guilt.

"Thank you again. I really appreciate this." With three neat folds I placed the apron back in the bag, which I carried with me as Fanny and I made our way out the door.

Mama offered one final warning: "You've got everything going for you, Pinky. Your life is perfect here in Tombstone, remember that. There's no point in shaking things up."

Fanny waited for me to speak as we drove toward Bluebonnet Drive. I was having a one-sided conversation in my head. All I could hear, over and over, was the word *queer*.

After we left the cul-de-sac, I asked, "Did Mama say 'queer'?"

"She's got such a stick up her ass," Fanny said. "And for what? Who cares?"

"They're not all queer. I mean, Mars is, but the rest of them . . ."

Fanny snuck me a quick look. "What? Are you serious?"

"About what?"

"I thought they were all gay. Or queer. I don't know. Are you sure some of those boys are straight?"

"What? Okay, not that this matters. Can you tell me what's on this flag? What could possibly be so offensive that Mama's in a tizzy?"

Fanny didn't answer as she waved to another car to go ahead of us. I pressed further.

"Does it say, 'Pinky Elizabeth Swear is an asshole'?"

Nothing.

"Do they have the C-word on it or something?"

Nada.

"Is it an A&M flag? OU? What is it?"

"I wish it were just an A&M flag," Fanny said. "Listen, it's not bad. It's a tad unexpected, but it's not that bad. There, take a look."

The top flag waved over Bluebonnet Drive, so high we could see it before we turned onto the street. It was a simple flag, and I recognized the picture of Sweet Potato Grace instantly as a larger version of the drawing I had made the day I formally met my friends at Peace Valley Park. Potato's angry face was squinting at the whole town of Tombstone.

My heart did feel heavy in my chest, I'll admit. Seeing Sweet Potato's face, even if it was poorly drawn, was a shock. My arms tingled from how badly they wanted to scoop my cat up (and promptly put her down, because she was not one for being held). The heaviness wasn't hot and angry, though. My chest wasn't being weighed down with ill will or frustration or madness. It was grief. Grief and love.

I was so focused on Sweet Potato Grace's mean eyes that it took me a minute to notice the flag beneath it. Right there, for everyone to see, waving over the town of Tombstone, was a rainbow flag.

Oh, damn it.

"Pinky pinky," Blaze hollered, kicking the front door open. He had a plate of eggs in one hand and a beer in the other. "Kegs and eggs! Happy birthday, my soul sister! You're just in time to join us for breakfast."

I stepped out of the car, keeping hold of the door as I straightened up. I scrambled for words as I debated what to ask first. I needed to talk to Mars, but perhaps it was too late.

"I will take you up on that another time," I said. "Um . . . uh . . ."

"Ah!" Blaze said, looking up at the flag. "Don't you like it? Isn't she beautiful?"

"It's a stunning flag, Blaze. But . . . what does it mean? I love it! But my Mama's worried there's something nefarious behind it."

"I like your how your words dance, Pinky," Blaze said, making a clicking sound with his tongue. It was the type of sound that would normally accompany finger guns, but Blaze's hands were full. "We wanted to help you honor your sweet cat. It was Mars's idea, if you can believe it." He winked. He *knew*. "That drawing of Sweet Potato Grace has a tighter grip on us than David Byrne's neckties. Mars suggested that there was no better image for welcoming friends to our little home. The way she didn't care what people thought of her? The way she lived for adventure? You might say Sweet Potato Grace is a bit of a role model for us. Mars really hopes you like it." Wink wink wink. Blaze was many things, but he was not subtle. Maybe that was why he liked playing the saxophone so much. "She's in the shower. Do you want me to get her? Do you like it? Honesty is the best policy, Pinky. If you want, I can tell her to take it down."

"No! No, I love it. I really do. I just know . . . people aren't going to get it. But thank you."

"Thank you for being born! Hey, I can't wait for the party tomorrow. Something to commemorate the rise of this great flag and the birth of our dear friend!" He raised his beer and yelled, "To Sweet Potato Grace!"

From inside the house, I heard a handful of echoes: "To Sweet Potato Grace!"

I turned to see Janelle Watkins's car slowing down as it drove past the house. She caught my eye and sped up again. I was losing track of the things I would have to explain.

"Okay, Blaze," I said. "I'll come around ten tomorrow. You enjoy your breakfast."

Before I could open my car door, Blaze cleared his throat. "Pinky?" His eyes had softened.

"Yeah?"

"You don't have to answer to your Mama. Or anyone else." He took a sip of beer and raised it high. "That's what Miss Sweet Potato thought, isn't it?"

It was.

✿

The drive to June's house wasn't any less awkward than the one to Bluebonnet Drive.

"Did you tell them?" Fanny asked quietly.

"I told Mars," I said. "But if everyone in Tombstone thinks they're queer already, no one will associate *me* with that Pride flag, right?"

"No. No, they're not reading into it that way. Their interpretation is much worse than just assuming you're a lesbian."

"What's worse than that?"

Fanny chuckled, then quickly corrected herself. "Sorry. Well." She slowed the car to a stop and looked me in the eyes. "They're convinced your funeral-crashing, old-people-terrorizing, robe-wearing, cat-worshipping barefoot friends are a cult."

NINETEEN

Wanda got me a tote bag during my teenage crafting phase that says, “Knit fast, die warm.” The bag outlived the phase. Inside it are always a few things: my phone, wallet, and keys, obviously; lip balm for wrinkle prevention (“Not that your lips are wearing out with use or anything,” Wanda would tell me once a month); cat treats, sealed tightly in a bag sealed tightly in another bag, for any stray animals I come across; and hand masks. If I could keep a mini fridge in my bag to keep the hand masks cold, I would, but I don’t know if that’s physically possible. Then again, I don’t know a damn thing about physical possibilities anymore.

Hand masks prevent wrinkles. Hand masks also prevent me from wringing my hands, a habit Nene Miriam says is for politicians and “sweaters.” It took about five years for me to realize that Nene meant people who perspire, not the garment, but the admonition brought me to shame regardless. Why couldn’t I be more ladylike when I got anxious? Why couldn’t I sit still and blend in?

The hand masks in my purse on my twenty-third birthday were lavender scented, but they did not calm me as they moisturized my hands at June’s house. As my friends picked at my

Birthday Frittata and gossiped, I tried to wrap my head around what Fanny had told me in the car. Was she exaggerating, or was this really the word going around town? Did people in Tombstone believe my friends were in a cult? Did people in Tombstone believe *I* was in a cult?

The small talk that afternoon went in one ear and out the other. June recounted her anniversary dinner with Michael. Ashley's toddler performed a tap dance while her niece threw up. The anecdotes everyone shared paled in comparison to what I'd just learned: The town disliked Mars and them so much that they were throwing the C-word around. (The C-word I can say out loud in Swear-It's, that is. *Cult.*)

Were they really so dangerous? Were they manipulating me? I will admit I was not as well-versed in the documentaries as my friends. There were more cult shows out there than alarm clocks for sale, and I'd heard my friends use the word to label everything from pyramid schemes to sororities. I couldn't tell where the barefoot folks would rank on such a spectrum.

"Pinky?"

June, Wanda, and Ashley blinked, waiting for my response. Rats. Exposed. I wasn't paying attention to the merits of cloth diapers.

"I'm so sorry. I've let my mind wander."

"Idle hands," June said.

"Heck," Wanda said, elbowing June in the ribs, "if I was spending time with that Blaze fellow, I'd be lost in a daydream too."

June was not amused.

"Why you keep making jokes like that, Wanda, I will never know," Ashley said.

"Pretty soon I won't have the chance to make any more.

Tombstone is ready to throw those yoga clowns out of town," Wanda said. "Sorry, Pinky."

Ashley and June hummed their sympathies.

"Um," I said, keeping my voice steady. "You don't really think that will happen, right? Sure, they look worse for wear with the bare feet and all, but they're quite nice once you get to know them. You met them. They didn't do anything crazy at the football game, did they? Besides get a little sick from the Frito chili."

"What were you doing in the parking lot?" Ashley asked. "My sister said Mars was making you do a strange ritual."

"She wasn't," I said. "I was shaking my stress away." My voice quieted as I heard my own words.

"People said it looked like a dynamic meditation," June said. "Have you watched *Wild Wild Country* yet? The similarities are eerie. And they were probably behaving at that football game because Scooter had a crowd around him. There were no other seniors for your friends to terrorize. You're smarter than this, Pinky."

"All this cult stuff sounds like a different language to me, June. I'm telling you, they're good people."

"The town wants them to be good people somewhere else," June said. "They have no ties to Tombstone. The moment we start allowing people like that to shake things up, the Oshos and the Teal Swans are going to come knocking."

"Maybe we can offer some commentary when they make a documentary on these folks one day," Wanda suggested. "Fanny would be perfect for that. She could get her big break."

"There's not going to be a documentary about Mars and her friends, because they're not a cult."

"You have to watch them, Pinky," June said gently. "Please. The point of those true crime documentaries is that anyone can get sucked into a cult."

"They're not a cult!"

"We didn't say they were," Wanda said, keeping her eyes away from mine.

"Who do you think the leader is?" Ashley asked. "People are saying it's the one with the yellow-tinted glasses. That one's Blaze, right? He looks charismatic enough to run a cult. Of course, we know *you* think he's handsome, Pinky."

"Who said I thought he was handsome?"

"About time she started showing interest in a guy," Wanda said. "Even if he does look like David Koresh."

June politely got up and walked into the kitchen, where she replaced her plate with a piece of paper. "Here," she said, handing it to me. My fingers squelched with hand mask goo as I gripped it.

The flyer featured two photos, side by side, that took up most of the page. The first was a mugshot of a spooky man with curly brown hair, serial-killer glasses, and a stare that reached beyond the photographer, myself, time, and space. Next to the man was a blurry, candid photo of Blaze at Peace Valley Park. He wasn't looking anywhere near the camera, much less giving a piercing, multi-dimensional stare. Heck, it could have been a photo of Sasquatch's skinny cousin on vacation. Yes, they both had long hair past their shoulders. Yes, they were skinny white men with glasses. Were the photos side by side to imply that they were the same man?

Underneath the photos were three words: WE'RE NOT WACO.

"Didn't your Mama ever tell you about David Koresh?" Wanda

asked. "Perfect example of a no-good, lying, dirty, Texas fool of a man."

"Mama got all her examples of no-good, lying, dirty, Texas fools of men in Tombstone," I said. I neglected to mention that one of the fools most frequently mentioned was Wanda's father.

"Another documentary to watch!" June said, revving up. "Janet Reno was the first female US Attorney General. She was a Democrat. And you know what she did when she was faced with David Koresh and his compound of hippies?" She didn't wait for me to answer. "Janet Reno blew them all up. Seventy people died. Babies died in Waco. But she had no choice, did she? That hippie freak David Koresh fought against the FBI for fifty-one days. With the Branch Davidians. He was having sex with all the children."

"That's how wacko-jacko a cult makes you," Wanda said. "They all believed they were doing the right thing."

"They're not a cult!" I said, trying to focus on the goo on my hands. Deep breaths, Pinky. "Christ on a bicycle, what are you insinuating? They're not having sex with children. They like to walk around barefoot and cut a rug in a parking lot and they made a nice flag of my cat. Are these crimes?"

"Cut a rug?" Wanda asked. "Now you're talking like an alien."

"Are they allowed to leave?" Ashley asked. "It's not a cult if they're allowed to leave."

"Are *you* allowed to leave *Tombstone*, Ashley?"

The scoffs bounced off the walls of June's house like a chorus from an experimental choir.

"All I'm saying," I said, "is that they're just a group of friends like you and me. I'm sure they'd love to come to a 'sewing circle' with us and do some crafts. They're more artistic than I am."

"Even Hare Krishnas need to embroider their robes," Wanda said.

June took a deep breath and put her hand on my hand mask. "We didn't want to have this conversation on your birthday, but we should have anticipated Wanda would open her big trap and let 'er rip. Sometimes you have to hear things you don't want to hear, Pinky. You're being defensive, but we want to protect you. Please know that. These people don't have good hearts. They've made a mockery and a false idol of your darling cat."

"It's not a mockery. And it's not a false idol! They don't worship Sweet Potato Grace!"

"Why do you believe that?"

"Why do you believe they do? I told them about Sweet Potato Grace. I painted that picture. I told them how much she means to me and—you'll never believe this—they listened. If I had known them before the memorial, they would have shown up there on purpose."

Ashley looked down at the floor. "I heard the flag of Sweet Potato is flying over a rainbow one, though. Which sends a message. A lot of questions are going around. What kind of cult are they running?"

"Not a cult," I said for the umpteenth time.

"Are they queer?" June asked. "Has Mars tried it on you? You can say 'no,' you know. You can fight back."

"Would Pinky even notice if she tried anything?" Wanda whispered to Ashley.

"Wanda," Ashley whispered back. "Please."

I took a deep breath. Nothing ran through my mind besides static and panic. So I perked up and crossed my hand masks over the poster, sloppily enough to stain it with goo.

"They're having a party tomorrow at their house. Ladies, you should see for yourselves how nice these little gatherings are. They mean no harm. Judge them for yourself. And if you see something nefarious, you can tell me all about it. I'll keep my ears and eyes open. I ask that you do the same with your minds."

My three best friends bit their respective lips and looked at each other for approval. I slapped on a dumb smile to move the conversation along.

"I'd appreciate it," I said. "Consider this a second funeral for Sweet Potato Grace, since you couldn't make the first one." That had to wrap things up, right?

I looked past June at the entrance to her kitchen to keep my face from cracking. If I held still, my friends would surrender.

"No good keeping your mind so open that your brains fall out," June said curtly.

"We'll come," Wanda concluded. "And see for ourselves. Ashley, you need a mom's night out. June, the best anniversary gift you could get Michael is time to himself. You can drive us, yeah?"

June nodded reluctantly.

"Good. We'll see you tomorrow, Pinky." Wanda winked.

She and Blaze had more in common than they thought.

TWENTY

Before I could open the door to June's minivan, the low hum of a podcast hit my ears. In June's opinion, there was nothing like "Could I Be a Tradwife?" to get the night started. She'd told us more times than I could count how much she obsessed over the hosts and their husbands. I took a deep breath and shook out my hands.

"Hello, Wanda. Ashley. Hey June, thanks for driving," I said, adjusting my seat.

June let the podcast drone on for a calculated few seconds before turning down the volume: "As members are cut off from their family and friends in the outside world, they begin to rely more heavily on the opinions of the cult leader. After enough time has passed, they lose all autonomy over their decisions . . ."

This was going to be a long night.

"Sorry about that," June said sweetly, switching over to her Fun Party Playlist. The dulcet tones of "Sweet Caroline" filled the van. "I just wanted to hear the end of that interview."

I imagined myself saying, "Was it an oral history of passive aggression in the southern United States?"

But June was operating the motor vehicle that was supposed

to take me to this party, and I didn't want to reroute her. My fellow passengers avoided eye contact. This was not a battle I wanted to fight, so I said, "What were you guys listening to?"

"Oh, just something Michael recommended. A lot of his co-workers are worried about the rise in cults. It's throughout the whole country, not just in Texas. I thought I would check it out."

"Okay, June."

"Do you want the name of the podcast? It's—"

"How about you send me a text tomorrow?" I snapped. "And how about we head over before the wine coolers get warm and word gets around that we're terrible party guests?"

✿

"Fridge is in the kitchen!" Blaze hollered from his usual post. The girls just stared as he winked and caught his breath from spinning around on the chair. "Man, this party's a hoot already!"

I saluted Blaze, immediately regretting the gesture, and showed my friends to the kitchen.

"Who knew so many young people lived around here?" Ashley said. "Are they from Bloat Hill? Gangrene? Midland?"

I shrugged.

Wanda suggested, "Maybe another time period."

"They do dress like the Manson family," Ashley said. "Plus the robes."

"And tradwives dress like they're in pioneer times," I said. "So what?"

"Pinky," Ashley hissed.

Before we made it onto the porch, Mika kicked the front door open with his bare foot, carrying a beer in each hand. He tipped his cowboy hat to us without spilling a drop. The gesture was impressive, but the sight of his bare foot was too much for June. She cleared her throat in disgust as I clapped.

"Ladies! Welcome!" he said. "Can I get anyone a drink?"

"We were just heading in to put these in the fridge," I told him, lifting my picnic basket.

"How's the weather?" June asked quickly.

"Pardon?"

"So cold," June said, nervously. "Feels like we're on a distant planet. Feels like we're . . . aliens." She awkwardly held her hand up, pointer and middle fingers diving away from ring and pinky fingers. "Take me to your leader," she said in an alien voice.

I'd never seen anything faze Mika until this moment.

"What?" I asked after a beat of silence.

"You know, like an alien," June said in her normal voice. She shot her hand down to her side. "No, really, though," she continued, looking past Mika to the indoor partygoers. "Who's your leader here, huh?"

June was never one for subtlety.

"Mika, please excuse her."

Mika shook out his curls underneath his cowboy hat. "Sure! Listen, ladies, whatever you need, let us know. Make yourselves at home here. We're a safe space for everybody, no matter your color, creed, or anything else." He caught the eye of some folks around the fire and politely walked past us. We continued to the fridge.

"How many hours did you spend in front of your mirror rehearsing that?" Wanda whispered to June, opening a wine cooler and taking a swig. "Everyone here is going to think you're on drugs."

"Everyone *here* is on drugs," Ashley said. "Pinky, have you ever seen anyone foaming at the mouth around here? Maybe while trying to talk to Jesus?"

"Christ," I said, not addressing Him but expressing my frustration. "I can't tell if you've never been around anyone on drugs or if the ones you know dabble strictly in bath salts. The only foam I've ever seen around these folks is the foam on top of their beers."

"People don't need drugs if they're brainwashed," June said. "It's wild how malleable the human mind is. You can convince yourself of anything: that dogs are immortal. Or cats. That polyamory is ethical. That"—she whispered this last part—"*Robin Williams is God.*"

A beat of silence passed.

"What the fuck are you talking about?" Wanda asked.

I tried to shake out my arms and wiggle my hips to loosen up before I gave my friends a tour of the house. We walked past the people playing California music around the fire pit and into the backyard, where others were dipping brushes in paint and continuing the project of jazzing up the fence.

"Landlord's keeping that security deposit," June muttered as we headed back inside.

"Is there anything positive you can say?" I asked.

"Well," June concluded, looking at the dancing strangers in the living room, "this wouldn't be the worst place to be held hostage. If I were Patty Hearst and these were my kidnappers, I would have stuck around, too."

In just a few months, the mission had gone from investigating the new folks in town to enjoying time with my barefoot friends to convincing my shoe-wearing old friends that I wasn't

Patty Hearst. June seemed intent on proving that I was, inspecting the items strewn about the two built-in bookshelves. I wasn't sure what she was looking for. A Buddha incense holder? A list of rules? An orb of sorts? Frankly, I was more embarrassed than a gymnast with a split leotard. At no place in our early education are Texas youth taught to look through a stranger's things like this. That's not what those "Come and Take It" flags are all about.

I was about to remind June that reading another person's mail was a federal offense when I heard a voice say, "Boo!"

When I turned around, Mars grabbed my hands and pulled me in so close that our noses were almost touching. My throat closed in panic and I tried to sneak a glance at my friends. They were too busy with the mail to notice anything amiss. I wriggled and boogied my way out of Mars's hands and her force field, pretending it was a dance move.

"June!" I called, hoping Mars would not raise an eyebrow at my friends' snooping. "Come say hello to Mars."

"Nice to see you again, Mars. Lovely home. You would never know the Beans boys destroyed the place by driving an ATV into the windows. Now, I have a silly question to ask you."

"June."

"What do you believe happens after you die?"

"June, would you stop it?"

"That picture of Madonna on a cross hanging on the wall just got me curious." Ashley and Wanda went over to examine it as June continued her sickly-sweet interrogation. "Reincarnation? Nothingness? Who's your Mother God? Do the names Ti and Do mean anything to you? Do you believe you'll be the last one left on Earth?"

"You'd be surprised," Mars said, leaning in. June leaned back. "Anyone who thinks they'll be the last one here is sorely mistaken. You wouldn't believe anything I said if I told you the rest, though. And that's okay with me. What's important isn't what I know, it's what I believe." Mars winked, then stepped back and raised her voice. "I believe in sunshine, lakefronts, and the eternal truth that pale ales are better than IPAs!" She bowed to the applause of a few partygoers. The twitch in June's eye muscle was visible, but Mars kept smiling. "We've got some arts and crafts going in one of the sitting rooms if you want to play with glitter or sniff some glue." She winked again. "I'm looking for some inspiration. Should I paint a picture of a donkey, a pe-can pie, or a field of daisies?"

"*Puh-kahn*," June said. Wanda and Ashley looked to June, then to Mars. If Mars tried to argue this one, the whole party was in for a hell of a lecture. But Mars kept smiling, her imperfect teeth shining in a way that made me jealous. I tried to look away from her lips.

"Have you ever stumbled upon a donkey's funeral, Mars?" Wanda asked.

"I haven't been to a donkey's funeral since the lot of us pitched a tent for dear old Mudge on that big farm in . . . now that I think about it, I'm not sure where it was."

"Do you and your friends travel together often?" Ashley asked.

"All the time."

"Are you allowed to leave the group if you want to?" June asked.

"June!" I said.

Mars took the continuing interrogation in stride. "You really don't like newcomers, do you?"

"It's just that Tombstone has never been a political town. We'd like to keep it that way."

"What's that supposed to mean?" I asked. "We have politics. We have a city council. I think."

Ashley sighed. "The flag outside the house," she said, as if reading from a teleprompter. "It's quite the political statement."

My mouth dropped open. "It's a flag of a cat. What the hell is political about Sweet Potato Grace?"

"That's not the flag we're talking about, Pinky."

"Don't get me wrong," June said. "There is nothing wrong with loving who you love."

"Excuse me?" I said.

"We know it's innocent. It's just that people here are a little uncomfortable. About the agenda behind it."

"What agenda?" I protested, a little too loudly.

June cleared her throat. "*We* are not saying that the people in this house are groomers, and of course *we* believe you're all nice people. But anyone in Tombstone who only knows y'all through the grapevine . . . well, they don't know. They might get the wrong idea. They might even think the top flag is sexual too! That it means you're furries, or that you worship cats."

"It was my birthday present!" I interrupted. "Don't read into it. Jesus on a tricycle. Can't you just leave it alone?"

Everyone shrugged, June last of all.

"Well, dames, this isn't really a conversation I feel like entertaining any further," said Mars. "I'm going to shake a leg and get my giggle water. Lovely seeing you again."

My cheeks were hot. My forehead was hot. I stood still as Mars walked away, wondering if I should ask for an apology from my friends. Whatever happened to keeping an open mind?

Then came the moment of looking around, as if the next topic of conversation were hiding somewhere in the crowd of dancers. The moment lasted too long. June hoisted her purse onto her shoulder and said, "Well, look at that. It's just about time to leave."

I swished around the wine cooler to see if I had even finished it. It was still half-full.

"Come on, Pinky. I think we've seen enough."

June really expected me to leave with her. I shook my head. "I'll get Fanny to pick me up later. She's started doing a lot of things at night so that the sun doesn't age her face." Admittedly, that was only half-true. But I didn't care. I just wanted to stay at the party until I could watch the stars move.

June looked satisfied by my answer in a way that made me shudder. "At least someone's taking care of herself. I'll send you that podcast episode tomorrow, okay?"

"June, I think we're—" Ashley started.

"I think I'm driving," June snapped. "Let's go."

My three best friends turned to walk out the front door. Only Ashley looked back, raising her thumbs to signal that I could text her for a ride if I changed my mind.

I stood there until Mars came back with one of her preferred pale ales. Her smile was wide and sparkling, and I couldn't help but laugh in what felt like defeat.

"Sorry about that," I said, still in bemused shock.

"Sorry about what? No one took away the speakers and no one stole the keg. What's so upsetting?"

"If only the rest of Tombstone were so forgiving," I said. "I don't know why my friends won't come around. I know you're not what they say you are."

"I'm not letting them ruin your birthday. Come with me." Mars grabbed my free hand and pulled me past the buzz of the dancers and into the backyard.

More flowers, cartoon characters, and squiggles of beautiful nothing had joined the murals on the fence. A handful of partygoers were in deep focus, adding details. I looked for a space to doodle Sweet Potato Grace snarling at the backyard. But those mean kitty eyes were already glaring at my friends as they pulled out of the driveway and headed across town.

"Here," Mars said, beaming.

"What am I looking for?" I asked.

"It's you!" Mars pointed to a corner of the fence.

Toward the top, a thin, white line traveled across a few posts. A faceless woman sporting a purple leotard and brown ponytail raised her hands to the sky as she balanced on the line. Below her, a faceless crowd held popcorn and mingled with an elephant, a strongman, and someone holding a big hoop.

It was me.

"When did you do this?" I asked.

"Today. I'm no artist, which may be apparent, but I did have time and a desire to make you smile on your birthday. Look at you! Spotlight's right on you."

No one had ever painted me before, or even drawn me a valentine. Fanny was the muse. Not me. Yet Mars saw me the way I saw myself in dreams I hadn't yet allowed myself to have.

"Happy birthday, Pinky," she whispered.

Like in the dreams I did allow myself to have, I slipped my hands around Mars's waist and squeezed, resting my head on her shoulder. No one turned their heads in disgust. No one gasped or paid any attention at all. I was suddenly thrilled that my friends had left early.

"I don't know if I deserve all this," I whispered back. "Thank you."

If Mars had a response, it was drowned out by the chirp of the sirens.

The Tombstone locals in the backyard perked their ears up in joyful confusion. Police, breaking up a party? What was this, a college campus? A city? A place where crime occurred? Tombstone shared a police force with Bloat Hill, and they usually only made appearances at birthday parties for firefighters and parades celebrating federal holidays.

At the sound of the sirens, it was also clear who *wasn't* from Tombstone. Mika ripped off a feather boa and turned around to wipe the glitter eyeliner off his face. Jean-Luc, who was sitting with his legs crossed, spread out and switched his martini for one of Charlie's beers. Charlie sat up straight and scooched away from Jean-Luc. Blaze disappeared. I felt a breeze at my side as Mars unraveled herself from me.

"What are they doing here?" Mars asked.

"I'm not sure. Is there a problem?"

"That's what I'd like to know."

"Listen, the cops are probably kids I know. Let me talk to them."

Approaching the gate were Parker Thomas and Andrew Frank, who'd graduated a few years before me. In third grade, Parker's younger brother Phillip once told me I smelled bad. This has nothing to do with Parker's path in life or his ability to enforce the law, but I'll never forget it.

"Evening, officers," I said as I approached the gate from the other side.

Andrew hit a vape pen and surveyed the scene. Parker jogged up behind him. He was much shorter. His whole family was quite short. Maybe that was why Phillip had made fun of me. But I'm no detective.

"Evening, Ms. Swear!" Parker said, twiddling his mustache.

"Hi, Parker. What brings you out here? I hope the music isn't too loud."

"Well, we got a call that there might be some minors consuming alcohol or controlled substances on the premises. Do you mind if we take a look around?"

"Should I get someone who lives here? I can assure you that no one underage is here. You can see that just by taking a peek."

"Is that right?" Andrew chimed in. "I know you see a lot of people go in and out of Swear-It's, Pinky. A lot of people who rely on us to keep this town safe. Just let us in and we can take a look around. Did you know the neighbors are trying to limit the number of parties they can have here each month?" He took another hit of his vape. It smelled like rotten limes and metal.

"Who's been complaining?"

"You know we can't tell you that."

Bluebonnet Drive is a street of houses spaced so far apart that I couldn't imagine even the folks in the next one over would be able to hear the music we were playing. So who'd complained? How would they know minors were at this party unless they'd been here themselves?

"Are you going to arrest anyone?"

"If we have a reason to, we might. Let us in, Ms. Swear, we're just going to take a look around."

I turned around so only the partygoers could see me roll my eyes. Making a fuss against the officers was not a good look, but I wasn't sure if they could legally search the house. What if everyone *was* on drugs and I was just naive? What if June was right?

June.

I whipped around.

"Was it June Ripple who complained, officers?"

"Pinky, come on now. We've never prevented you from doing your job at the store. Can't you just let us do ours? We've never known you to make a fuss."

The two officers walked past me, taking a look at the faces of the partygoers who stood around the fire. How old was Blaze or Mars or Mika anyway? Early twenties? Late twenties? Thirty? I couldn't ask them. I couldn't even find them.

Parker put his thumbs in his belt loops and hollered: "Anyone under the age of twenty-one needs to get the heck out of here, got it? Go now and we'll leave you with a warning."

They repeated this speech in the living room and the backyard. This only turned up one offender, who followed them out of the house looking guilty. The dire consequences were a tip of the hat and a clap on the shoulder.

"Tell your little brother his throw is improving, Martin," said Andrew. "And tell your mom we did good by you in this here cult house. Don't make a habit of this, you hear?" With a wink, the current QB1's older brother was free to go.

They came back to me in the front yard, as if I was in charge or something.

"It's not a cult house," I said quietly.

"What's up with the back fence?" Parker asked. "There are symbols."

"Is it a crime to paint a fence?"

"I'm just asking a question, Pinky. Come on, now."

"Looks like weird hippie stuff to me," Andrew said.

"Where are the actual tenants?" Parker asked. "We'd like to have a conversation with them."

I sighed. "I'm sure I can find someone. Give me a minute."

Mars wasn't in the living room or out back. She wasn't in the craft room or kitchen or downstairs bathroom. The whole houseful of barefoot residents, in fact, was up in Blaze and Mika's room, where I found them peering through the blinds.

"What are you all doing up here?" I asked. "Scared of a little police officer?"

"Pinky!" Mars said, clearing her throat. "*Scared* is not the word I'd use. We just don't trust them, that's all."

To my knowledge, Parker and Andrew had never so much as drawn their service weapons on anyone, ever. Tombstone had never been that dramatic.

"They're alright. Trust me, I've known them all my life. Mars, would you mind just coming with me and introducing yourself? Honestly, if you're nice about it this is probably the last time you'll see them. They're called out to handle stuff in Bloat Hill way more than anything in Tombstone."

"Do I need an ID?"

"What? Why?"

"I . . . do I need one?"

"I don't think so. If you do, I can reason with them. Parker owes me." I still think of his younger brother when I put on deodorant.

Downstairs, Parker had cracked open a beer and was talking to some of the Bloat Hill partygoers. I was pretty sure that wasn't legal either. Mars shimmied her shoulders to make herself look taller and let me lead the way.

"This is Mars, y'all. She lives here. You had a question for her?"

"I'm sorry for the disturbance, ma'am," said Parker. "You live here?"

"I do," Mars said.

"Are any of those fellas you live with your boyfriend? Or are you the boss of the place?"

"I wouldn't say that any of us are the boss."

"Communists," Andrew said, chuckling.

"Can you just get to the point, sir?" I cut in. "I'm sure you're tired. No one here is underage. You could tell that just by walking through the place."

He turned back to Mars. "Alright. You relay this message to everyone who lives here, okay? I do apologize that we have to meet under these circumstances. My partner and I have been meaning to make a stop down here since y'all moved in, but we . . . never got around to it. So I'm going to tell you this now, straight up. I'm sure you've figured out by now that people in this town don't like their routines being disturbed. To them, a too-loud party or a disruption at the movies is just as outside the law as theft or arson. So if you want to avoid trouble with me, you've got to keep things quieter around here. If you want to play obnoxious pranks or start a cat-worshipping cult or make some sort of political statement, best go to another jurisdiction. Okay?"

"They've never—"

"Miss Swear, you too. I don't know what you've been watching on TikTok or what people are saying over at Blinn these days.

All eyes are on members of the force and we're being just as discriminated against as anyone waving one of those rainbow flags. The best way for us all to get along is to just keep our mouths shut and play nice, okay? There's no need to take sides here in Tombstone or shake things up. That's not what we're about."

Was this the moment to say something? Oh, how I wished I could open my mouth and let an argument fly forth like a dove at a wedding, but I stopped before I could embarrass myself. The two police officers grabbed beers for the road and tipped their hats to the partygoers. At least they were gone for the night.

"I'm so sorry, Mars," I said as the patrol car sped down the street.

"For what?"

"For . . . that was so rude. And condescending."

Mars shrugged. "Sure. But I've seen cops do much worse. They were actually pretty cool. Maybe we could shake it out?"

So we grabbed another drink, danced around to the now-slightly-softer music, and shook out the stress and the condescension and whatever memories from the past had scared Mars and her friends like dogs in a pound.

When our legs felt like gelatin and our bodies were humming, we twirled into the backyard and watched art fill the fence and stars fill the sky. The flags flapped lamely above the property. With the beers and the confusion and the music I had lost all sense of which way was up, and I relished the opportunity to squeeze Mars around the waist again while we faced Bluebonnet Drive. We weren't being political. We were just two women with smiles we could wrap around ourselves over and over again.

Mars squeezed me back and planted a kiss on my forehead. Again, no complaints from the partygoers or the stars or whatever lived above them.

"Do you want to go inside?" she asked with a wink.

I did.

TWENTY-ONE

I feel tempted to describe the glow in my cheeks and the quiver in my legs the next morning, but let me remind you that the night I spent with Mars was not my first rodeo. She wasn't the first woman I had ever romped in the hay with. I was familiar with the natural eruptions that could take over a woman's body when she was touched by someone who actually looked for the shudder-spots, although I'll admit I'd been through a few calendars since I put my boots under anyone's bed.

I woke tumbling into a universe made only of Mars, eyes opening slowly, sleepily, blissfully. Every morning before that one, for so long, I'd woken with a crooked start to the mechanical whirring of Potato's automatic feeder and the fear that I had forgotten to fill it up the night before. The first sounds of my day were the rickety crunches of Potato's teeth as cortisol started running through my veins. I wouldn't take those mornings back for anything, but I have to admit that waking up in the mother-in-law suite was usually about as pleasant to the senses as instant coffee.

This morning was different. I slept through 6:00 a.m. like a train passing through Tombstone and through the sunrise, too.

My phone was dead and Mars had no clocks in her room. I looked over and saw Mars's lips, pouted like a movie star's. The morning revealed itself to me in the outline of her neck, her shoulder, her slender arms covered in blonde hair. The morning revealed itself to me in her body, tangled among tie-dyed bedsheets. I found myself wondering where she'd gotten her collection of toe rings.

I sat looking at the bare room—hardly anything in it but some pearl jewelry on a thrifted nightstand—until Mars stirred and gently rubbed my thigh. She started singing "Good Morning to You," to the tune of "Happy Birthday." I closed my eyes, needing nothing else. Especially not an alarm clock.

When Blaze called for Mars and me to grab breakfast, she assured him we'd be down in "two shakes of a lamb's tail," but the only things shaking when we made our way downstairs were my calves.

Standing at the base of the stairs on Bluebonnet Drive, I felt just as naked and exposed as I had literally been five minutes prior. But what was I going to do? Run away? I would have to face the music sooner or later. The boys knew I'd slept over, and if they hadn't guessed what I'd told Mars before, they surely did now.

A card table adorned with a picnic blanket held the morning's feast. Back at Blinn, when the haze of my few-and-far-between frolics with women wore off, the world lost its technicolor and the gray hues of secrets and anxiety took over. This morning was different. It couldn't get any brighter. Oranges welcomed Mars and me to the table. No one had their claws out, just fingernails to peel back the skin of the fruits and let their scent freshen up the living room.

Mika came to the table with a big plate of scrambled eggs.

Instead of asking me where I'd been, he leaned down and wrapped his arms around Blaze. They kissed. With tongue.

Was it contagious? No, that wasn't true, despite what Mrs. Lindsay had told us in sixth-grade health. I guessed that Blaze and Mika had simply been as hesitant to share their flirtations as I was.

"No fruit left for me," Mika said, disappointed.

"Plenty of fruit left for you, toots," Mars said. "Just look at him."

Blaze hadn't flinched at Mika's wet embrace. His eyes kept sparkling. "Also, I saved you an orange."

Mika sat down next to him and started peeling it.

"Pinky pinky," Blaze said, leaning his elbows on the table to look at me, "do people still go camping around here?"

"Why wouldn't people go camping?" Mars asked, looking up from her orange.

"Air pollution. Guns. Better stars inside." He leaned in to look very seriously at me. "How close are we to virtual camping?"

"Oh, please don't tell me people believe the stars are better inside," Mika begged me. He took my hand in his sticky, citrusy one. "Do you want to go camping with us? Outdoors?"

"Camping sounds grand," I said. "When are you going?"

"Maybe today, maybe tomorrow," Mars said. "It depends on your schedule, if you like. It'll be a gasser."

"You don't have to schedule this around me."

"Yes, we do, darling. We don't make appointments. Time is irrelevant."

"Then how does anyone know when to meet you?"

The whole table giggled.

"When would we be coming back?" I asked.

"Two days? Three?"

"I can probably get my sister to cover a shift or two at the store, but no more than that."

"Do you mind sleeping in a van?" Jean-Luc asked, taking his place at the table.

"I'll think about it, okay?" I said. "It does sound fun."

Mars placed her hand on mine, minding her rings. I started to flinch, as the table was full of people, then remembered that none of them cared.

"Sleep on it tonight, pickle, and let us know. We'd really like you to come with us. We have some plans that we'd like you to be a part of."

"Can I know what these plans are?" I asked.

Mars giggled. "Certainly not."

In her eyes shone the memory of the night before. I nodded, cleared my dry throat, and wondered if a day was enough notice for Fanny to cover my shifts.

✿

A stretch of postcard-perfect gravel road bounded by grass and sky stretched before me as I left 101 Bluebonnet Drive on foot. No concrete for a mile or so. The few industrial buildings along the route would be quiet in the morning hours. I had all the space in the world to get a sense of myself and observe who I was, inside and out. I took off my flats and held them as I walked in the grass.

Mars could have driven me home that morning. Ashley. Fanny. Tex Trombone, the taxi driver of Tombstone. I had options, but I wanted to walk and feel my bare feet on the earth.

It had been a while since I remembered that my body had a shape and that one could trace its lines and curves to make an outline of me.

Inside, I was buzzing. My spirit was humming like a neon light on a summer evening at Fun Earl's. But the energy inside me wasn't industrial. Despite my best efforts to tame the butterflies and waterfalls, I recognized an entire natural ecosystem blooming within me. And just like Earth spun for and around the sun every day, I was pulled to Mars. I had enough light inside to nourish whatever was growing and living and humming within my spirit. And my spirit needed to move, to dance, to celebrate, to live. I was a creature of love, as they say.

I enjoyed my barefoot meditation right up until I turned onto Lee Street and saw the long row of doors with identical fliers stuck in the middle.

Solicitation is not a facet of everyday life in Tombstone. If you need your windows replaced, you call Wanda's uncle. Heidi Granger's dad is the King of the Roach. Father McGillian, the only accepted transplant from Ireland by way of New York, is the one trusted source for all questions Jesus Christ-related. None of these men have any reason to ring anyone's doorbells. Fliers haven't been left on my Mama's door since the former mayor of Bloat Hill tried to organize some sort of Memorial Day event for the neighboring towns. Talk about sandwiches left uneaten. Not one person from Tombstone attended.

I thought about all the craft supplies June owned. Did she make the posters? Or did one get stuck on her door the same as everyone else's? It didn't matter. What mattered was that I needed to put on my shoes and get these fliers off these doors as soon as possible.

I felt like a damn cartoon character, running up and down porches and snatching fliers. That morning was a Sunday, and most people were visiting Father McGillian at church, but I did worry that I saw at least one pair of eyes peeking out from behind their blinds. Better they see me than this flier.

By the time I'd zigzagged my way through the east side of Tombstone to my house, I had collected close to thirty fliers. Expired Trees Print Shop probably hadn't seen this much business since before the advent of the internet. Exhausted, I threw the fliers down on the end table in the living room and fell into Mama's chair. Five minutes went by before I could feel the chair under my butt and the carpet under my feet. I failed to notice the sound of Fanny's little toes walking down the hall. When she said my name, I yelped.

"Sorry! I didn't hear you come in."

"I have hollow bones like a bird and toes like marshmallows."

"I hope that's not what you put on your dating profile."

Fanny shrugged and took her spot on the couch, grabbing the top flier off the pile on the way. "Who the hell is this?" she asked.

"This guy apparently caused a big standoff with the government way back when."

"Wouldn't people around here like that kind of thing?"

"He also molested children."

"Did you know Texas has more child marriages than any other state?"

"Well, apparently people have been saying this cult leader looks just like Blaze. I don't get it. Why's this town being so cruel to them? They're not out to terrorize seniors, corrupt anyone, or do anything besides have a few parties at their house. I just don't get it."

"If you sat at home all day hearing that the world was ending because of colorfully dressed, happy queer people, you'd be upset with them too." Fanny sighed. "They're shaking things up, Pinky. You know how much people around here hate that. Plain and simple. They'll do anything to fight off people who want to shake things up."

"But they're spreading lies."

"Yeah, that's what people do when someone makes them uncomfortable. Remember when Jimmy Beans told everyone Wanda ate dog food? And when Wanda told everyone Jimmy peed on the floor in homeroom?"

I looked at the dark mirror of the silent TV. I had definitely been a part of spreading that rumor in tenth grade. "They want me to go on a camping trip with them."

"That sounds fun."

"It does, but I don't think I can go."

"Why not?"

"I have work. I have Swear-It's. Have you noticed Mama's just been lounging around in her pajamas in the morning now, thinking I'm going to work seven days a week?"

"Exactly why you deserve some time off."

"Do I?"

"Pinky, Jesus, loosen up. When was the last time you had fun with your friends?"

"Which friends?"

"Your barefoot friends."

"Last night."

"When was the last time you had fun with the Sewing Circle?"

"College?" I was being facetious. Or was I?

Fanny sniffed as I made her point for her. "Listen, Mama's

working the store today. I'll take your shifts tomorrow. When are they leaving?"

"They said whenever I can make it. Fanny, are you sure this is a good idea?"

"Why?"

"Do you really feel comfortable running the place?" I couldn't tell my younger sister that Mama didn't have faith in her to do squat, but I didn't need to.

Fanny started laughing, a laugh deeper and wider than I had ever heard from her. It was maniacal. "Do you want to know why I serve terrible coffee?"

This felt like a trick question.

"Do you want to know why I mess up the math sometimes, or wobble around as I'm moving the inventory?"

I kept my mouth shut.

"Because if you do something poorly, no one will ever ask you to do it again. But I'll make an exception this time. Go with your friends. Clearly, you've been stressed." She held up the flier. "Being in Tombstone isn't helping. Fresh air will. You'll come back from a nice, long weekend with all those beautiful barefooted people and the cash register will ding as it does, just as you left it. I promise."

"Are you sure?"

Fanny handed me her pinky, an oath we hadn't made since I broke Mama's favorite vase and blamed it on the wind. I wrapped my little finger around hers and we kissed our fists. By the end of the hour, my bag was packed.

TWENTY-TWO

I should have known we'd be driving somewhere that didn't have cell service. Texas stretches eight hundred miles from east to west. The highway from Waskom to El Paso is an eleven-hour journey that requires diligent preparation and a military-trained bladder. Booker to Brownsville, north to south? If you don't have a plan or a cup, you're not going to have a comfortable ride. At some point along the journey to forever, your cell service is going to drop out and you're going to find yourself wishing you had at least texted someone (besides your sister) about your whereabouts. I was wringing my hands in the front seat of the van as soon as we turned off the highway and onto the dirt road. I hadn't packed any hand masks to distract me.

"Pinky pinky, what are you flipping your wig over?" Mars asked, placing one of her hands on mine. She kept the other one on the wheel and her eyes on the bumps ahead. "I can feel your energy hitting my cheek like snowflakes in a storm."

Mika and Blaze sat in the middle row, snoring with their mouths open and hair entangled. Jean-Luc and Charlie were playing Go Fish, giggling at every round.

"I just realized that nobody knows where I am."

"Well, that's not true."

"I guess. My sister knows I'm camping. But she's usually too busy looking in a mirror to gossip, so no one *else* will know. She's the one person in Tombstone who's too busy to gossip."

"Sounds like you couldn't have told a worse person that you were heading off into the wilderness with a bunch of cult members," said Jean-Luc.

Mars shook her head and laughed. I had brought over June's flier that morning as we packed up the van. When I explained the impact of the Branch Davidians on the town of Waco, I only received shrugs in return.

"A government setting fire to their own people?" Blaze asked. "Never heard of it. Not in Philadelphia, not in Waco."

"This tends to happen to the misunderstood," Mars said, crumpling up the paper and throwing it in the trash. "And Blaze tends to grace a lot of fliers. I guess he just has one of those faces."

"Looks too much like Jesus?" I said.

"Nah. Too pale," was Jean-Luc's response.

I thought about the town gossip that swirled around the fliers. "Y'all don't . . . worship my cat or anything, right?" I asked.

Mars didn't laugh this time. "No, toots," she said. "We don't."

I looked at my phone. Still no signal. "Maybe I should just turn it off until we drive back."

"The view outside of the window square is much more beautiful than the view into your phone square. Look up. Look out. Take in the sky."

Mars was right. It was fire pits, music, and marshmallow weather. The air was cooling down and a gentle breeze glided clouds across the blue Texas sky. I can't tell you much about the sky in other states or countries, but I can speak to the Texas sky.

The next time you're in Texas, take Mars's advice. Put down your phone and look up. The Texas sky is not like the sky in paintings or on TV, I'm telling you. Paintings only show rectangles or lines of blue. The Texas sky doesn't have limits. The Texas sky runs in all directions, stretching and stretching beyond anything you can comprehend. Try and find the end of it. You can't. If you let your mind follow the sky, you'll find yourself thinking about the happenings underneath it in Booker and Brownsville, Waskom and El Paso. You'll feel so small.

I rolled down the window of the van and took a deep breath, as if I could pull some of the sky down into me. Who were the people in Booker, Brownsville, Waskom, and El Paso? I felt a sense of kinship with all of them. Was someone buying an alarm clock? Was someone camping? Was someone far away looking up at the sky and wondering about me? No—why would they, after all. Or maybe they were?

I am so small. But they are, too.

Have I always been this small? I asked myself. Have I always been this free? I rolled up the window and tossed my phone into the back seat between Blaze and Mika, who didn't stir.

✿

The sky didn't end as we approached a tall fence with a locked door another two hours later. Blaze and his dried drool hopped out of the car and punched in a code until the fence opened. The small cabin was tucked half a mile of crackling road behind the fence. Longhorns and donkeys roamed the property, weaving between oak trees that held squeaky swing sets and a zipline that looked like it would snap at the lightest touch. I felt my heart sigh.

"Blaze, you said you lived on a compound. Is this it?" I asked.

"Ha!" Blaze slapped his knee. "Not at all. Where I grew up's a lot closer to a cult than any of these shenanigans your neighbors have been talking about. But I managed to escape from it with Bobby, Tip, and Dolly a long time ago."

"Why don't you stand up for yourselves back in Tombstone, then? I think if people heard your story, they'd let up on the cult rumors."

"We're already up the creek without a paddle, Pinky."

I didn't like his resignation, but I would be lying if I said I didn't understand it. "How'd you find this place?" I asked, taking stock of the property.

"Believe it or not, this is our very own slice of paradise," Blaze said. Mika gave him a pinch on the butt and Blaze hopped in the air.

"Friends of ours own this place," Jean-Luc clarified. "It'll be here until the aliens claim it. If you ever need it, Pinky, we can give you the code."

"You mean if I wanted to drive four hours outside of Tombstone all by myself?"

"Why wouldn't you?" Jean-Luc said. He paused, watching my reaction. "I mean, Tombstone is a nice place and all, but doesn't it feel . . . claustrophobic sometimes?"

"It's something-phobic," Blaze said, opening a beer with his teeth. "Sorry, Pinky."

"I'm going to get a fire going," Mika said, arms already full of firewood. "Blaze, baby, can you get the food organized? Ladies, you just take a load off. I forget what year it is, Pinky, but I still treat women like delicate creatures. Hard habit to break."

An acorn hit Mika in the arm, straight off a slingshot that

Mars was holding. "I can't believe they still have this here," Mars said, examining the toy. It was rusty, the type of thing you might see in a store of vintage odds and ends.

"You've been here before?" I asked, taking a seat in a rocking chair on the porch. "I thought y'all were new to Texas."

"We're new to Tombstone," Jean-Luc said, hanging off the tire swing in the front yard, "but just a few hours' drive from here is Marfa. Last time we made our way to Marfa, we took refuge in this place. Took a heck of a lot of traversing, what with the maps we had back then."

"Pinky, let's grab a beer," Mars said. "A strong one. I'm no delicate creature, but I'm happy to take a load off after driving."

That's what we did. We just relaxed. Mika had the fire going before we finished our first beers and dinner was cooking while we drank our second. Blaze strummed his guitar, letting the California music send the birds flying above to check their maps. Jean-Luc and Charlie entertained themselves by playing around on the tire swing, then the rickety zipline. Watching them all felt like a weight off my shoulders. This was all we needed to do tonight. This was it, and this was pleasant.

"Feeling better?" Mars asked, cracking open another drink and clinking it with mine.

"Don't get me started on how I feel," I said. "The second I think about my responsibilities in Tombstone is the second I'll want to hop in the van and drive it right back to the store."

"How many things can you be responsible for, Pinky? You deserve a vacation."

"I can't just walk away from the family business."

"Taking two days to go camping is hardly walking away. But also, you sure can, if you want to. Is Swear-It's *your* store?"

"It's Mama's store. Soon to be mine. I'm the only person she trusts with it."

Mars leaned back in her chair, looking at where the sky decided to keep going. "I traveled the world for years to avoid what I thought were my responsibilities. My mom's happiness, my father's rage. Living in a society where men required sex and women were required to give it to them. But when I found myself on a train in Europe haggling for a ticket or on a country road in Argentina hitching a ride, I started to realize that I was only truly responsible for me. And that responsibility alone required a lot of moxie."

"What did you do once you made that realization?"

"I went back home for a spell. It didn't work out. I tried to tell my folks that I was going to be the woman I was, but they weren't having it. So I flew the coop. I found Blaze, I found Jean-Luc, and they found their boys. We don't owe each other a damn thing. Point is, your Mama could hire someone else. She could."

I left the conversation at that.

The hot dogs were charred and the marshmallows toasted, nothing burnt or gone to waste. Every star made its appearance in Texas that night. I couldn't tell whether they hung above us to stand guard or to illuminate the love that looped tighter around Mars and me, Jean-Luc and Charlie, and Blaze and Mika as we continued to drink beer around the fire. Mars and I even snuck a kiss or two under the moonlight. The boys didn't cringe or cry out or notice at all.

How many other women in Texas were kissing the woman of their dreams? If they were in Booker or Brownsville, Waskom or El Paso, would they feel as free as I did right now?

TWENTY-THREE

"So where exactly are we going?" I asked from the back seat. For our second drive, Mars and I were in the last row, with Blaze and Mika in the middle and Jean-Luc and Charlie in the front. I hadn't spent so much time in a car since Ashley's parents tried to take her, Fanny, and me out to South Padre Island for a weekend. Fanny threw a fit so wild we just took a picture near the entrance and drove all the way back home. We were not invited back to the beach house after that, but Mama didn't mind. Fanny was precious cargo, didn't the rest of the town know?

"To Austin!" Mika said, unhelpfully.

Austin was a big city. Beyond its animal shelter and a few bachelorette party stops that old college classmates posted on Instagram, it was like a foreign country to me. But if Mars wanted to go, I did too.

Blaze started singing "Road to Nowhere" in response to my question, which was charming but equally unhelpful. He and Mika seemed more excited than anyone else—so much so that they both wore pleated skirts and black lace gloves for the occasion. Their feet were bare, of course, and their toenails were painted bright pink.

"You're as helpful as a compass in a magnet museum, boys," Jean-Luc said.

"Okay, okay," Mika said. "We're going to a gay country night! It's all Loretta Lynn, Randy Travis, and bedazzled homosexuals. You'd think, in 2003, Texas might have a few more gay clubs nearby, but drive to Austin we must."

"2022," I said gently.

"Must we, really?" Jean-Luc sighed. Charlie squeezed Jean-Luc's cheek in his fingers and shook it. Jean-Luc loved driving, but he loved complaining more.

"We'd go to the ends of the earth for a rainbow boogie," Blaze said, trying to chomp at Mika's hair-touseling fingers. He was unsuccessful.

"Do we need any codes to get in?" Mika asked.

"Codes?"

"2022, Mika," Mars repeated. She looked at me and whispered, "This is the farthest he's ever been."

"From what?"

"The seventies." Before I could ask her to clarify, she said, "We'll figure it out. Reviews online of Giddy Up Chuck's say it's a gay bar. We don't have to sneak around."

"Where did you have to sneak around to get into gay bars?" I asked.

Everyone looked in different directions.

"In other countries?" I offered.

"Sure, darling," Mars said. "That sounds about right. If the pictures of this bar are accurate, it looks as though we're in for a gay ol' time."

✿

We were. Giddy Up Chuck's stood proudly on the outskirts of Austin's downtown area, where people crisscrossed the streets between music venues in search of cigarettes or to join queues. Its neon sign featured a purple background and a cartoon pony. You couldn't help but smile while looking at it. From the outside, the place looked more like a fairground than a dance hall. Before we could enter, we had to pass through a small parking lot next to a fenced-off area with three food trucks. Young people sat on benches eating tater tots and leaning into each other, laughing out loud.

"We're in!" Mars said as we received stamps on our hands. "And here just early enough that they're not carding people." She lowered her voice. "Do you mind grabbing drinks, Pinky? I'm afraid most of us don't have proper identification. We're all of age, though, you know that. We'll give you cash."

"Sure, Mars. Why don't you . . ."

I couldn't finish my question once we made it past the person stamping our hands. A wooden ramp zigzagged from where we stood to the entrance of what I assumed was the bar, a modest concrete building lit with all the colors of the rainbow. To our left was another path leading behind the bar to where groups of people vaped, drank, or admired each other's outfits on a turf field. To the right of the bar there was a big top, a huge pink parachute floating over a dance floor of gravel with a stage behind it.

We were a far cry and a loud laugh from Fun Earl's.

"This might be a sandals night, boys!" Jean-Luc said.

Everyone at Giddy Up's was stylish. (This was another way in which it was different from Fun Earl's.) And from what I could tell, everyone was gay. At first, I thought we had stumbled upon a costume party. Someone was dressed like an elf; another person was wearing a cape. Sparkly cowboys and glittery cowgirls mingled nearby. This was my first time at a proper gay bar, and in my T-shirt and jeans, I felt sheepishly underdressed.

No one would dare dress like this in Tombstone unless it were Halloween. I wanted to take a picture, to commemorate this other world I had stepped into. I wanted to be able to cradle the whole scene in my hands like a kitten. But as I patted myself down, I realized I'd left my cell phone in the van, which was parked a few stops away.

Oh, what the heck? The neon lights were so bright I was sure I would see them in my eyelids for the next several weeks. Who needed a picture?

"Yee-haw!" Mars yelled, taking in the fairground-like decor. "This is what I'm talking about."

Jean-Luc and Charlie had already run to the dance floor, where they were twirling each other around under the parachute. Blaze and Mika stood arm in arm on the ramp, waiting on me. I remembered I was supposed to buy the drinks.

"I'll meet you back here in a minute?" I said. "Just give me your orders."

"Anything liquid!" Mika said, tousling Blaze's hair again. "Now, this is what I was hoping we'd find when we realized we were in Texas."

This was still Texas. Tombstone and Austin stood within the same scraggly borders of the Lone Star State. I'd once heard someone in Tombstone condemn Austin as the blueberry in a bowl of tomato soup, but I felt happy to be amongst the little fruits.

The liquid I chose for the group was called a Golden Ticket: a mixture of kombucha, whiskey, and lavender with a spicy ginger candy pierced by a plastic sword. I wasn't one for fancy cocktails, but it sounded delicious and did not disappoint. Neither did the second one. Or the third.

The big draw of the event seemed to be the playlist: country songs from the nineties. I'd grown up hearing all these songs on the radio, but the dancing crowd didn't exactly resemble the crowd at a George Strait concert. The cowboy hats were all covered in sparkles and the boots were all bright pink pleather.

Patrons stopped their conversations to line dance when the DJ, a man in a bright pink crop top who sported a fabulous mustache, turned on "Copperhead Road." The lines snaking on and off the stage brought me right back to Rip Ripple's gym classes. But the uniforms here were tight tank tops and neon and faux fur, and all the students were grown adults. Women danced around the DJ and men gave each other flirty winks that sent the crowd hootin' and hollerin'. Giddy Up Chuck's felt like a drag queen's version of Texas.

As a matter of fact, a drag show turned out to be the next attraction, and it was a show to die for. One queen lip-synced to "Three Wooden Crosses," complete with her smoking three joints fashioned as empty crucifixes. Another performed "Angel from Montgomery" and brought the whole party to hugging and swaying together. After the show, the music flowed on. When the first notes of "Forever and Ever, Amen" bounced from the speakers, I wet the tips of my fingers with the tears that came to my eyes.

I looked over at Mars, who swayed, absorbing the lyrics. Blaze and Mika were sitting on a wooden bench nearby, looking into each other's eyes. Jean-Luc and Charlie were nowhere to be found. Everyone on the dance floor was grabbing someone to boogie with. Which couples were romantic? Which were just friends? It didn't matter. All types of love tangled in the air. Women sang to women, men to men, people to people.

Being queer wasn't different here. It's what the whole place was about. Every paint color and drink and piece of furniture. It was a home unlike any I had ever stepped into, one that welcomed me instead of craning its neck in judgment at the idea of me. This was life outside of the closet, and the fresh air felt sweet on my lips. I tried to steady my hand as I held it out to Mars and asked for a dance.

Mars blushed—a real, red, sweet blush—and put her hand on mine. I could tell she was overwhelmed too. That wherever she'd been before Tombstone was nothing like this. Me, I'd never imagined that a single place on earth could hold so many rainbow lights and so much freedom. Inside us was something we had locked away. Here, together, we could share it with a dance.

We could even share a kiss. I hadn't kissed a woman in public before, not until the end of "Forever and Ever, Amen," when Mars gently kissed my lips and rubbed the tears off of my cheeks with her thumbs. I started laughing, thinking how much of a mess I must look. And then I kissed her again, a big pouty kiss with both my arms around her neck.

When the song changed to something more poppy, everyone broke off from each other and lassoed themselves into new entanglements under the big pink parachute.

"Come with me," Mars said, grabbing my hand and pulling me away. We passed by the bar into the outdoor area with turf on the ground. Folks wearing rhinestone jean jackets and lace tank tops sat with us and smoked cigarettes, giving their bedazzled boots a rest.

"*I'm glad you came to the bar with us*," she said, slurring her words a bit. This was the first time I had seen her as toasted as a marshmallow over a fire in October.

"I'm glad too," I said.

"*This is special*."

"It is."

"*No*." She grabbed my face with her two hands. I must have looked like a fish. Despite my silly face, Mars's eyes were serious. "*This is really special, toots. Can you grasp that, pickle? Just a few decades ago, people couldn't dance like this out in the open. Blaze and Mika couldn't wear their little skirts.*"

"Oh, I'm sure they could wear skirts in other places. Not Tombstone, maybe, but other places."

"*Not where we were*."

"Where?"

"*Before. Before Tombstone. And before that. Things were so different in the twenties. Everything was hidden behind codes, secrets. You had to know someone who knew someone who was running a gay club. You'd think by the seventies people would have come around, but . . . nope!*" She flicked her hand in the air. "*Obscenity laws.*"

"What are you talking about?"

Mars started giggling and pulled me into a rusty old photo booth nearby. We were alone. She leaned in and whispered:

"*Do you want to know why life is so easy for us? Why we don't take things so seriously?*"

"I've been thinking about that quite a bit, yes."

Mars slipped some cash into the booth's money slot, plucked

the sword out of her drink, and sucked on her ginger candy. Her lips puckered at the spice, which put her in the perfect position to kiss me on the cheek. The photo booth started taking pictures. I looked forward and smiled as she rested her forehead drunkenly against my face and laughed.

"*We're time travelers*," she said.

Mars looked ravishing in every photo, smiling ear-to-ear as she tossed her blonde hair around. In the last two squares on the strip of photos, I look wide-eyed and confused.

TWENTY-FOUR

Before I recount the goings-on that took place after that magical night at Giddy Up Chuck's, I must admit that my brain had been tickled to exhaustion by those Golden Ticket cocktails. This explains why the idea of time travel didn't send me into an immediate existential spiral of confusion, disbelief, and quick breathing. I was drunk. And every time I opened my mouth to speak, I could taste a combination of ginger candy and watermelon lip balm that was more distracting than any suggestion of alternate dimensions or universes. My priorities weren't straight, maybe, but neither am I.

"Well, I told her," Mars said, putting a sailor's hat from the trunk over her face and lying down in the backseat. It was two in the morning and the bar had closed. We would make it back to Tombstone before I had to open Swear-It's, and I could hiccup out enough questions between glugs of water to fill up the entire drive home.

"Told me?You mean—the thing you told me in the photo booth?" I asked. My words were coming out like the meat from a sloppy joe, but I'd heard what I heard, and what I heard was absurd.

"No need to tiptoe, Pinky," Blaze said through his own hiccups, settling into the row in front of us with a sleeping Mika on his shoulder. There was a little lipstick left on his mouth, but most of it had been smeared all over Mika's face. "Time travel. It's out in the open. We figured Mars would tell you, since she's been so smitten with you lately. That hasn't happened since the seventies. Or was it the forties? Maybe the forties—or the 1400s . . ."

"So you all . . . think this is real?" I asked.

"Yes, I am very smitten with you," Mars said, giggling.

"No, the time travel. Is this a drug code or something? Are you just talking about drugs?"

"Trust me when I say I haven't done drugs in five hundred years, Pinky," Jean-Luc said. "Although, people today may not consider leeches to be drugs. But—and try to keep an open mind—the truth is that we literally travel through time. Anyone can do it, did you know that? But only if they know how. Mars trusts you, and we trust Mars. Although normally we *discuss it with each other* before spilling the beans."

"Oh, please," Blaze said, popping some leftover tater tots in his mouth. "If Pinky's not coming with us, I think the beans will remain in the bag. Right, friend?"

Mars lazily tried to smack Blaze on the shoulder but couldn't reach. Blaze handed her a tater tot to ease the tension.

"Quite the change of heart, Blaze," Jean-Luc said. "Jimmy, Tip, and Dolly threaten to tell this little town and you tell them to go back to Marfa. But you're okay with Mars just whispering sweet somethings at gay bars?"

"Oh, pish-posh, you scaredy-cat," Blaze said. "You know those three have been plotting something since we scooped up Mika.

They're jealous." He looked at me. "I got in trouble for telling some folks about our journeys a few jumps ago. Although folks in 2022 can probably put the pieces together better than those goofballs in 1946."

"1948," Jean-Luc corrected him. "Remember? The Olympics. The Swedish track team?"

"How could I forget?" Blaze asked, cracking a smile. He switched to a whisper as he covered Mika's sleeping ears. "Don't mention the Swedish track team in front of Mika, Pinky. He joined us after our time with the athletes. Runners aren't famous for their flexibility, but . . ."

"Oh, dry up, Blaze!" Mars said. "Pinky doesn't want to hear your drunk rambling. The only reason you could tell the Swedes about time travel is because they barely spoke English. Let's stick to what we agreed on after the theater. Lay low. I'm not telling anyone besides Pinky about our romps in the timeline."

"Pinky speaks English, unlike those Scandanavian fellows, so we all have some explaining to do," said Jean-Luc.

Blaze settled in. "Okay, Pinky. Let 'er rip. What questions do you have?"

Where was I supposed to begin? Thoughts were swimming through my brain like eels at a roadside petting zoo. Mars and the boys said a lot of kooky stuff—our first interaction was a business card asking me to join a circus, for George Strait's sake—but this was the kookiest thing of all. I ran my fingers over the business card in my purse. The edges were real. But what else was?

"What do you mean by 'time travel'?" Strong start.

"It's not exactly the time traveling you might have seen in

movies or television," Jean-Luc explained. "Or maybe it is. I don't think I've ever watched television in the 2020s."

"Is it like *Back to the Future*?"

"Oh, god, no," Blaze said. "We have no control over where we end up. One time, we washed up on the shores of Pangaea and the only friends we could make were jellyfish."

"Another time," Mars slurred, "we got dumped in the middle of Czechlo . . . whatever it's called now, but it was Czechoslovakia then. Let me tell you, Blaze's tank top was quite the scandal."

"It's not my fault!" Blaze said. "I left my coat at Studio 54. Have you ever tried to get a coat back from Studio 54?"

I had not. "How long do you stay in each place?"

"Depends on how conducive it is to setting up a circus or hosting a party," Mars said. "We didn't stay long in Pangaea. The Middle Ages are quite stinky, but it's where we found Jean-Luc all those jumps ago. The 1970s were fun, but our long-gone friends caused a bit of a ruckus and we had to leave after a few months. Longest we stayed anyplace was a whole year back in 2076. Just wait until you see what happens to . . . you know what, never mind."

"We're still trying to figure this all out," Blaze said. "We've only known each other for a handful of years, total. I think. I've lost count. I left the compound when I was nineteen and I think I'm about twenty-five now? Twenty-six?"

My head was spinning into the philosophical. "So which religion is the most accurate one?"

Everyone shrugged.

"Did man walk with dinosaurs?"

Everyone shrugged again.

"Where is Amelia Earhart?" The van fell silent. Only after Jean-Luc cleared his throat did Mars clarify why.

"She's a doll from my past. Awkward situation."

"Oh." I shuffled through a few thoughts, figuring out how to react to Mars's statement.

I was left frozen until Blaze proclaimed, "Pinky pinky, now it's out. You're Eleanor Roosevelt's kissing cousin, twice removed!"

"Can you go back and stop the release of the nuclear bomb?" I continued, changing the subject. "Find Abraham Lincoln and tell him not to go to the theater? Sounds like you've got a lot of work to do if you time travel."

"We all ask that when we first start jumping," Jean-Luc said. "What should we do to change the world? How can we save everything? What course of action will end the presence of evil throughout all humanity? We've done a little bit, with Mars whispering in FDR's ear about the New Deal and all, but there's only so much a few individuals can do. What we choose to do with our circus is spread kindness where we can."

"The circus? You have an actual circus?"

"Wherever we go, that's the circus."

"It's all one big circus," Mars said, "when you can't choose where or when you end up."

"Where did you travel after talking to Franklin Roosevelt?"

"Oh, god, where did we go? Was that 3000 AD?"

Blaze shuddered. "No, but that was not a good time."

"What happened in 3000 AD?" I asked.

"You don't want to know," Mars said.

"You'll be dead anyway," Jean-Luc affirmed.

"Thanks."

"I think the closest we got to saving Abraham Lincoln was

popping up in the 1800s in what's now known as East Asia," Blaze said. "Boy, that was a tough one to get out of."

"Can't exactly hop on the old internet back then and just ask for directions back to Washington, DC," Mars said, patting my head.

"We couldn't do that in the forties either," Jean-Luc said, "but somehow you made it from Sweden to DC to Argentina in just a few hours. Must be nice to know a lady with a plane."

"Why were you flying to Argentina?"

"Because we were tired of Sedona," Mars said. "You have to know where to go in a given time period in order to time travel. Marfa, Sedona, Capilla del Monte, this one waterfall in the Gobi Desert, Uluru . . ."

"But you don't know at all where—I mean when—you're going to land?"

"It's not up to us," Blaze said. "Trust me. I've been doing this longer than anyone in this van. I still have no idea why I pop up in certain time periods or in certain places. But I have noticed a pattern."

"Which is?"

"Usually I meet someone who needs a little kindness. Jimmy and Tip and Dolly found me when I was escaping the compound. Mars was a lost lamb in the Jazz Age before we scooped her up and hit fast-forward to the forties."

Mars blushed.

"People come and go," Blaze continued. "Sometimes we see them again, sometimes we don't. Sometimes our kindness is welcomed and sometimes it isn't. If we don't know who to help, we just put on a circus and have a grand old time. But it was pretty clear when we saw you in that parking lot that you might need a little kindness. I hope our Sweet Potato Grace flag helped you honor your kitty and feel a little solace. Even if it's supposed to be evidence that we're a cat-worshipping cult."

"I appreciate the kindness, Blaze," I said, holding back tears by squeezing his business card. "I think it's quite kind that you lead with kindness."

"Kindness is timeless," Blaze said.

"Like denim," Jean-Luc continued.

"Like pearls," Mars said.

"Like bare feet," Mika said confidently.

TWENTY-FIVE

After Joe Clark's no-good nephew crashed his truck into the Exhaust 'n' Rest, Mama preached a sermon to Fanny and me about the dangers of alcohol, even though we were a decade away from being able to obtain a driver's license. The details of that sermon have washed away with the tide of every other sermon Mama has preached, but one phrase sticks in my brain:

"Remember this, girls: Beer weighs you down, tequila makes you lie down, and whiskey makes you feel so down you either write a country song or ruin your life."

I will admit I didn't feel like writing a country song when I woke up in the van that morning. I didn't feel like doing much of anything besides leaning my head against the window, closing my eyes, and waiting for Jean-Luc to make a stop at my house so I could get ready for work.

"Rise and shine," Jean-Luc said as we passed the modest sign at the Tombstone town limits.

"Back already?" Blaze yawned. He gently shook Mika awake.

Mika sat up with a start and an exclamation of "No, David Byrne, *you* stop tickling *me*," before he came to and realized where he was, issuing an apology.

"Having that dream again?" Blaze asked.

Before I could lift Mars out of her dreams, I saw Kim and Tom Bailey in front of Swear-It's.

Kim was the face of KMNZ, the local news station. Her husband, Tom, worked the camera. They had both gone to Tombstone High School and graduated a year above me. Two nights before the wedding, Tom had told Ashley's older sister (his ex-girlfriend) that he was still in love with her, but that part of the story is usually omitted when they reminisce about their romance during the morning news.

That morning, Kim was set up in front of the store windows, which were covered in fliers comparing Blaze to David Koresh and a *new* flier that showed a full-color picture of Sweet Potato Grace's flag.

"Jean-Luc, stop the car!" I said. He swerved and pulled over, throwing Mars into my shoulder and waking her with a start.

"Everything okay?" Blaze asked.

"No. What's *she* doing here?"

"Has your Mama mentioned anything groovy happening this week?"

My phone. My phone was off. I scrambled to turn it on and sat slack-jawed as it powered up, connected to the universe, gathered my data to sell to whomever, and started buzzing. The buzzing started and it didn't stop. Ten missed calls from Mama. Fifteen from Ashley. Sixty from June—dramatic. A slew of text messages, including one from Fanny that said, "Can you remind me where you said you're going again?"

Fantastic. Everyone thought I had been Patty Hearst'd.

"Y'all, just drop me off right here. I'll handle this. Tombstone doesn't need any more photos of you to put on posters."

"Are you sure, Pinky?" Mars asked, stroking my shoulders. She leaned over to kiss my cheek but I put my hand up. Tombstone *especially* didn't need any footage of an alleged female cult member giving me a smooch. Mars sat back, issuing a meek *oh*, looking through the ghost of a once-familiar sorrow. I didn't have time to tell her we weren't in Austin anymore. I opened the door to the van and waved goodbye to my hungover, silent friends.

Fanny didn't pick up my first call, as usual. But when I called again, I heard her groggy, "Hello?"

"Fanny?"

"Pinky?"

"Yes, Fanny. Did you not see who was calling you?"

"I don't have anyone's phone number in my phone."

"But I'm your sister. You know what? Never mind. Can you pick me up?"

"Where are you again?"

"Well, I'm in front of the store. The whole window is covered in some dumb fliers, and Kim Bailey is here. What's going on? Did you not tell people where I was? Why is everyone so upset?"

She sighed, as if failing to do the simple task of sharing my whereabouts had caused a large inconvenience for her.

"You were gone for twenty-four hours, so June Ripple submitted a missing persons report. I did try to tell her that you were with your new friends, but she wouldn't listen. Wanda said something about you being Patty Burst? I don't know why they fear you've gone to Broadway, I'm the one in the family who can tap dance."

"Patty Hearst was a woman who got kidnapped, Fanny," I seethed. "Why didn't you tell my friends I went on my own?"

"Have you ever tried to tell June Ripple she was wrong, Pinky?"

Point taken.

"Well, I'm safe," I said. "I'm alive. We just went camping for the weekend. Can you pick me up from the store? I need to shower before we open. And before that, can you tell Mama I'm not dead in a ditch or robbing a bank with the Symbionese Liberation Army?"

"I can't spell that."

"I was joking, Fanny."

"And I'm not joking when I say that you need to tell Kim to go eat dirt. Is she that great of an investigative journalist if her husband still has a profile on Match.com? I'll see you in ten minutes, Pinky."

I hung up the phone, not fully trusting Fanny to do what I'd asked her to do. But I had no other choice. Sometimes you just have to trust your sister.

Now, Mama raised me to be better than the woman I was while I waited for Fanny. I didn't take two steps toward Kim before my old sneakers betrayed me and skidded, sending me tumbling onto the pavement. Thank Dolly Parton no cars were on the road, although I could have used her assistance getting up. I didn't think to check my hair. I barely had enough room in my head to pick myself up, brush myself off, and process the fact that a van full of my new friends had just told me after a few whiskey cocktails that they traveled through time, seducing Olympic athletes and national heroes along the way.

What would *you* do if your friends told you all this? Put on lipstick? Finger-brush your hair? Check to see if the stamp from Giddy Up Chuck's had rubbed onto your face as you slept, giving the appearance of a bruised cheek? I can tell you right now, you might be too distracted.

If I'd had a moment to take a deep breath and find a mirror, perhaps I wouldn't have looked like a vagrant or a victim on local television. But I cannot go back to that moment and brush my hair, wash my face, or fix my posture. I cannot go back and ask myself, "How do I look? Presentable for the morning news?"

Kim saw my stumble and waited patiently for me to join her in front of the camera. I wanted to make a statement. Tombstone had to see that I was alive and well right then and there. Fanny didn't gossip, after all, although at that moment I wished she did.

"Hello, Tombstone!" I said as I ran into the frame next to Kim. She was amused, but I didn't give her space to ask any questions. "Hello, Mama," I continued. "Hello, June. Hello, uh, Nene. I'm fine. I'm alive." I caught my breath and doubled over, flipping my hair back when I stood up straight again.

"Kim, you're getting this, right?" I looked into the camera. "Good to see you all! Guess what? I'm not in a—um—well, let's just say I'm fine. I'm better than fine! I'm ga—garrulous, is that the right word? What I mean is, I just went camping with some friends, and *someone* overreacted. I will respond to all of your texts soon, and please calm down, everyone. Calm down about my, um, friends. They do not worship a cat."

Kim's bright smile twisted a knot in my stomach.

"Well," she said to the camera, "there you have it. More on this story in the evening news hour. Back to Emily for the weather." Tom stepped away from the camera, offering Kim a thumbs-up and me a look of pure bewilderment. I knew the camera had stopped rolling because the corners of Kim's mouth dropped out of position.

"Pinky Swear," she said, her words dripping like salsa onto the first breakfast taco of the morning. "I can't believe it. The police can call off their search, I guess."

"This is ridiculous, Kim. I went camping with friends for a weekend and the whole town turned upside down?"

"I think *upside down* is a little dramatic. One disappearance doesn't cause a whole panic. Unless it's Mayor Johnston, or Scooter. Or me, of course."

"What makes you as special as Mayor Johnston?"

"Who else would report the news?"

"I'm confident the town gossip train would keep chugging along just fine without you."

"Harsh. Those cult freaks are doing a number on you, aren't they?"

"They're not!" I started to yell before I lowered my voice. "They're not a cult and they're not freaks, Kim. They're just . . ." What did I want to say? Time travelers? "Lord on a unicycle. What's the big deal? People are allowed to move to Tombstone. What are people calling the FBI on, bare feet?"

Before Kim could answer, Fanny honked the horn. "Pinky!" she yelled. "Get in the car. Before Kim's low-budget news team gathers any more material."

"Nice to see you, little Fanny!" Kim shouted, waving politely. "Enjoy your debut on television, Pinky."

A frame of Kim's sly smile greeted me on the living room television after I got home and showered. At least Kim's Botox had worn off enough that she could show emotion again. Mama sat on the couch, Fanny next to her, while I stood in the doorway and winced at my hungover, chaotic plea to the town. We watched the clip in silence. It wasn't the *ums* or the *ahs* that would get

Mama's goat. It wasn't calling Mama out on national—well, statewide—well, local—television that would boil her soup. No, it was the hair. My hair had been styled by the headrest of the Volkswagen, and that would really steam her vegetables. My hair was beehived by upholstery. You know how they say "the higher the hair, the closer to God"? Not in this case. God wouldn't let this mess near the gates of heaven. Heaven's Gate was my only option. My mascara was streaked underneath my eyes and lipstick was smeared up to my earlobe. I looked like a street-walking, gum-popping, heel-clacking hussy of the night. If I was inching closer to God, I was only inching closer to a smitin'.

The coffee brewed and its aroma offered a smidgeon of roasted solace as the segment ended and Emily Granger gestured wildly at the weather report.

"Who was sitting next to you in that van?" Mama asked, turning the television off.

"Why does that matter?" I asked.

"I want to know who you spent your weekend swooning over."

I looked at Fanny, who tried to look confused by the question. Nene Miriam was looking at her blanket, but I knew she could still hear. I couldn't answer truthfully. She wouldn't understand.

"What do you mean?"

"You don't just run off with a bunch of barefoot fools because you like to look at their toes. Which one are you swooning over? I worry because I want to protect you."

"I know."

"Tombstone is as safe a world as I can make for you."

"I know."

"I don't know these barefoot folks, but Tombstone doesn't

think they're safe. Texas doesn't have casinos for a reason, Pinky. We don't gamble here."

"I know." But did Mama *know?*

"It's getting worse out there because of people like them. In Texas, sure, but everywhere. I've been hearing about it every day on the news. You're not as young as you used to be, Pinky. It's about time you started thinking about your health, your safety, your place in this town. You know what's right and what's wrong. If you get hurt or develop a reputation, Swear-It's will fall into disarray. I'll rot in this old house alone. Do you really want that? Do you really want me to end up like Mrs. Lindsay, that old, miserable bat? Do you want your Mama to suffer because a bunch of . . . barefoot folk . . . want to make some sort of political statement? Next thing you know, they'll get us all canceled!"

"I don't think that's how being canceled works," Fanny offered, but she shut her trap when she saw Mama's eye twitching. Fanny chose her battles wisely.

What was I supposed to tell her? That, in this case, "people like them" meant more than being queer? She wasn't going to believe me if I told her my friends were time travelers. I still didn't know if I believed it myself.

I just nodded and left for my shift.

✿

The shift at Swear-It's was the same as always, once I took down the posters and threw them in the trash. The Tuesday routine didn't change, apart from every customer making a point to express their relief at my safe return—and trying to weasel a little gossip out of me.

"Pinky, thank goodness you're home! I was shocked to hear the news. You're not a senior. Maybe you look a little older than your age, but I didn't think that would get you terrorized!"

"I saw your clip on the news, Pinky. I prayed for your safe return. Have you got one of those robes for yourself? The ones those barefoot people wear?"

"So glad to see you home safe, Pinky. Now, have you seen this golden cat your friends have? Sounds exactly like a golden calf, but a cat. I'm just curious."

Feeling different is like watching the world from behind a two-way mirror, with my mirror being the register at Swear-It's. I didn't need sympathy. I didn't need looky-loos. I needed answers. Clarification. Direction. I wished Roger were still alive. He wasn't the judging type. He'd hear me out about what my new friends told me and give me solid advice. I didn't think I could find it anywhere else.

That night, when I unlocked the mother-in-law suite, I stuck my foot in front of me. I didn't mean to. It was a reflex. Sweet Potato Grace had tried to dart out whenever I opened the door, but upon being blocked by my foot, she would greet me by using my shoe as her personal scratching post. I looked down and slid my foot back. The silence in the room felt visceral, like a physical pressure stuffing into my ears. How was the room still this empty, months after she passed? I sat on my bed looking at what I knew was real: photos of Sweet Potato Grace.

Outdoor cats don't live as long. That's what the vets reassured me whenever I brought Sweet Potato Grace in for a visit. Keeping her indoors was the responsible thing to do.

But Potato wanted to be outside. She wanted open spaces where she could sink her claws into local squirrels and eat scraps.

She was a gambler. Sweet Potato Grace wanted to do what was natural, but there I was, trapping her inside and giving her the same smelly food twice a day, every day. What had I done? Had I ruined Sweet Potato's life, instead of saving it?

No, no—outdoor cats don't live as long. And I couldn't change the past. The past was frozen solid.

If my friends were telling the truth about time travel, what did it mean about life? Death? Could you come back to see your loved ones again?

When Blaze said I could see Sweet Potato Grace again, what did he mean?

"Sweet Potato Grace," I said into the stale air of the mother-in-law suite, "where are you? What am I going to do?"

TWENTY-SIX

Ashley didn't launch into a story the moment I picked up the phone. She was polite. That's how I knew something was wrong. That, and I hadn't heard from her in the week since my "disappearance."

"Pinky, hi," she began, seeming to hope I would interrupt her. When I didn't, she just cleared her throat. "We're getting together at June's tonight. Are you available? June will be providing an assortment of cheeses."

"What's the occasion?"

"Oh, nothing, just the usual. It's BYOB, but . . ." A beat of silence went by. "Well, I just wanted to hear about your time with the . . . uh . . ."

"The cult? The freaks? The stain on Tombstone's grave that's terrorizing our seniors and kidnapping our future grocery store owners?"

"Pinky, please."

"I'm not a freak, Ashley. You know that. Or do you? Where have you been? The last time you didn't answer your phone for this long, you were doing that Motherbosses Against MLMS retreat at Port Aransas."

"No one thinks you're a freak. It's just . . . a lot of people around town don't 'get' your new friends. And I can't blame them for being suspicious, especially after you left without telling anyone."

"I told Fanny. What are you suspicious of? Don't you trust me?"

"I'm staying neutral, Pinky. I'm not educated enough on the conflict."

"What?"

"I've heard the things people are saying at the preschool and in different social circles. They think I'm next to be recruited because I'm friends with you. I see where everyone is coming from, though, and I'm going to listen to what June has to say *and* what you have to say."

"What does June have to say?"

Ashley's hesitation flooded me with anxiety.

"*What does June have to say, Ashley?*"

"I don't know, okay? But I've got to warn you," she said, lowering her voice. "She's got something prepared. June has gotten high off her own supply because the whole town is cheering her on. You know how she likes people cheering her on."

I refused to let her enjoy that attention at the expense of Mars's or my reputation. Did that make me a bad friend to June? Or a good friend to Blaze, Mars, and the rest of my barefoot friends?

"Let me guess. She's got a PowerPoint presentation about how Mars is in a cult."

Now, I made that comment in jest. The Sewing Circle had sworn off PowerPoint parties after COVID, when Ashley started on the first of thirty slides about her great-great-great-great-

great-great grandfather who fought as a Confederate soldier. Wanda took control of the remote, and no more presentations were allowed.

"Ashley," I said firmly. "Did June put together a PowerPoint presentation about how my friends are in a cult?"

"You might want to have a rebuttal prepared," she said. "I'll pick you up in an hour." She hung up the phone and the countdown began.

I half expected to walk into June's house and see a projector like the ones wheeled into classrooms when it was time to talk about bodily functions and abstinence with reference to that old diagram of the uterus. (The "Texas Longhorn," as Mama used to say.) The same shame washed over me walking into June's that day as it did when I walked into Ms. Lindsay's health class.

But June's living room was not arranged for a formal debate or a sex education lesson. Chairs were not arranged in a circle for my intervention. Podiums were not placed in front of the TV. Wanda was lying on the couch with her legs kicking up in the air like usual, and Ashley was putting her toddler down in the guest room where the toddler usually slept. I could hear her taking deep breaths. She wasn't one for being caught in the middle of things.

Then I saw June taking a baked brie out of the oven. Oh, this would be bad after all. June knew that I *loved* baked brie.

"Our local celebrity," Wanda said, keeping her eyes on her phone as I walked in. "Did you see any peacocks while you were in Austin?"

June sighed. "I don't think Pinky's involved with Buddhafield. They're in Hawaii now." She looked at me, trying to keep a smile on. "You didn't see any, though, did you?"

She walked over to give me a cordial, vapid hug with her

oven gloves still on. Her smile was bright as a daisy and she smelled like one, too. This was her going-out perfume, the one she wore for confidence. She wanted to smell sugar-sweet before sinking her teeth into my skin like a cottonmouth. Or was it a copperhead? Either way, I could see June's tongue starting to split in two.

"Please, sit. Do you want some wine?" June said.

Emboldened by my recent appearance on the news, I took the offensive. "No, I'm not thirsty. I've been drinking too much Kool-Aid." Wanda's phone hit the carpet with a *thump* and Ashley's head popped into sight from behind the guest bedroom door. Time stood still as I waited for June's counterattack.

She dropped the smile. "That isn't funny."

"Oh, yes it is," I said. "I get what's happening here. Let's just get to it."

"Nine hundred people died at Jonestown. Three hundred were children." She placed her Minnie Mouse oven mitt over her heart.

"How many times did you google those numbers while I was taking an innocent camping trip with my friends?"

"Nine hundred is nothing to joke about."

"Well, Blaze doesn't have that big of a following yet. So you can relax."

Ashley put her hand on my shoulder. "Can we call a time-out?" she asked. "I would at least like some baked brie. Maybe we could give it time to cool down before we start throwing it at each other?"

"Hot," Wanda said. She's never been particularly helpful.

Ashley turned to June, giving her a look that told me they'd discussed their discussion before discussing it with me. "Tell

Pinky your concerns, June, and she'll tell you hers, and we'll all have an open and honest discussion that ends in the best possible outcome for our lifelong circle of friends."

If only it were that easy.

June removed her oven mitts and sat down, smoothing her apron. That meant a monologue was coming. I'd sat through hundreds of June's monologues—or were they soliloquies?—over the years and knew when to brace myself. If a spotlight had come on and illuminated all the dust flying around her face and she'd started belting out a German aria, I wouldn't have batted an eye. June yearned for melodrama. Worst of all, June yearned to be right.

"Pinky," she began, looking into my eyes with artificial sympathy, "I've been doing some reading. About cults. What I've found sounds too much like your new group of friends for my liking. If you would like, I want to share some of what I've read with you."

"I wouldn't like," I said, only to receive a throat-clearing of a warning from Ashley. No one had even asked how I was doing that evening. Interventions should start with a temperature check, at the very least. Not that I've ever hosted one. Are baked bries commonplace?

"Are you going to recite me a poem?" I asked.

"This is serious," June said. "We care about you. These people. Where do I begin?" She shuffled the contents of a manila folder that she had ready next to her chair.

"Dishonoring the family unit," she read. "I'll start there. People in a cult dishonor the family unit and isolate you from your family and friends."

"What kind of dressing would you like on that word salad?"

I was ignored.

“These people brought you out camping for a whole weekend. You had no service, your Find My Friends wasn’t working . . . you could have been killed out there and they wouldn’t have been held accountable.”

“Except they would, because you know where they live.”

“What if they’d killed you and then kept on driving to Oregon?” Ashley asked.

“They didn’t. They all like you girls, you know. If you hadn’t been so quick to leave their party, they would have invited you to go camping too.”

June started to protest but chose another battle. She continued to move through her list.

“No financial transparency. If their budget is not clear, or they are independently auditing themselves . . .”

“When was the last time you audited your friends, June?”

“They don’t have jobs. They don’t have an account at the bank. Don’t scoff at me, Pinky, Michael checked. Have you ever loaned them money?”

“I haven’t given them a dime,” I said. “I bought a Lone Star here and there. So at most, they’re swindling me out of a beer or two.”

“So far,” Wanda said.

“I bought them all drinks this weekend and they paid me back in cash.”

“How did they get cash?” June asked.

“They run a traveling circus.” I sounded *real* confident with that answer.

“Why did you have to buy drinks for them?” June asked.

Shoot. What was I going to say, that they were time travelers and didn't have the proper dates on their IDs? The truth was stranger than fiction, and my fists were clenching tighter than the Hulk's.

"The day they ask me for anything more than gas money," I said, "I'll come straight to your house and bake you a big ol' cake with your face on it. I'll put some delicious icing on top, and in another color I'll write, 'June was right. Pinky was wrong.'"

"Pinky," Ashley warned through gritted teeth. Strike two.

"Until I see them walk on tightropes, I won't believe they actually run a circus. We've done our research, Pinky. They have no jobs in Tombstone. Heck, they could be drug dealers or prostitutes for all we know."

"Sex workers," Ashley, Wanda, and I said together. June claimed to be right, not politically correct.

"And what if they are?" I said. "What if—"

"There you go," June said, pointing at me and looking at Ashley and Wanda. "Leaders are extremely charismatic, to the point where they have significant influence over their victims. Look at what that Blaze has done to you, thinking it'd be just peachy to have a bunch of drug dealers and sex workers hanging around Tombstone."

"And what Wanda's sister does isn't sex work?" I asked.

"She just sells pictures of her feet," Wanda said. "Doesn't count."

"Yeah," I said, "because the guys that buy them are all cobblers making shoes."

"But you do agree that Blaze is their charismatic leader?" June asked. "We've been going back and forth on whether it's Blaze or Mars. Mars seems to be the one you're closest to. Are your old friends not good enough for you? Or are you pushing us away because we don't share their"—she looked down at her notes—"exclusive definition of 'truth'?"

"They're all pretty charismatic, and that's why I like hanging out with them." I failed to acknowledge that their version of truth included time travel and a sapphic Amelia Earhart.

"Are we *not* charismatic?" Wanda asked.

"That's a great question, Wanda. Believe it or not, Blaze and them remind me a lot of y'all. Except with them, I'm allowed to share my opinions and disagree. With you, I cannot. Seems a lot like you're the cult, doesn't it?"

Strike three.

June stood up. "Pinky, you have done nothing *but* dissent since those barefoot freaks came into town, and we haven't said boo. Now things have gone too far. Just rewatch that clip of you on the news. You looked crazed. Did you sleep at all? What did you do on this camping trip? Dynamic meditations? Bioterrorism?"

"What did *you* do this weekend, flip through a thesaurus and choose words to throw at me? I have no idea what those terms mean."

"No, I rewatched *Wild Wild Country*. The parallels between your new *friends* and the Rajneeshees are eerie."

"Bless you."

"Thank you." One more thing: June didn't pick up on sarcasm. "A group of shaggy-haired hippies moving into a sleepy town? That's the whole first episode of the documentary. Next thing you know, they're going to poison our water supply and commit bioterrorism."

"Blaze told me he didn't want to feed the longhorns 'people

food' because he didn't want to find out if they were allergic. I highly doubt they have any desire to poison anything."

"They treat the longhorns better than they treat the old folks in this town?" Ashley asked. "And don't try to paint them as animal activists, Pinky, seeing as they interrupted your cat's funeral."

"What does Sweet Potato Grace have to do with any of this?" I could feel tears pricking my eyes but tried to snort them away, as if I were a little longhorn myself.

June's voice got very low. "Cults prey on the vulnerable," she said quietly, avoiding eye contact with me. "You are very vulnerable, what with grieving Sweet Potato Grace and all. I'm sure they picked up on that. Cults prey on the weak."

"I'm not weak," I said quietly. I had no way out from my corner. I had to do something drastic if I was going to shut June up.

"Then why are you hanging around them so much?" June asked, a final jab of a question.

I threw back my shoulders and looked June in the eye. There was still something in me that needed to get out. Maybe it was a cop-out to drop the bombshell at this particular moment, but I didn't care. At the very least it would give them something else to gossip about.

"Because I have a crush on Mars," I said. "That's why."

Wanda sat up.

Ashley looked at me, then at June. She bit her lip, worried about whatever June was going to say next.

June stepped back. "How do you know that?" she asked coldly.

"June!" Ashley said. "Stop it. We're Pinky's friends. Let her talk."

"We *are* Pinky's friends," June repeated. "More than those people are. They don't know you like we know you."

I looked at Wanda, who looked away. Ashley started walking back to the guest room.

"We've known you since elementary school, Pinky," June continued. "We've known you your whole life. You kept this from us for fifteen years?"

"Wait, so you're a lesbian?" Wanda asked.

"She's not," June snapped.

I smacked June square on the cheek.

"Pinky!" all three of them yelled, filling June's house with their shock.

I picked up a paper plate, threw a hunk of baked brie on it, and walked straight out the door.

TWENTY-SEVEN

Adrenaline coursed through my veins as I gnawed on baked brie. My skin was hotter than all the days of summer combined. I needed to keep walking. I needed to sit down. I needed to yell and shake and figure out if smacking my lifelong friend was justified, or if my friends were just doubting me in a normal way. I would figure that out later. I was in such a state of fight or flight that I couldn't even enjoy my brie.

June's house was a short walk away from Peace Valley Park, which is usually empty on weeknights. Rowdy teenagers did not stand a chance against Brenda, Brenda's cranky old neighbor Jim, the Tombstone grapevine, or the paddles of parents who still believed in a good whooping for sneaking around at the Devil's hour. The only frequent visitor to the park at night was Brenda herself, who went to check for wounded animals that needed a place to rest and heal.

I had not brought enough brie to share; fortunately, Brenda was Tombstone's resident vegan. Another reason Mama believed she was single.

"I don't want to startle you, ma'am," I said as I approached. "It's me. Pinky Swear. Looking for strays?"

Brenda lifted her head and her headlamp shone directly in my eyes. "Whoops! Sorry, honey." She turned it off. "Yes, come have a seat. Tina Clark saw two little kitties in a tree earlier today, but I can't seem to find them or their mama. How are you? I heard you had quite the weekend with Blaze and your new friends."

I winced as I sat on the bench under the pavilion. "Did you see that on the news? I didn't realize how awful I looked. We drove through the night after going to a bar, and I didn't look in a mirror. I was so panicked—I just wanted to tell everyone I was safe, and Kim Bailey was ready to embarrass me."

"It's a shame how Tombstone has been treating those folks."

"My friends think they're forming a cult to worship Sweet Potato Grace."

"Heck, I'd join that religion."

I didn't laugh, but what I'd told my friends had left me feeling lighter. Nothing was holding me down. I had left a weight behind me at June's.

"I told my friends I was . . ." Repeating the feat wasn't easy, though. I took a deep breath. "I told them I had a crush on Mars."

Brenda sat down next to me. She put a hand on my shoulder. "And what'd they say?"

"June doesn't believe me."

"June Ripple?"

"Yes, ma'am."

Brenda sighed. "What a bitch."

As much as I wanted to protest, I didn't want to go against Brenda's better judgment. I wanted to change the subject. "Do you remember Roger?"

"Roger Lindsay?"

"Mmhmm."

"I haven't heard that name in years. May God have mercy on his soul, for Roger certainly got none while he was alive."

"I've been thinking about him lately. He was the first gay man I ever met. Only one I ever knew for a long time. Or should I say, the only out gay man I knew? He was so kind."

"He was the wittiest, sharpest, and smartest man in Texas. And yes, he was so kind. But his mother was a nasty old woman. Right until the very end, just said terrible things about him. Most people would move to Timbuktu just to get away from her. But Roger stayed. Fed her, bathed her, changed her . . . I told him he should just wheel her in front of the nursing home and leave the old bat to bloat on her hill. Nope. Sweet Roger, he stuck around."

"Why?"

"I don't know. He was a good son, I guess. Or a naive one. Part of me thinks he wanted to change her. He had hope that one day, a cosmic switch would flip and she would accept who he was. But that doesn't always happen, Pinky. People are people, and people can only change themselves. I can't believe they let that woman teach health class for thirty-six years."

"Kids at school were pretty mean after he died."

"Oh yeah?"

"One said Miss Kitty ate his face off."

"Kids are awful. That's why I never had them." In the dark, I couldn't see if she winked or just had a lash in her eye. "Well, there is one good thing that came out of Miss Kitty sauntering out of Roger's house all those years ago."

"What's that?"

"Well, before I managed to catch her and spay her, she had a few kittens." Brenda knew every cat in Tombstone and their lineage. "I managed to bring most of them to the rescue or the shelter in Austin, but one was very stubborn about being outside."

"Hmm."

"She quickly developed a taste for whatever leftovers they had at Lethal Peppers BBQ."

Then it clicked. I was thirteen when Miss Kitty had her kittens out of wedlock. Sweet Potato Grace was ten when she died.

"Are you telling me Sweet Potato Grace is Miss Kitty's kitten?" This piece of her history felt like the very best belated birthday present.

"Yes, ma'am. Sweet Potato Grace was a special cat. Nasty, but special."

"And you never brought her in?"

"It's funny, Pinky, she's the only cat that's evaded me. But something also told me she was searching. She was looking for adventure, just like Roger, until it was time to come home. Maybe she knew you were her home all along. The universe is funny like that."

"It really is." Fanny's car swung into the parking lot. Its lights shone on Brenda and me. I was being summoned. "I hope you find those strays, Brenda."

"Thanks, Pinky. Off to go camping again? Or . . . where were you?"

"Not this time. No detours to Austin, either."

"Austin! Oh, I'm glad you mentioned it. Sweet little Max found his forever home in Austin."

"He did?"

"Yup. It was a risk, taking him there, but it paid off."

"I'm glad it did."

Fanny honked her horn. I had a few more questions to ask Brenda; I set them aside for the next time I would see her.

Except I never did.

TWENTY-EIGHT

Over the next few days, I had nothing to do after work except count all the things in the mother-in-law suite that weren't mine. The signs weren't mine, the furniture wasn't mine. Everything was picked by Mama or Nene to please strangers. For almost three years I had lived between the same four walls, and the only things I could claim for myself were a few weeks' worth of clothes, a scratched-up couch, and the skeleton of an automatic feeder that fed dust to pillbugs. I finally took out the batteries the night I slapped June and took her brie.

Counting things also kept me from thinking about the barrage of questions I had about my friends, my family, and what the heck I was still doing in Tombstone.

To the things I claimed for myself, I added my time. I missed monthly brunch with the Sewing Circle and our movie night too. Ashley called twice, but I ignored her. I'm sure she thought I was busy performing blood rituals in a cult and strange sex acts with Mars. I wanted to perform normal sex acts with Mars, but even though she called me three times, I didn't answer her, either. I couldn't bring myself to go to the house on Bluebonnet. I couldn't organize my questions—they floated around like dust just out of my reach. How did these folks find out they could time travel? How did it work? Was what they told me all a dream? Was it a lie?

It was true that their story might explain why they were clumsy with cell phones and the vague way they answered questions about their backgrounds. It explained Mars using outdated geography terms and not knowing who Lady Gaga was. They often had the wisdom—or was it serenity? Apathy?—of people who had witnessed the future. But it hurt my brain to think of the logistics of time travel. And my heart had already been hurting something fierce for months.

On the other hand, the people closest to me believed my friends were a cult. They also thought my friends worshipped my dead cat.

I followed my routine like a good Tombstone woman, going to work and going straight home, for over a week before Fanny finally knocked on my door and got me out of bed.

"I think your friends are gone," was all she said.

The image of Sweet Potato's mean pout greeted me as I pulled into the driveway on Bluebonnet, but the rest of the property looked empty. Chairs were stacked neatly in the corner of the lawn and thrifted furniture was piled up in front of the fence. Inside, the house was bare. Light outlines of pennants and posters and memorabilia marked the walls in the sparse living room. God, those could have been the real things, I found myself realizing. Everything was possible. Anything was possible. And yet, I wasn't overwhelmed.

"Anyone here?" I called out.

I received no answer, but Charlie was in the kitchen. He was wiping down the fridge until it shone. When he saw me, he gave me a glare so sinister I thought the Devil was burning up his eye sockets from within. He opened his mouth to start shouting, but Mars ran into the kitchen just in time and put her hands on his shoulders. She gave him a nod that calmed him down and he returned to his task.

Mars's eyes darted around, as if the right question were on the walls. But there was nothing to steal her focus.

"Pinky," she said. "I hadn't heard from you. How are you?"

"Well, I'm not so sure. Is this a bad time?"

She grabbed my hands timidly and gave me a quick kiss on the cheek. "Let's go into my room?"

Her room matched the rest of the house. Only the bed remained, with a sheet and a single pillow on top. There was so little to get lost in now.

"I'm sorry I haven't been by the house," I said. "I've had to wrap my mind around a lot. What's going on, Mars? Are you moving out?"

A twitch of seriousness pinched Mars's brow. "Did you tell anyone, Pinky? About our secret?"

"The time travel? No. Everyone already thinks I've got a screw loose because I'm friends with you. If I were to start going on about time travel, I'd be supergluing my own coffin from the inside. I wouldn't do well in a padded room on the other side of Texas, Mars. Best to keep my mouth shut."

Mars must have had this conversation before, but she didn't want to show it. "You're not wrong about that, doll. Makes sense you're in a tizzy. People usually do one of three things after we tell them about time travel. One, they disappear forever. I thought at first you might have done that, given the missed calls. Or did the calls not go through? Was this a situation where I was supposed to text you?"

"No, sorry. I was just taking it all in."

"I understand. Two: they try to expose us as freaks of nature and we have to run ourselves out of town. The boys believe you've taken the second option, so I'll have to tell them otherwise. Are you sure you haven't told anyone? Not a soul?"

"No. Why would you think I did?"

"Well, then we're getting run out because people here are suspicious. Quite the paranoid town you've got."

My tonsils tumbled over themselves but no words came out.

"Our landlord told us we have to go," Mars said. "By Friday. He's received a bunch of complaints."

It was Wednesday.

"Tomorrow morning, the town's holding a hearing to outlaw being barefoot in public. It's a silly law, but we get the message."

I thought fast. "I could take you to a mall, maybe? They've got plenty of shoes—"

"The point is that people don't want us here and they're making that clear. If we tried to stay, they would only get more suspicious. We don't need that. We don't want that. Who wants to be in a place where everyone is all up in their business?"

"That's certainly a question for anyone who chooses to stay here."

Mars pulled me into a hug, and her cinnamon candy wrapped us in a bubble of warmth. Why couldn't June have given me a hug after I told her about Mars?

"Don't you want to fight for yourselves?" I asked.

"That's noble. But, pickle? We can travel through time. And

it's the bee's knees. I hate to say it, but sometimes we just like to head on over to Marfa."

"I don't want to live in Tombstone if you're not here," I said.

"Well, then it seems like you'll have to find another place to live."

"What? I can't do that."

"Why not?"

"This is my home. I haven't even thought about plans to leave, I've been so distracted lately. And useless, it seems. I've spent months trying to make this town like you, and . . . I failed."

"You didn't fail, pickle."

"I did too."

"Trying your best is never a failure."

"I haven't tried *everything* yet."

Mars sighed but let me speak.

"I'm going to go to the hearing tomorrow. I'll stall. I'll get them to postpone the law, and you can stay here for a few more weeks, and maybe the town will see that you're harmless."

"God, you're so earnest."

I preferred to be Pinky.

"We're all packed up," Mars said. "I trust you, but I don't know if I can convince the boys. They want to leave tomorrow."

"They have to at least give me a chance to try! A town can't just kick folks out like this. It isn't right."

"A group of people will do whatever they like to another group of people that they don't like. We're no different from animals in that way. We just have cars. And cell phones. Sometimes."

"Just give me one more day, Mars. Please? If things go sour, you can finish packing up and leave. But if they don't . . ." I couldn't think of anything beyond kissing Mars square on the lips. Her lip balm tasted like watermelon from the State Fair, and I knew I would do whatever it took to make sure she could stay in Tombstone.

Mars said, "How can I argue with that?"

I smiled. "I like you a lot."

"I like you even more, Pinky Swear. You're the loveliest woman I've met this side of 2000. Would you like to stay the evening?"

"Want to help me write an argument for the hearing tomorrow?"

Mars smiled. "I'm not sure we'll have time."

Mars was very convincing.

TWENTY-NINE

That night, I wrapped my arm around Mars, wiggled under the single sheet she still had on her bed, and set the last alarm I might ever need to set on my phone. Seven o'clock. Enough time to bike home, take a shower, and start writing the speech I would make at the town hall meeting.

With each turn of my bicycle's wheels, I felt my determination dwindling. Mars and her friends had only lived here for a few months, and the target on their backs had only grown during that time. If this rule didn't pass, wouldn't the town just find another way to kick them out?

Overlapping fliers desecrated every door I passed on my way home. Every image of Sweet Potato Grace's face was a bee sting on my butt. My poor dead cat didn't deserve to be wrapped up in a mess of my own creation. Neither did my friends, my Mama, or anyone who had to answer for me. Today was the day that ended. I was going to answer for myself.

"Breakfast?" Mama said curtly, sniffing as I swung open the door.

"That would be lovely."

Politeness ensued.

Everyone in the house had been too distracted to make a good breakfast. The coffee smelled sour and the eggs tasted bland. Every time my fork clinked the plate, my teeth rattled. We could have eaten a whole coop's ovulation before Mama or I would speak a word. Nene would pass away before the silence would end. To save her skin, she caved first.

"Are those foot people going to come around for dinner any time soon?" Nene finally asked.

Fanny snorted, but her unladylike behavior did not receive a scolding from Mama. Her fish weren't worth frying that day.

"That cult is coming nowhere near our house," Mama said, looking Nene in the eye. "They're getting kicked out. Today's the day."

"They're getting ready to leave anyway, Mama," I said. "No one wants to live in a place where they're unwelcome."

"And whose fault is it they're unwelcome?" she mumbled.

"The whole dang town's fault! Everyone who's going to that meeting to run them out."

"The town is simply responding to the terror that's been inflicted on us, Pinky Elizabeth. On our seniors. And this is for your own good, too."

"Nene Miriam isn't terrorized," Fanny said, stabbing a yolk open with her fork. "Besides, people in small towns terrorize each other all the time. Why is this so different?"

"Do they?" Mama said.

Mama's eyes were still on Nene, whose head was bobbing and whose mouth was dribbling egg. She looked tired, not terrorized. But she had enough energy to open her mouth and say, "The Women's Club said they're all homosexuals."

Fanny's eyes bulged. Nene continued chewing her food.

"What's wrong with that?" I asked slowly.

"Let's not talk about *that* over breakfast," Mama said.

"About what? People being gay? It's sure no reason to kick them out of a town," I said. "Surely you can't believe it is."

The clock ticked and tocked three times.

"Mama?"

"Well, it's certainly not helping them any."

"What do you mean?"

"It's not helping, Pinky. They should have kept their mouths shut and they'd have avoided a lot of trouble here. Now people won't shut up about how they're flaunting their fruitiness all over town. Next, it'll be men invading the women's bathrooms. We can't bring politics into Tombstone."

Too late for that.

"Excuse me for one second," I said. I got up, careful not to lose my footing on the slippery slopes Mama had dragged into the kitchen. I opened the screen door and walked toward the mother-in-law suite.

For a moment, I asked myself what would happen if I just kept walking. Past Peace Valley Park, past Bloat Hill. Past Texas.

But I didn't. I wasn't going to disappear without giving Mama one last chance. I put on my pearls and grabbed the crisp black folder that was collecting dust on my dresser. The last part of my speech was almost five months overdue. A lot about me had changed since I wrote the eulogy, but the message was the same, wasn't it?

Mama didn't have a full question for me when I walked back in and stood before my family. Fanny seemed resigned to whatever would happen next. Nene kept eating her eggs.

The second part of my speech was on a separate page, tucked

behind previous drafts and photos of Sweet Potato Grace that spilled out of the folder and onto the floor. No one flinched. No one picked them up, either.

"Before the barefoot folk—my friends—stumbled upon the funeral, I was going to make an announcement. Now seems like the appropriate time to do it." I began to read from the paper. "I want to share something that has been on my heart. I know this is a speech about Sweet Potato Grace—well, it was—but as I stand in front of my family and friends, I feel a very complicated mix of grief for my cat and love for you all. I love that you give me boy advice, June—just pretend my friends came to the funeral, Mama—and that you want to help me set up my dating profiles, Ashley. Mama," I said, looking up quickly, "you have raised me to be a woman who does not need a man to pay her bills. As it turns out, I don't need a man for anything, least of all matters of the romantic. I am attracted to women." I cleared my throat and added, "And I like Mars a lot. And she likes me, too."

There was another paragraph of apologies and backtracking, but I didn't read it. I just lifted my eyes to look at the breakfast table beyond the folder.

Mama had her elbows on the table and her hands over her face. She exhaled sharply, and when she peeked through her fingers, she just said, "Why did you feel the need to tell us this? After what I just told you?"

"It's important to me, Mama."

"Not important enough to say months ago, apparently. Why now? Are you telling me this now to upset me?"

"It's up to you whether or not you're upset," Fanny mumbled.

"It's up to me whether or not you live in this house," Mama said back.

Fanny didn't deserve to be hit in the crossfire. I shook my head to reassure her that I was fine, she didn't need to defend me.

"Mama, I'm sorry you're upset. I've thought a long time about telling you this."

"Well, you should have thought a little longer. After everything I've given you, you'd put our business in jeopardy like this? After everything we've already been through. There's nothing wrong with keeping your head down, Pinky. Even if that means making sacrifices."

"What's so wrong with being gay?"

"You haven't told anyone else, have you?"

"Only June, Ashley, and Wanda."

Fanny snorted. "So the whole town's going to find out in, what? An hour?"

I prayed that if I waited to respond, Mama would come up with a positive word to say. But my patience was starting to shrink thin as a wafer. My chest was squeezing in on itself. Fire ants could have been running across my feet and I wouldn't have noticed, because my whole body felt like it was burning.

Nene broke the silence: "Mars sounds like my good friend Lisa."

Fanny let out a sharp guffaw and started collecting the plates.

"Mama," Fanny said. "I know you have the best intentions for us. And I know things usually fare better when they don't change, but this doesn't change anything about Pinky."

Mama wasn't convinced. "Everything was just fine before the LGBT cult came in and started worshipping our cat."

"How many times have I told you?" Fanny said. "You can't call them a cult."

Mama turned to me. "I don't want anyone else in Tombstone to hear about this. This conversation does not leave this room, you hear me? People are already wary of going to Swear-It's because you're so closely tied to those people. And without Swear-It's, we'd lose everything."

"Fanny's right," I said. "They probably already know."

"Then take it back! Say you got confused."

"No," I whispered. It was more a statement of fact than it was a protest. My mind went back to Giddy Up Chuck's. I was who I was outside of Tombstone. I wasn't going back into my closet to suffocate.

"What did you say to me, Pinky?" she said.

"No. I've had it," I said. "This is ridiculous. So what? So what if I'm gay, so what if my friends are queer, so what? So was Roger. He had a business. He supported himself. He was gay and everyone knew it! So are a lot more people who I bet left this town because they felt alone. People in Tombstone want to run out the barefoot folk because why? They sang in a movie theater? They wear funny clothes? They're gay? They're *fun?* My friends are the best thing that ever happened to Tombstone, and no one can handle it. Whatever happened to 'love thy neighbor'?"

Fanny stayed as still as she could, not bothering to wipe the spit that flew from my mouth and Mama's off her rosy cheeks.

"You know what else?" I continued. "Because I'm on a roll, Mama. My friends don't worship Sweet Potato Grace, but they love her more than you ever did. And they love me for me."

"Who you are is not—"

"So give me a reason to stay," I said.

Fanny sat frozen, knife and fork still in hand. The universe hung in the balance. Then Mama looked me dead in the eyes. (It's possible she was just doing the trick of looking between a person's eyebrows to feign eye contact. I can't say for certain.)

"You're going to stay here and you're going to keep quiet. And not embarrass me."

"Well, that settles it. I guess I'll be quitting, then. And I'm leaving, too."

Mama scoffed. "I bet. You'll be back as soon as you realize how complicated you've made things."

I turned the doorknob on the hallway closet, pulled out a suitcase that had only been used once, and shut the door. The suitcase was supposed to be Fanny's, but she didn't mention it. She just whispered, "Don't forget Sweet Potato Grace."

I wouldn't. The last thing I grabbed was the box of her ashes. They sat on the dashboard as I drove to fight for my friends.

THIRTY

The lawn in front of Tombstone's city hall smelled like a football game that morning, though the constant waving of signs kept the aroma of burgers and chili from lingering. Even if Tombstonians were dead serious about the barefoot folks' removal, they did not succeed in dampening the overall energy of the event. I was in for something much livelier than a snoozefest on policy, it seemed—more tailgate than town hall. The whole town was there, apart from Mama, Nene, and Fanny. But Mama was never one for bureaucracy, so she wasn't missing out. "All governments are made up of queso-dribbling, woman-lassoing, cold-blooded amphibians," she was fond of saying. "Mayor Johnston is our only hope."

The protesters' signs and memorabilia for sale were ridiculous. Did we really need a three-foot-tall Kool-Aid man with an "X" through his sugary smirk? Janelle Watkins sold shirts that featured a bare foot next to a frowny face. Every bag of Frito chili came with a sheet of talking points about why bare feet should be banned in Tombstone, as if everyone didn't know why they were at the town hall in the first place.

June's comparisons of my friends to the Rajneeshees, who

were apparently known for wearing all orange, must have gotten out around town. A number of folks had taken it upon themselves to wear orange in protest. But since we were in Texas, the only orange they appeared to own was burnt orange, which threw me off when I first arrived. Truly, if a stranger had arrived in Tombstone with no context, they would have assumed a UT game was on.

June and Wanda matched the orange crowd and protested side by side with them. We made eye contact but said nothing. I didn't have time to start an argument. The meeting was kicking off in a few minutes, and I needed to go over all that I had to say to the town. I'd see them inside.

"Pinky!" Ashley waved her arms from a different part of the crowd, calling me over without looking at June or Wanda. Her eyes were puffy. She wasn't wearing orange.

I braced myself and walked over to her.

"How are you doing, Pinky? I'm sorry I haven't been able to come over, I've had to pick up extra shifts at work." She lowered her voice. "I let June know that we can't feed you to the gossip monsters. I told her to focus her efforts on the barefoot people for now, and we'd figure out how to talk to you about your . . . preferences . . . later."

"Thanks," I said, unsure if I meant it. "But it's okay. Mama and Nene know, now. You can tell the whole town if you want."

Ashley's relieved face made me question how many people in June's orbit already knew. "How did they react?"

"Terribly."

"Oh, Pinky."

"I don't know if Tombstone is the place for me anymore."

Ashley's lip quivered and I wanted to take everything back. All I could see was Ashley, ten years old and crying over a skinned knee. Fifteen years old and upset that Tommy Beans kicked dirt in her face after she beat him in the pull-up contest. Nineteen years old and embarrassed after her first keg stand.

"You can't leave, Pinky."

"I don't want to."

Her voice became more resolute. "You *can't* leave."

"What else am I supposed to do? Mama doesn't want me to be out of the closet, and then what? I'm going to never date? I'm going to end up alone? I'm going to end up like . . ."

I couldn't say Brenda, but Ashley could read my mind.

"If you leave right now, in the midst of all this mess, it will be pretty tough to come back."

"Ashley."

"You know it as well as I do. Leaving will just make everything worse."

"That should be painted on the 'Welcome to Tombstone' sign. Then maybe Mars would have driven straight through this place on the way to Marfa."

"They're going to have to go back to Marfa, Pinky. Or wherever they came from. I'm so sorry, I've got to get back home to the baby, but I just wanted to come tell you that I still care about you. I still support you. You're still my best friend." She pulled me into a hug, her tears hitching a ride down my cheek.

"Even if I leave?" I whispered.

Her shoulders sank. "Do you think it's worth it? To leave everything behind?"

"What will I have if I can't be myself?"

"I just don't understand," Ashley whispered.

I pulled away and looked in her eyes. "I don't know if I understand anything anymore. But I think I'd like to try."

"And that means leaving," she said.

"And that means leaving."

Ashley squeezed my hands. "Forget what June said, Pinky. I believe you. About what you said about Mars. And I still love you."

"Thank you. I love you too, Ashley."

"I hope you find what you're looking for." She started walking away, squeezing my hand until she had to let it drop.

✿

The only updates Tombstone's city hall had seen since the 1950s were the installations of a few window air conditioners. The air was still stuffy inside, and attendees fanned themselves in their metal seats, buzzing with gossip and impatience. I found a chair in the back of the room and watched June and Wanda seat themselves up front.

Mayor Johnston was chronically late, on account of her (alleged) man on the side, who lived out past Bloat Hill. She arrived a few minutes after I snuck in through the back doors, but the crowd didn't stop their murmurs.

"Oh, settle down," she began. "We can handle this cordially."

"How we handle it is by kicking those no-good hippies out of here!" someone yelled from the middle of the room. The murmuring took a cheery turn. People agreed. They wanted this to happen. I wanted to slide down the wall and become a pile of Jell-O. Why couldn't I? If people could time travel, why couldn't I become Jell-O?

Mars had assured me that the barefoot folk wouldn't be attending the meeting, but that didn't stop me from looking for them. They would want to plead their case, right?

But they had more experience with this kind of thing than I did, and they didn't seem to think the fight was worth it. There was no sign of them. I felt even more hopeless.

The line to make public comments formed as Mayor Johnston beat her gavel. All heads were nodding along to the testimonies, happy to hear the accusations and passive-aggressive jeers. Only twice did I hear folks ring the old bell of "They're terrorizing our seniors," but I heard plenty more:

"Walking barefoot in a grocery store is unsanitary."

"That political statement flag has no place so close to Tombstone Elementary."

"They have a golden cat. Do you hear me, people? A false idol. They are worshipping a dead cat."

Six crazy people stood and spoke into the microphone, all leading up to the grand finale: June. My lifelong friend. A person who had stood up for me for fifteen years was now about to speak out against me.

She didn't utter two words before my protest interrupted her. I don't remember yelling, I swear it on all Swears. But they say my impassioned *Hey!* rang from the brick walls of the city hall's auditorium. Then all eyes were on me. Only a few blinked.

"I . . . I'm sorry, June," I said, adjusting my shoulders to stand up straight. "Pardon my outburst. Please."

"No! No," June said politely, adjusting her shoulders too. "It's quite alright. Do you have something to say?"

I looked at Mayor Johnston, who looked at June, who spoke into the microphone: "You know what? I'll let my friend take things from here."

The whole town watched me walk to the microphone. At first, I stood there slack-jawed. I wasn't going to keep anyone's attention by catching flies with my open mouth, I told myself. Or was I? No. I had the floor. Twice in one day, I had to make a speech.

But this was not the Our Lady of the Obituary Youth Group Talent Show of 2009. This was not a eulogy, either. This was a question: *Do you trust me, Tombstone?*

"Well," I said, clearing my throat, "if you didn't know, the cat flying over the house on Bluebonnet Drive is Sweet Potato Grace."

"Cats can't fly!" yelled Ginger, a gas station attendant and Wanda's godmother. Wanda smacked Ginger's arm with her purse. It was an interruption that I would not allow to become a distraction.

"The cat on the flag. Sweet Potato Grace. She never appeared to be happy. In fact, if you ever met her on the streets of Tombstone or through my Instagram account, she looked downright mean. All the time. She didn't just *look* mean, either. The first time I tried to put her in a crate, she gave me such a scratch that I needed a bandage." I rubbed the place where the scar had faded into my thumb. Despite the imperfection, I hoped it never went away.

"I say this all because Sweet Potato Grace warmed up with time. She was misunderstood, yes, and she certainly disagreed at times with the indoor lifestyle I was giving her, but she came around. Many nights, she slept right in my bed. She appreciated the food and the water and the treats I gave her, but best of all, she knew she was loved and she liked being doted on."

I was straying from the point, no pun intended. Time to bring it back around.

"First impressions aren't always what they seem. Sweet Potato Grace had a hard time adjusting to life inside, even if that life meant she was safe from coyotes and could have three square meals a day. Three square meals, appropriately portioned out, of course." Dr. Senior, the town veterinarian, was present at the meeting.

"Over time, Potato learned not to scratch and not to bite. She learned that she could greet someone at the door, but there was no escaping. Our neighbors at Bluebonnet Drive have scratched and bit, *so to speak*, the town of Tombstone. *I was using a metaphor there.*" Those last words were drowned out by the grumbling of the crowd, followed by bangs of Mayor Johnston's gavel. "To be clear," I continued, "the residents at 101 Bluebonnet Drive didn't actually bite anyone. But they're like a cat that's used to living outside. It's just a metaphor. My friends have good hearts, and no one knows that better than me. I've spent more time with them than probably any person in this town would allow themselves to. They're smart, decent, kind people. They only want what's best for Tombstone and its constituents. If you give them time and compassion . . . oh, please. They're my friends. This law would be a big disappointment to me."

I closed my eyes, bracing for impact. Did people hurl tomatoes in 2022? Could I dare to expect thunderous applause? But I got neither. I got something worse: sympathy.

Mayor Johnston had kind eyes. "Oh, Pinky," was all she said, as if I were Sweet Potato Grace, my snout covered in barbecue sauce and fleas. She scanned the room. "Can someone please contact Ms. Swear? Please."

June stood up again, raising a hand to assure Mayor Johnston she had a handle on the situation. She came and laid that hand on my shoulder. Murmurs erupted into full-on conversations. The noise rose as June led me to the door.

Janelle Watkins said, "Get her home to her Mama. Save her from the cult!"

Joe Clark yelled, "Goddamn homosexual barefoot lizard people!"

Ginger chimed in with, "They're scratching and biting the seniors!"

June led me out of the room like we were two-stepping. I could feel the tension in her arms and the strength of her core. The worst part was, I was so frozen I just kept walking in front of her, sweetheart-style, until we reached the auditorium door. June let me go and I walked out.

"Go home, Pinky."

"June, I don't have a home anymore. My Mama—"

"I don't want to hear about it. I'm setting a boundary. This is for your own good," she said as she shut the door.

Outside, a slow cooker simmered next to unopened bags of Fritos. I ripped open the first one I saw, filled it with chili, and took a few more bags for the road.

THIRTY-ONE

Thank John Prine himself that the city hall was just a few turns away from the Exhaust 'n' Rest. As I sat in the car scraping up the last of the Frito chili, I tried to sort through all the noise, fog, and pressure that was filling my skull.

Mars and her friends weren't a cult. I knew that. Did I? Yes, I knew that. They were free to leave. But when they left, they left the universe. Right? No. Mika had said they might see Jimmy, Tip, and Dolly again. Was that what he'd meant at the party? Had I missed them talking over my head about time travel this whole time?

I had. I really should have brought a notebook every time I hung out with them.

I normally had a hard time believing in the impossible, but the town hall meeting had just introduced me to an impossible version of the town I'd grown up in. My third-grade teacher, the one who taught me how tolerant and kind the citizens of Tombstone were, was at that town hall meeting. June, whom I've known since elementary school. She led the charge against my friends.

What if the town was right? What if I was wrong? What if

leaving did mess everything up? Was I being selfish for coming out?

The Exhaust 'n' Rest was even more deserted than usual. I could have stood in the middle of that empty parking lot and screamed at the top of my lungs and no one would be gossiping about it that afternoon. No one was standing outside to smoke a cigarette. No one was walking their dog. I was alone in a corner of the universe, in a corner of time, next to the A-frame of an abandoned building and a punched-in sign advertising $1.25 gas from another time. Above me the Texas sky stretched out, bright blue with freedom and bliss.

I am so small, I thought. Like a tiny pickle in brine.

I shut off my car and leaned back. The lever beneath the seat pushed me away from the steering wheel. Same coping mechanism as always?

Yes, I thought.

I inhaled, ready for a big scream, but nothing hurled itself at the windshield.

Instead, I found myself laughing.

Bubbling, dancing laughter. I couldn't stop. The vibrations of my laughter shook the asphalt beneath me in one of Tombstone's two gas stations, which was one of 145,000 gas stations in the United States, which is one of over 190 countries in the world, which is one of however many planets in the universe, or the galaxy.

Admittedly, I'm not an astrophysicist, but why should I be? What do they know about time travel?

Did Mars travel in a time machine? How did it all work? Was I being scammed? Who knew? Who cared?

Mars could be a liar just like my third-grade teacher. But if

Mars was a liar, and my third-grade teacher was a liar, and June, who said she'd always be my friend, was a liar, and Mama, who said she'd love me no matter what, was a liar, then what the heck was I doing trying to please anyone anyway? My stomach hurt from laughter. Did Jesus laugh like this to get his six-pack abs?

"Sweet Potato Grace, you and me are the only truth-tellers left!" I hollered to the box of ashes. I kept laughing. *Everything* came back to Sweet Potato Grace. I imagined what she'd do if she were in the car with me. I imagined her watching me laugh hysterically in an abandoned gas station parking lot. And then I laughed some more.

If Sweet Potato Grace had had everything she wanted, she'd have roamed free forever. I didn't give Sweet Potato Grace that chance, but I could give myself that chance. Couldn't I? Did I deserve that much? I didn't know! I kept laughing.

I played hyena until I noticed that I wasn't alone. A car had pulled up next to me and the driver was patiently waiting for my giggles to evaporate. The car was Mama's, but Fanny was the only person inside.

"How did you find me here?" I asked, rolling down my window and wiping tears from my face.

"I have you on Find My Friends, dummy," she said. "I watched you drive out here. I thought you might be leaving Tombstone forever."

"Fanny, I *am* leaving Tombstone forever." I was anticipating a frown, a pout, a burst of tears.

Instead, she gently smiled. "Good for you, Pinky."

"What do you mean, good for me?"

"You hate this place, Pinky. You were so happy to leave for college and so sad to come back. I can't pretend I know everything you want in this life, but I do know you want to get out of Tombstone. You've wanted it for way too long. Do it."

"What about Mama? Aren't you worried about her? And the store?"

"People shouldn't have children to solve their problems, Pinky. If Mama needs someone to run the store, she can put out a 'Help Wanted' sign like everyone else."

"She won't be happy about that."

"Tough titties."

"Fanny!"

"Tough titties! I mean it. All my life, I've watched you dream about places other than Tombstone. Go see them. Your bags are packed, Pinky. Get out of here."

Her blessing took a weight off my shoulders. "But I don't know when I'm coming back," I said. "I don't think I can right away. I think it'll be a while."

"Where are you going?"

"I don't know yet."

Fanny nodded, looking down at her dashboard. I wasn't sure if I could answer the questions Fanny would have about time travel, so that can of worms remained shut. The only thing I knew was that I would do what *I* wanted for the first time in my life. The fewer people I had to answer to, the better.

After a moment, Fanny looked up at me with a peaceful smile. "I trust you, Pinky. I'm sorry I didn't come to the meeting today. And I'm sorry I read that diary entry you wrote about Elizabeth Stewart in seventh grade without your permission."

"There's no need to apologize. I already forgave you."

Fanny looked at her lap, laughing to herself. "You're quick to trust and quick to forgive."

"For all the grief Mama gave me about it, I kind of like that about myself."

"Good. Never apologize for it."

I thought of Blaze and his saxophone, the incense rising behind him. A smile crept to my face, nudging the corners of my eyes. I felt myself shining.

"I like that idea," I said. "I'm not going to apologize for anything anymore! Although I do feel the urge to say I'm sorry I yelled at you for stealing my makeup when I was twelve."

"I'm sorry I stole your makeup."

"Thank you for forgiving me after Mama said your face was too sensitive for makeup and I didn't defend you."

"I do have sensitive skin," Fanny said. "Thank you for still playing the violin after I said you were bad at playing the violin."

"I should apologize for playing the violin. I *was* bad at playing the violin."

"Thank you for being a good sister."

"Thank you for being the best sister," I said back, and I meant it. Fanny *was* the best sister.

"Mama hates her sister for leaving Tombstone," she said. "I don't hate you for leaving Tombstone, Pinky. Not at all."

"What about Mama?"

"What about her? She's fine."

"I'm going to try to come back and make things right someday. I just need some time."

I looked at the box of Sweet Potato Grace's ashes. Suddenly, I didn't like the idea of stuffing her in my suitcase to gallivant into the unknown. I didn't like saying goodbye to her again, either, but at least I had some practice doing that.

"Can you hold onto Potato for me, Fanny?"

"I will," Fanny said, reaching out to grab the box.

"And can you tell Nene Miriam I love her, and Mama too?"

She squinted at me.

"Tell them, Fanny. I want them to know. If there's one thing Sweet Potato Grace taught me, it's that you can love something even when it's not the sweet little thing you expected it to be."

"I'll tell them. I can't make them receive what you're giving them, but isn't that why you're leaving anyway? I love you, Pinky. Now, go make out with that pretty blonde barefoot lady."

"You don't think there's any chance they *are* a cult, do you?"

"I haven't always been a good sister, but I would never let you go on the road with a cult."

"Thank you, Fanny."

"You're welcome." She rolled up her window, put on some sunglasses, and left the Exhaust 'n' Rest but stayed under the infinite Texas sky.

I looked up and wondered if Sweet Potato Grace was looking at the Texas sky too, wherever she was.

THIRTY-TWO

I got to Bluebonnet Drive just in time, ironically. The orange Volkswagen was packed, with a suitcase or two bungee-corded to the top. Blaze was tying them down, a cigarette hanging from his mouth.

"Pinky pinky," he mumbled. "Good to see you." He jumped down and gave me a pat on the shoulder.

"You're leaving right now?" I looked into his eyes. There was that twinkle again—that gosh-darn twinkle. If I hadn't been so concerned with the logistics of their departure, I might have stopped to ask why that twinkle was brighter than usual.

The front door swung open and Mars ran into the front yard, breathing heavily. "Pinky!" she yelled. "I've been trying to reach you." She took my hand in hers and gave me a big smack on the lips. If I had been on the fence about leaving before, I was convinced now.

"Blaze and everyone decided we're going to Marfa," she said. "And I wish I could explain everything, but . . . Blaze, how much time do we have? Can I talk to Pinky quickly? I've got a lot of sweet nothings to share with her."

"We've got all the time in all the universes, pal," he said, giving us some space in the yard.

"Mars, I tried to convince the town to let you guys stay here. Honest. I tried, and my speech was the best I've ever given. But I don't think it was any use."

"Doesn't matter, doll. We're leaving to jump right now."

"What?"

"Blaze's decision, but I agree with him. We don't belong here. And not just because we're a bunch of barefoot homosexuals who wear robes and sing in movie theaters. There's something to be said for staying and fighting in a place where you don't belong, but that's not us, Pinky."

"Would you want it to be?" I figured I would ask one last time.

"We've tried before. We didn't come to Tombstone to try again."

I nodded.

Blaze interrupted us for a moment, presenting me with the folded white fabric of a flag.

"I don't know what your plans are, Pinky pinky, but I wanted you to have this. I hope you know that you're the best dang cat mama I've ever met."

"She's the cat's pajamas, too," Mars said.

I nodded my thanks to Blaze and hugged the flag to my chest.

"Hey, Mars?"

"Yes, toots?"

"What's the third thing?"

Her eyebrow arched. "What do you mean?"

"Yesterday, you said that when people find out about you,

they do one of three things. One, they disappear forever. Two, they tell everyone. I haven't done the first two things. So what's the third?"

Mars smiled. "Very few people choose it, Pinky."

"I've been braver than usual today."

She wiggled her fingers in excitement. "Well, I think you already know that third thing, doll. Come with us. If you want to come with us to Marfa, you're welcome. Let's jump. Let's party! Let's start a circus!"

Blaze turned the key in the ignition and music blasted through the speakers. David Byrne's voice sailed across the sky.

"How do we do it?"

"Shh." She put her finger to my lips and I tasted strawberry juice. "I don't have time to explain all that, but we've got quite a bit of time until we get to our next destination."

"Are we going to the future?"

"We'll set our sights that way, but we can't guarantee it. Don't tell Blaze I said this, because he's ornery about getting run out of town, but we do alright anywhere we go. At least, we do for the first few weeks."

"Do I need to take out any money?"

"No, pickle. If we go to the past, our money's worth quite a bit more than it is today. If we go to the future, our accounts are fat and happy."

"Do I need to . . . wear any special type of clothes?"

Mars giggled. "Only if you think you've got a good guess at where we're going to end up. That's why we stick with jeans, they're—"

"—timeless," we said together.

"There you go," Mars said.

"Why all the Talking Heads music? Is David Byrne a time traveler too?"

Mars shrugged. "We just think they're groovy. Boy, are we relieved when we find out we've landed in a time after the eighties."

"I presume we're bringing the van with us?"

"Yup! Maybe we'll ditch it. Maybe we'll keep it. Who knows? But throw your bags in and say goodbye to the car you've been driving."

I nodded, tentatively, as if a nod could say, "I don't know why the heck I'm agreeing to this." And you know what? I don't know why I agreed to it. I took my time walking to the van, but not before I took off my shoes and unfolded the flag with Sweet Potato Grace's face on it.

"Can I hang this off the side?" I yelled.

"Pinky pinky," Mika responded, bringing a small suitcase out of the house, "that sounds swell. Let's go, boys!"

Have you ever taken the time to notice how grass feels on your feet? Oh, I'm sure you've walked along the grass barefoot before. Everyone has. But have you *really* stopped to feel what's going on under your toes? The tickle of each blade, the itchiness of the life underneath. If you explore a little deeper, you're walking on dirt, on Earth, on one tiny planet in an infinite number of universes.

My shoes are off, now. I'm going to start living in the world. Where in the world? When in the world? I don't know. I'm going to leave that up to the universe. Not Mama, not Nene, not anyone from Tombstone. Just chance, fate, Jesus, karma, the roll of the dice—whatever you want to call that guiding force. Texas doesn't have casinos, so I've never been one to gamble.

Until now.

Acknowledgments

So many beautiful people, and a few special cats, made this book a reality.

Thank you to Katelyn, my sigh of relief.

Thank you to Christine, Feliza, and the Lanternfish team. I'm glad I met you in Kansas City, and that you encouraged me to share my very silly book.

Thank you to my parents, who bought me a rainbow cake.

Thank you to my siblings, I love you a whole lot. Emily, I'm sorry I didn't share my makeup.

Thank you to Grandma and Nana, the best storytellers.

Thank you to Yvonne, Sara, JM, Caitlin, Olga, Joy, Melissa, Aunt Lisa, my mother, Tim, Brenton, Mark, Candiace, Anna, Erica, Sean, Doug, Paul, Patrick, Brian, Melissa, Casey, Andrew, Emily, Parker, and everyone who took the time to read the early drafts of this book.

Thank you to all of my friends. You're all hot.

Thank you to all of the queer people who made it possible for me to hold Katelyn's hand in public. You're all magical.

Thank you to Austin Pets Alive, and to the kind volunteer who drove two nervous grey FeLV+ kitties from Lake Charles, Louisiana. Funny Business and Pinky Swear found their forever homes.

And finally, thank you to the Cat Distribution System. You brought me Sweet Potato Grace, you wonderful force. I'm forever grateful.

About the Author

Megan Okonsky is a ghostwriter, novelist, and murder mystery party host. Known for her conversational voice and wit, Okonsky specializes in helping business leaders uncover their "hero's journey." As a novelist, she writes about cats and queer joy. Her work has appeared in *Reductress* and *Mantra Wellness*, and her short story "The Five Stages of Grieving My Attention Span" was a finalist in Southern New Hampshire University's 2024 Fall Fiction contest.

Okonsky is a proud member of the Writers' League of Texas and the Association of Ghostwriters. She lives in Austin, Texas, with her wife and their cat, Funny Business.

PHOTO CREDIT: KATELYN STEWART